PRAISE FOR THE AUTHOR

'Full of realistic emotional twists. The characters' reactions to the challenges they face are frank and unmelodramatic; there is a refreshing honesty about the numbness that comes from discovering an infidelity, and the shame that comes with perpetrating one. Equally affecting are the counterpoised sources of sadness in Jill's life. Her marriage has faltered because she and her husband can't have children and yet she must be a mother to her own parents in their old age; it's a poignant combination.'

—*The Telegraph*, UK

'What really goes on behind closed doors? Carol Mason unlocks life behind a marriage in this strong debut.'

—*Heat Magazine*, UK

'Mason's writing is absorbing. While reading a spicy bit about Leigh's affair while taking the bus to work, I rode past my stop.'

—Rebecca Wigod, *Vancouver Sun*, Canada

'This poignant novel deals with honesty, forgiveness, love and the realities of modern-day marriage.'

—*Notebook Magazine*, Australia

'There is a fresh and vital edge to this superior debut novel. Mason has much to say about relationships. Her women have resonant characters and recognizable jobs, which give depth to their messy lives. A bittersweet narrative and ambiguous outcomes make this much grittier and more substantial than standard chick-lit fare.'

—*Financial Times*, UK

'It's got the raw realism of someone writing about a world she knows. A grand little book for the festive fireside.'

—*Evening Herald*, Ireland

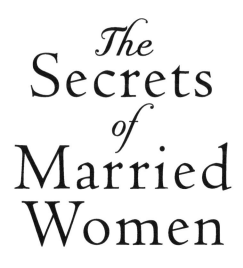

The
Secrets
of
Married
Women

ALSO BY CAROL MASON

After You Left

Send Me A Lover

The Love Market

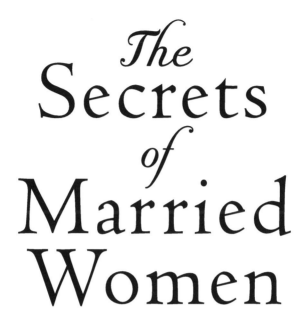

The
Secrets
of
Married
Women

Carol
MASON

LAKE UNION
PUBLISHING

This is a work of fiction. Names, characters, organizations, places, events, and incidents are either products of the author's imagination or are used fictitiously.

First published in Great Britain in 2007 by Hodder and Stoughton, a Hachette Livre UK Company

Published by Lake Union Publishing, Seattle

www.apub.com

Amazon, the Amazon logo, and Lake Union Publishing are trademarks of Amazon.com, Inc., or its affiliates.

ISBN-13: 9781503942066
ISBN-10: 1503942066

Cover design by Debbie Clement

Printed in the United States of America

For my mam, and not forgetting my dad, who would have been so proud.

CHAPTER ONE

'How do I look?'

I am powerfully aware, as I stand here before Rob in my best going-out wear, that I don't want to go. My feet already hurt and all I've done is put high heels on, not actually walk in them. I'm tired; this day has felt so long I can barely remember when it started. And I'm frustrated with myself. Why do I always commit to things I don't really want to do? Make plans with people secretly hoping they will cancel? Though tonight is not about my wants. I must remember that. Tonight is about Wendy.

'Great,' Rob says. His eyes haven't once left the television.

I stare into the top of his head as though he is a foreign species. 'So you don't think this skirt is too short, do you, by any chance?'

'Nah. It's fine,' he says, with such cheerful certainty.

'Rob?' I feel like pinging him with a high heel. 'I'm not even wearing a bloody skirt!'

Aha! That got his attention, didn't it? A dirty big grin spreads across his handsome face. 'I was just testing you.'

'I give up.'

Our six-month-old puppy, Kiefer, who is sleeping curled up adorably on one of Rob's feet, raises his head and yawns, sounding almost human. I give him a quick tickle behind the ears, and Rob says, 'Can you scratch my ankle while you're down there, please?'

I flick my middle finger against the top of his head. 'See you, then.'

At the front door I slip into my Burberry-type, three-quarter-length trench coat, knowing I'll feel better once I'm in the car. I'm only thirty-five; I don't know why leaving the house on a rainy night has to be so hard.

'Going, going . . . gone,' I shout to Rob, hearing, through my attempted good humour, the slightly fallen note in my voice that I can't seem to shake lately. I wonder if he even registers that Fridays used to be our date night. Our rule was we could go out with other people, but it had to be together.

'Have a good time,' he calls back, then adds, 'Knock yourself out, but not literally.'

I park on a side street down at the Newcastle Quayside, squeezing my Jetta between a black BMW 7 Series and a Mercedes convertible, whose alarm goes off although I swear it wasn't me. Nonetheless, I scurry off without looking back. It's drizzly, but the bar where we're meeting for drinks is close by, so I try to live dangerously and forgo the umbrella. I never know why Leigh has to always propose the newest, trendiest, loudest hotspot. I can't help but feel those days of caring that I've been to all the *in* places are long behind me, much like wearing gorgeous but insanely uncomfortable shoes.

When I go in, I immediately see her standing at the bar – perhaps because, sadly, she's one of the oldest people in here. I am a bit surprised to see that she's wearing an asymmetrical little emerald dress that's about four inches too short and so tight that I can actually see her protruding belly button even from a distance – an odd outfit choice, for both her and the occasion. Her long hair is newly coloured and is a shade too black for her very pale face. And when Leigh isn't smiling her expression is strikingly severe; almost as though she's angry at her own thoughts. I notice she's already halfway through a glass of red. When she sees me, she perks up and gives a little wave.

'I know. I'm early. Jill, if I hadn't got out of there, I swear I'd have left him in a puddle of his own brains!'

We suddenly become almost conjoined. Leigh always stands fractionally too close, invading your personal space. You will back up a step, but she'll then take a step forward, until eventually she will have you pinned to a wall, if you're not careful.

'Can you believe, when I left this morning there were only two things on his to-do list and he didn't manage either of them!'

'Poor Lawrence!' She's beginning the husband-bashing early tonight.

'Poor me, you mean! He's driving me mad! When I told him he could take a year off, I didn't mean literally! I just imagined he'd get more done with his time. But all he seems to do is sit around all day reading Eckhart Tolle and saying he wants to find himself!' She chuckles, despite herself, and I do too.

The stress of teaching eight-year-olds was making Lawrence's obsessive-compulsive disorder intolerable. Leigh thought it might be better for all of them if he stayed home and took care of one child rather than thirty.

I quickly order a drink because I sense I'm going to need one.

'Look!' I say. 'There are two free seats.'

I pay for my wine and we edge our way over there, taking care not to spill our drinks.

'I don't want to have to ask him to do things all the time,' she yammers away as she follows me. 'He's not a child. I just wish he'd be a bit more proactive sometimes. More of a man! You know, even when Lawrence hugs me, I swear he leans on me rather than supports me.'

This conjures up a funny picture and I try not to laugh because I can tell she's deadly serious now. Leigh will never sugar-coat reality. This is a quality you have to get used to when you meet her. And you're either going to like her for it, or you're not. Admittedly it can be a little bit terrifying, especially if she's telling you something about yourself that you don't want to hear.

We plonk ourselves in the two overly deep, white leather armchairs.

'Seriously, though . . .' She crosses one very slim bare leg over the other. 'I am really resenting his lazy 'hind these days! I mean, I work long hours, putting up with all kinds of petty egomaniac bullshit, and he gets to stay home and watch *Judge Judy*. A big drama for him is if the supermarket is having a two-for-one and he forgot to clip the coupon.'

'Well, his world is quite narrow now, admittedly, compared to yours.' Leigh has a fantastic job earning a packet marketing a trendy line of locally made leisurewear made popular by a famous footballer's wife.

'It's more than that. I'm going off him in a big way. It's so depressing . . . Last night in bed we were kissing, he was trying to get me going, and I felt nothing! I might as well have been kissing the sheet.'

Hmm. This conversation is taking a dark turn. We've had many a chuckle about Lawrence's unusual obsession with Christmas, or about how he comes to bed after checking forty times that the front door's locked only to leave the back door open, and how she wants to smother him with his pillow. But this is different. She's being more unkind than usual. I don't quite know what to say.

'Well, all marriages go off the boil a bit, Leigh.' I try hard not to think of my own. 'There are times when you think you're so well matched and other times when you don't know how you even got together in the first place.' The music – some *X Factor* diva – is grating on my nerves. I can't project my voice over it.

'I don't care about all marriages, though; I just care about my own. I know people say you should look at somebody who's got it worse than you – the poor chap with no legs when you've got two, and a fine pair at that . . . but I just think I'm not even forty and I'm already losing it for him, and it terrifies me. Mind you, nothing seems to put him off sex, but that's men for you.'

She sends a dour gaze across the black expanse of the Tyne and I wish Wendy would hurry up as I'm not quite in the mood for this tonight. It's one thing to poke a bit of fun, but I don't believe in jumping on the bandwagon when friends criticise their loved ones. Rob is far from perfect; he leaves his banana skins in the plant pot and his underwear on the floor. It's fine for me to find fault with him, but woe betide anybody else who does.

Leigh can be two different people – she's either fun, funny and forthright, or she's almost suicidal and she won't tell you why. We met when I was nineteen, in my first job working in accounts for Marks & Spencer; she was one of their buyers. We bonded in the staff canteen over our uncanny ability to ape the same co-workers. We would spend our entire lunch breaks chortling and whispering like a couple of naughty schoolgirls; once we got going, we were unstoppable, which is embarrassing now, thinking back. Who did we think we were, anyway? It was certainly more a testament to our maturity level than to the actual shortcomings of any of our subjects. And yet, when we weren't being idiots, we could talk about really serious things: our deep, dark teenage disappointments, world politics – though admittedly to a lesser degree. I had never had a friend I felt as close to as Leigh. But over the years I've come to see that she is a bit of a mixed blessing. You can be open with her and she will sally along with you quite happily, or you can find yourself treading carefully because you sense she's lying in wait for an opportunity to have a go at you – perhaps something that inevitably comes with knowing someone too well. Familiarity breeds contempt, as my mother always used to say. And you never quite know which Leigh you're going to get until she doles one of them out for you and you think, *Ah . . . this Leigh today.*

'It's just a spell,' I say finally. 'You have to look to his good points – of which there are many.'

'Wendy's going to be half an hour late, by the way,' she says now. 'Neil was late getting home from work, apparently, and she wanted to make sure he didn't think she was running out on him.' I can hear friendly exasperation in her voice. We both find it oddly intriguing how Wendy's first thought is always to consider what Neil wants over everything else. *Funny,* I think. *Rob seemed more than happy to get rid of me.*

Leigh sets her eyes on two burly twenty-somethings in brilliant-white T-shirts who are walking past us clutching beers. 'Oh, to choose all over again! A clean slate. Hmm . . . A *young* clean slate. With massive, bronzed biceps.' There's a devilish twinkle in her eye.

The lads look from me to Leigh. One of them says something, and by their laughter I doubt it was complimentary.

'What was *that* about?' Her face clouds. 'Were they mocking me? How dare they?' She dangles over the chair arm and says 'Oi!' after them.

'Oh, who cares?' I take a sip of my drink. 'They're kids!'

'Well they're not going to look at us with *this* around, are they?' Her gaze follows a girl's pert bottom in hot pants that have the word *Fatz* – Leigh's brand – written on them in pink sequins. 'Not even baldy by the bar, who looks like he got that suit free when he bought the tie. Mr Divorced in Polyester. It's so depressing!'

I shake my head in exasperation. 'Why do you care what two teenagers or a lonely heart with a hair weave think of us?' Sometimes the people I know best are the ones I least understand.

'Because our days of attracting anyone worth having are over!'

'Well, someone should just slaughter us and serve us up as dog food.'

'I know,' she says, and I think, *Good heavens! She thinks I'm being serious!*

'I've been stalking a few of my exes on Facebook.' She says this furtively and hurriedly. She'll want the conversation over before Wendy gets here.

'Which ones?'

'There's too many to name.'

We chuckle.

'Haven't you ever done that?' She quickly adds, 'Oh, no you won't have, I forgot. Because Rob was your only boyfriend.'

'But that doesn't make me a bad person,' I joke. It's odd, though. Sometimes I can't picture a time when I wasn't married. I mean, I know it's not quite been ten years yet, but I do sometimes wonder whether there was life before Rob, or was there Rob before life. And I'm sure he must think the same way, which is even more of a disturbing thought.

'But you'd never leave Lawrence and you'd never have an affair,' I remind her. 'You've always said that.'

'And that's all true. No one knows me as well as Lawrence. I couldn't contemplate starting from scratch again with a new man. Besides, affairs are so tacky. And I can barely be bothered to have sex with my own husband, let alone anybody else's.'

I see Wendy coming through the door and think *Hallelujah!*

'Anyway, I did all my screwing around years ago.' We both wave so Wendy sees us in a sea of bodies. 'Though I'm sure it's different for you. You've only ever been with one man so you could be forgiven for being curious. Plus I have a lot to lose. Remember, I have a daughter. You don't understand what it's like when you're a mother, Jill.'

Leigh sometimes makes tactless comments that make me feel like I'm a member of a very limited club of childless pariahs, and it wounds me more than I can ever let on.

'How is Molly these days?'

She doesn't get to answer because Wendy is upon us, all smiles, the way Wendy always is. Consistent. A bright-side finder. Three cheers for straightforward, happy people!

'Hiya!' She playfully air-kisses us and I smell the lovely orangey waft of Hermès Eau des Merveilles. Her former chin-length black bob has been recently cut shorter. It suits her, I tell her.

'Oh no. It's awful! Neil hates it.' She grabs a stool that frees up as the couple of girls next to us leave. 'He hasn't said anything, of course, but it's all in the subtleties.'

'I always think you have to be really skinny and young, with fantastic posture, to pull off a really short hairdo.' Leigh eyes her over the top of her drink.

I'm about to say *No way!* But Wendy dismisses it with, 'You're right. She took way too much off. But it'll grow soon enough!'

She settles herself on the seat and immediately tells us she won't drink until we get to the restaurant, as she has a headache. 'It's been quite a night trying to get out of the house.' She fans her face for dramatic emphasis. 'The lads decided they wanted to go see a film, and then Neil got home later than normal. You know, the murder at the university.'

'So you drove them to the cinema? Couldn't Neil have done that?' Leigh asks. 'It's not like you have plans every night.'

'No. He came home and he was stressed and he was ready for a Scotch,' Wendy says, as though it needs no explaining.

Leigh gives me *that* look.

Neil is a superintendent at Northumbria Police. His impenetrably handsome face regularly graces the nightly news. Wendy and Neil have been married seventeen years. Wendy always loves telling the story of how Neil was a twenty-five-year-old police sergeant who stopped her car on Christmas Eve and offered her a free ice-scraper, and like an idiot she put her mouth on it and blew because she thought she was being breathalysed. They have two sons.

'So what's it like working together then?' I ask. Just over a week ago, Wendy began working at Leigh's company and I've been dying to hear how it's going.

'Go on, you can be honest,' Leigh says playfully. 'I won't be insulted.'

'No! I love it!' Wendy says. 'I know it's not as though I'm running the company, but you can't imagine how great it is, after all these years as a mum, to finally have another dimension to your life, you know, to learn new things, use your brain . . .'

'It's overrated,' Leigh says. 'Trust me.'

'Maybe to you because you've achieved so much. But what have I done all my life?'

'You taught yoga,' Leigh points out. 'Your classes were an accomplishment.' She chuckles, 'Completing one certainly was.'

'Oh yes, but it's not nearly the same. I was just teaching something I could do with my eyes shut.' She playfully pinches a small roll of flab on her belly. 'Shame the years of exercise didn't pay off.'

'Neil always seems to like your curves,' Leigh tells her.

'There's no accounting for taste,' Wendy says, and smiles.

I always think there's a fine line between being modest and selling yourself short.

'Wendy's doing a great job,' Leigh says. 'I'm very impressed with what a fast learner she's being. In fact, I'd better watch my back!'

'Maybe it's because you're such a good teacher.' Wendy blushes; she can never take a compliment.

I'm pleased she seems happy. I must admit I'd had my misgivings. Friends working for friends. When does that ever end well? Especially when Leigh is such an alpha female, and Wendy is so pliable, and the last person to stand up for herself. It could only work because Wendy lets so much roll off her back and Leigh, at her core, has a good heart – a quality Wendy cuts people a lot of slack for.

'Don't get too happy,' Leigh says. 'It rarely lasts.'

We chat for a while, then finish our drinks and walk over to the restaurant. We arrive just as the hostess is about to give our eight thirty reservation to someone else, despite us being only five minutes late. Leigh makes a big song and dance about it, of course, and Wendy and I look at one another. Why bother? We've got our table!

We do this every year. Same date. Different restaurant. It goes much the same as all our nights out over food and booze; we never come out to be glum. Except that at one point early on, usually between starter and main course, there is a natural break in our chirpy patter, and we give it over to Wendy. Wendy will say pretty much the same thing she's said for the last three years because, really, time ticks on, but there is never any more you can add, or anything you can take away. A mother's love and the loss of a child can only be fully known by those who have gone through it. I am not a mother, but the day I saw Wendy's baby pass away in her arms was the day a switch was flicked within me and I wanted to give life, care for life, raise a child to an adult, with a force I never knew was possible. So this is the reason that a part of me was selfishly not looking forward to tonight. It's a reminder of what *I* don't have either.

Wendy smiles at us, and it's the only time it ever looks like she's trying too hard. Wendy doesn't do maudlin – not in public. And we are her public despite being her friends. After everything that has happened, she somehow manages to hold herself together. Wendy is the most dignified person I know. But I will always remember her words at the funeral. 'Losing a baby feels like the end of an unwritten story. I've spent hours visualising her life from birth to old age. What might have been. I've created a wonderful life story for her in my mind because she was denied one. I've missed her more, and on deeper levels, than you would ever think it possible to miss someone who only lived twenty-two days. I will never stop missing all that she never became.'

I have played this over and over in my mind. And part of me wants to add: *It's the same when you know you can't have one . . .*

'Neil still doesn't approve of this, you know?' she says now. 'Our getting together like this.' Someone has suddenly dimmed the lights. It seems prophetic and timely. Leigh and I softly hold eyes in the candlelight. This is possibly the closest Wendy has ever come to saying anything negative about Neil, except when she once confided to me that he disapproved of her keeping a lock of the baby's hair. 'It's just his way of coping, of course.'

'Men don't like to be vulnerable,' Leigh says, with an all-knowing expression in her eyes. 'They've got to act hard, or they're being wimps. But sometimes they genuinely do prefer to just forget.'

'But you made sure that at least the three of us would never forget her,' Wendy says to her.

It was Leigh's idea to celebrate Nina's birthday every year. She said, that way, we'll remember that she lived, not just that she died. We won't let her become a memory that goes unmentioned. I have to admit that after Nina's death it was Leigh who stepped up as a friend, even though I had only introduced them a year before. I, who had known Wendy longer, who was supposed to be the better friend, just became sort of ineptly mute, and faded into the background.

'Every day I think of her, you know? She will always be part of my family, even though I can't see or touch her. I can't have a conversation with her . . .'

Wendy will never let go, and while this is probably the right and proper thing, a part of me is in Neil's camp – sometimes it's easier to close a door on your pain, especially when keeping it open won't rewrite history.

She reaches for our hands so that for about thirty seconds the three of us, who are not normally touchy-feely with each other, are joined in a circle. 'Thank you, my treasured friends. You two were closer than family to me at the time. And you still are. It means so much to me that we do this. That I have people I can remember her with.'

I sneak a look at Leigh's wistful expression. 'We have to band together,' she'd said to me that day as we left the hospital. 'It's all we can give her. Being there and not conveniently backing away when we think we have her permission.' She'd suddenly seemed so strong and so selfless – a side to her that I'd never witnessed before. I'd looked on in awe at how she had thrown herself into recruiting all of Wendy's friends, next-door neighbours and distant family to organise a meal schedule. 'When you're going through hell, the first thing you do is forget that you have to eat,' she'd said. Every night, she'd seen to it that someone dropped off a warm casserole, or a cooked chicken at the door. Of her own volition, and from her own pocket, she'd had Sainsbury's deliver groceries – essentials like milk, butter, bread, cooked ham, wine and beer – once a week. She'd even paid for a cleaner to go in and rally the household into some sort of domestic order when Wendy was incapable of coming downstairs from her bed. Despite Leigh not being the most generous of people with her money, she'd never once shown Wendy a bill. It was a display of practical generosity that had left me feeling furious at my own inadequacy. Why had the death of Wendy's baby almost sent me over the edge too?

'To Nina.' Leigh raises her glass and Wendy and I follow suit. And we hold them there, touching, mid-air, for one or two seconds longer than usual. I am sure we are all saying the brief and silent prayer that people who never pray find themselves saying when the moment calls for it.

'Who is, and always will be, my daughter and greatly, greatly loved,' Wendy finishes.

Neil came for Wendy at ten p.m. sharp. Through the window we saw his black Audi truck idling across the street, a flash of prematurely silver hair and the sleeve of a cashmere jumper – even snatches of Neil leave you in a mild form of awe. The expression on his face, glimpsed briefly as Wendy opened the door to get in, was inscrutable, yet I sensed he wasn't pleased. 'Neil will never argue or fight,' Wendy has often said. Leigh trots off to her car – her parting words to me are, 'I feel so much better than I did earlier! I feel bad for saying all those things about Lawrence. Sometimes you have a gripe and you don't even know why . . .' She seems genuinely regretful, and I am glad for Lawrence that he will live to see another day.

I stand still for a moment to stare across the river, suddenly finding myself in no real hurry to get home. On the other bank, the floating party boat where Rob and I met is still there – or some updated version of it. It always fills me with a bright nostalgia: the covert passage of time. But tonight I can't connect with it. I am somewhat deadened to its positive significance.

It's refreshingly chilly and spitting with rain, a fine mesh visible only under the halo of the streetlamps. I breathe in the oily Newcastle dampness. I have always liked this part of the city, especially at night: the Blinking Eye Bridge lit up with blue lights; the Baltic Centre for Contemporary Art, a converted flour mill, floodlit against the night sky. And the Sage Centre for Music that reminds you of a stainless steel seashell. Out of nowhere in the silence, a group of girls jig past me, linking arms and performing their drunken version of the cancan. I listen to their voices, diminishing the farther up the street they go, until the void comes back again. I start walking in the direction of my car now, aware of the clack of my heels on the cobblestones, as light reflections from the Sage Centre bob on the river and cars drum noisily over the Tyne Bridge.

The lovely silver Mercedes SL 500, whose alarm I may have set off, is still parked behind me. I'm about to get in my car when I notice something under my wiper.

It doesn't look like a parking ticket or a flyer. I pull out the somewhat soggy piece of paper and read: *I saw you scratch my car. So instead of compensation, how about a drink?* And under that is the name Andrey and a phone number.

When a motorbike whizzes past me and I feel the draught from it, I'm aware that I'm standing there, a little baffled. How strange! I read it again, the words sitting there in my hand.

An invitation to wrong-doing, from a complete stranger.

I cast around me, to see if anyone's watching.

There is no one, of course. It was probably some chancer, a clever bugger, lads out on a stag night. I can practically hear them laughing as they take off up the street.

Still, though, I'm oddly flattered.

I don't know where to put it. I don't want to litter, so I slide it into the front pouch of my bag. I drive home with the radio burbling low, enjoying the peace of the dark road ahead of me, aware of feeling somewhat sprightlier of spirits. When I get in, Rob is sitting in the same chair, though the dog's coat is damp when he comes to greet me so he must have had him around the block recently for his nightly walk.

'Good time?' he asks, looking like he couldn't care less.

I think about telling him about the note, but something about it feels desperate.

'Surprisingly, yes,' is all I say.

CHAPTER TWO

'Rob can only keep it up for about thirty seconds,' I tell Wendy on the phone while I sit at my desk at work. I'm personal assistant to the Head of Finance for Newcastle Football Club. The girls who sit across from me nearly fall off their chairs.

'You and your dirty minds!' I look at them over the top of my glasses. 'I'm talking about running!'

We are training to run 10K. It's the new 'us'. It's healthy, it's bonding, it's the perfect way to exercise Kiefer.

'Glad you clarified that, Jill girl,' Leanne says to me. 'Otherwise that would account for a lot about you, wouldn't it?'

'Really?' I cover the mouthpiece with a hand. 'Like what?'

I try to tune back into Wendy. Wendy is my running guru. Without her I am the most unmotivated person I know.

'It gets easier surprisingly fast. You'll be stunned by your progress in no time.'

'The hardest part is putting one foot in front of the other and keeping going. I'm still trying to work that part out. But we followed the programme, just like you said.' With our own variation. 'Run one minute, dawdle for six, right?' I joke with her.

The girls are laughing at me.

'We'll stick with it, though! My pledge to you!' Once we pick it up again in the dark nights, when the neighbours can't see us. As Rob said, it's getting too warm to be doing all this extra sweating. Besides, running isn't good for big puppies; it can displace their hips. 'Oh, you don't want your hip displacing, do you now?' I rubbed the top of his head. Apparently he was talking about the dog.

I see my boss coming and duck into my shoulders. 'Gotta go. Adolf's doing the goose-step, two-step.'

'I'll see you in yoga tonight, right?'

Oh, it's exhausting, this business of trying to age gracefully! 'Now, Wend, what would I do without a friend like you, driving me to be a better person?'

'I'll loan you my large bottom then you'll have no problem finding the motivation.'

I'm just about to knuckle back down to work when I receive a call from my dad on my mobile.

The anguished draw of breath. 'Jill! She's gone!'

My heart sinks. Not this again. 'Oh, Dad!' I can't stand hearing him panicked and vulnerable. 'Calm down. Take a breath. Tell me what happened.' My work friends send me sympathetic looks. My mam has vascular dementia and my dad can't cope. He's becoming more and more helpless, but tries to shield this from me in case I press the issue of putting her in a home.

'She's still in her dressing gown. Wouldn't get dressed this morning. I'm sure the door was locked, but maybe I left it open when I went to put the rubbish out. Sometimes I forget myself . . .' I can tell he's seconds away from crying, which is always shocking to me. My father was a manual worker. Like Atlas, I always thought he could put the sky on his shoulders and carry it. I never, ever imagined him raw-boned and out of his depth. The reality of where we are is sometimes hard to take.

'You know that somebody will find her, Dad. Just like last time. She'll be home before you know it. There's no need to panic.' The village where they live is so small you couldn't run away if you wanted to. 'But I'm on my way, anyway. I'll be there as soon as I can.' Though it won't be fast. Not with rush hour.

We used to have a very understanding department head, until he dropped down dead in his office about a month ago. This new guy, Michael Irving, goes around like he's got a large, splintery plank up his bottom, and he's always watching me as though he has something on me. He walks past my desk in his slip-on tan shoes with leather tassels that have all us girls giggling. I tap on his door. When I go in, he gives me a cautionary look over the top of his glasses, and I haven't said a word yet.

'I'm afraid . . . I'm sorry, but I'm going to have to leave early. I have a family emergency.'

'Another one?' he says, as though I get them every day.

'I'll make the time up.'

'I believe that goes without saying.'

It doesn't help that I was late in this morning because that hound Kiefer tried to take our neighbour's bunny for a ride around our garden in his mouth. I had to streak across the lawn in my underwear trying to catch him, but he just thought we were playing a game. By the time he took my threats to kill him seriously and I'd got the bunny back in its hutch and got dressed, I was fifteen minutes late in leaving the house. So it's two nails in my coffin in one day.

'I'm sorry,' I tell him. He says nothing.

It strikes me, suddenly, that he could show a note of sympathy. He could cut me some slack; he knows my situation. My heart begins a soft hammering. 'You know, Michael' – it takes a lot of effort for me to say this – 'I have worked here four years. I have an impeccable record of attendance, punctuality and efficiency. I regularly work overtime without pay, and I never once complain or say I can't do it. I don't have children, so luckily I'm not always disappearing to take them to doctor's appointments, nor am I taking days off when they're home sick. But I do have aging parents. My mother is seventy-five and she suffers from dementia. She ran away from the house today, and she won't know where she is, or where she's going. She probably won't even know *who* she is, for that matter, if it's a bad day for her. And my dad has a heart condition and he can barely cope. So if I occasionally have to leave the office to go and be a good daughter, then I'm afraid everyone is going to have to cope with it.'

My heart is leaping from my body now. It's possible he might sack me. I feel it in the air. He starts moving paper, as though I'm not there. His face has coloured slightly, though, and a fine sweat has broken out on his brow.

'See you Monday,' he says, without looking up.

My heart is still racing when I get into the car. Of course because I'm in such a hurry to get through to Sunderland, there has to be an accident on the Tyne Bridge. I switch on some music because there's no point in stressing over things you can't control. The passenger of an A1 Windows and Doors van that's idling beside me catches my eye and winks. Next, his buddy is leaning over and doing the same thing. I try hard to tune them out. She's going to be fine, I tell myself, because I think you have intuition for bad things happening and my gut tells me it's not going to be this time. But still I worry because I am a worrier by nature. Even when I have little to worry about, I worry. I worry about whether they're sleeping, eating, going to the toilet. Whether they're warm, getting fresh air, turning the oven off, closing their windows at night, and not answering the door to strangers. I was an only child to 'old parents', as I always thought of them when I was growing up because everyone else's were so much younger. The only downside of this is that I am going through the caregiver dramas now, rather than in fifteen years' time when most of my peers will.

Somebody toots a horn. Traffic ahead is moving again. The two men in the van pull argh-she's-leaving-us faces and wave like a couple of half-wits. I also pull a face, crossing my eyes and lolling out my tongue. On the way, I ring Rob to tell him what's happening and to bitch about Irving and my day.

My mobile rings as I'm pulling up at their front door. 'We found her! Mary Jennings found her sitting in the bus shelter. She said she was going on holiday to Harrogate of all places! You needn't bother coming now, love. We've survived another one!'

'Look out of the window,' I tell him.

When he does, I wave. 'Oh,' he says, sounding sheepish.

I push back an overgrown rhododendron bush by the gate and walk up the path, recognising that I'm a tad irritated about having to leave work, and hating myself for it. My dad opens the door. 'Guess what? Your mam gave Mary a good hiding for bringing her home!' My dad finds it funny that such a ladylike woman has taken to smacking people for the smallest of reasons. Then the smile disappears and his face takes on that look that comes right before he crumples. 'Oh, Dad!' I go to give him a hug but he swats at me, saying 'Get off!' We're not supposed to be soft in this family.

My mother is sitting prettily on the sofa now, dipping Jaffa Cakes into a cup of tea and staring, bewildered, when the biscuit disintegrates in her fingers. Every time I come through that door I die a little, until she recognises me, then I'm reborn. It's called my reprieve from the inevitable. She looks at me benignly, then smiles. 'Hello, Mam,' I say. A former registered nurse, my mother never was benign, nor was she razor-tempered, like she can be now. She was hardworking, fiercely loyal, caring and independent. She was gentle to my dad's strong. They rarely fought, and you never got the sense that they needed to. They were well-balanced and well-matched in all things, in the way they orchestrated their marriage, in their opinions and likes and dislikes, and especially in their humour. 'I married out of my league,' my dad would often say, with such pride, as though he'd hit the jackpot. My mother's parents were business owners and quite well off, and my mam went to college. In Dad's eyes, that meant their daughter should have done better because my dad's family were hard up and my dad had very little education. 'Make sure the man you marry thinks *he's* the lucky one,' my mother would often whisper to me, 'not the other way around.'

I kiss the top of her fragrant head. I will often hear her words of advice even though she can't speak them to me any more; they remain there, her pearls of wisdom, helping me become who I am, directing my course and nudging me to be better. Despite the fact that much of who my mother was is gone, I am just so thankful that she's still with us in pretty good shape and form. I make a point of cherishing every minute I have with her. I want to scream at the world, *Be thankful for their consistency and their presence, because the downturn happens so quickly that it takes your breath away.*

She looks me up and down, admiringly. 'Long skirts look very nice on daughters,' she says. My dad and I smile. We go into the kitchen and make tea in the old brown teapot we've had since I was little. We talk. About the weather. About next door's cat digging up the flower beds. About the latest local headline news. Sometimes, through my heartbreak, I can accept that this is just one of the inevitable unfortunate paths that life takes and I try to force myself to emotionally disengage slightly – preparing for the inevitable day when they won't be there – so that my falling apart will somehow be more tempered. But it is so hard. So very hard to love less, care less, be less of a messed-up emotional disaster than you actually are.

We talk about everything except the one thing we should be talking about. 'Things haven't been so bad lately, you know!' my dad says, apropos of nothing, perhaps anticipating what I am about to say. 'I know there was a spell where it wasn't looking too good, but she seems calmer in herself lately. She's settled down. Sometimes we even talk like we used to, and she's eating better too . . .'

My dad will not give up on her, even to his own detriment. In some ways I see Rob in him. When my dad loves, he does it with a force that allows for no compromise, ever. 'It's really only been this one episode today, otherwise she's been much like the old Bessie. The other day she even asked when you'd be home from school! She wanted to have a sandwich ready for you because she said you'd be hungry.' His face floods with warmth and pride. Until he realises.

There is a moment when hope seems to peel away, when it dawns on both of us what he has just said.

'Oh,' he says. 'You don't go to school, do you. You're thirty-five.'

I can't look him in the eyes. I want so badly to un-hear it that I have to gather teacups and clatter them in the sink. 'Don't worry, Dad. It's all right. You're just under a lot of stress. It's normal to get a little confused when you've got so much to cope with . . .' I can hear the cataclysmal cracking of my own voice.

'I don't know why I said that,' he says. 'I'm sorry, love.' Then he adds, without humour, 'If I'm not careful you'll be locking us both up next.'

I stay for a couple of hours, valiantly trying to cheer him. He takes me down to the bottom of the garden and shows me the work he's been doing on his vegetables, the runner beans he has planted, the cabbages, carrots and peas. He tells me at length about his experimental peppers and avocado. All the things he tried to interest me in as a child – his world, the things he derived pleasure from – and I would never listen. But now I make a point of it, trying to make up for the small offences of my teenage past, recognising how little it would have cost me back then. Then he waves me off at the door. He looks at me with that pathetic little face that I will see repeatedly in my mind.

I am barely around the corner, out of the sight of neighbours, when I have to pull over and ring Rob. I rarely cry, but tears come so profusely now, I didn't know I had them in me. 'It's not fair,' I hear myself saying. 'I can't have it happen to him too!'

'Of course it's not happening to him too,' my husband assures me through my stammers and sobs. I don't know where this meltdown is coming from. 'He's seventy-five, Jill. He can barely take care of himself let alone your mam. You've got to forgive him the odd slip. Hell, I forget things all the time and I'm half that age.'

'Do you ever think your wife's still a teenager?'

'Only when you give me reason to. Which, come to think of it, is quite often.'

'Bastard,' I say, my sniffle being replaced with a weak smile.

'Cheer up now, OK?' my hubby softly scolds me. 'I told you I don't want you upset when you're driving or next time I see you you'll be wearing a toe tag on a gurney.'

Rob always has a remarkable ability to talk me down from a crisis. He's like some giant safety net that I know will always be there when I fall. 'Well if I am, will you make sure they give me a nice-looking toe tag? A lively one that matches my nail polish.'

'I'll see what they have in stock.' He chuckles, then says, 'I love you, you know. And guess what? When all else fails, you've still got me.'

Something in his tone says he doesn't think that's a very tantalising prospect.

I text the girls and tell them I won't be at yoga, then I start to drive home in a mental fog. Wendy rings me minutes later. 'Everything all right?'

I tell her briefly. 'Oh,' she says. 'I'm so sorry. Never forget you're a fantastic daughter and you're doing all you can.'

'Thanks,' I say, and I ask her how work was today.

'Well, OK. Sometimes Leigh and Clifford act a bit like an old married couple. It's bizarre.'

Clifford La Salle is Leigh's gay, eccentric boss who founded the *Fatz* empire and interviews a person by asking to see what's in their handbag.

'Does he really pass wind all the time and light matches to hide it?' I've always wondered if Leigh exaggerates.

'He must have a gastric problem.'

'Oh no!'

'Poor man.'

'Poor you! But other than that – you're still liking it then?'

'Oh yes. Definitely. When you think, but for the grace of God I might have got that job at the call centre.' Wendy walked out of one of the rare interviews she's had when a very jumped-up nineteen-year-old kept insisting she prove she's had experience of dealing with people.

'I must go,' I say, feeling thankful for the spot of cheery conversation. 'Rob thinks I'm a calamity waiting to happen when I try to talk and drive at the same time.'

I collect Kiefer from Pause for Paws, where we leave him on days that Rob can't take him into work. As I drive down our street, he hangs out of the window barking at the world, grounding me in the moment, somehow. In my kitchen I set out the ingredients to make my quick Thai chicken curry. I can't instantly find the scissors so I try to open the bag of rice with a sharp knife. It pierces the tough plastic – and my finger – just as Rob walks in.

Upon sight of his lord and master, Kiefer's tail thrashes a tune on the parquet floor. 'All right there, my angel?' Rob strokes him and Kiefer jumps up and has a fit of hysterics. There are three of us in this marriage, so it's a bit overcrowded. Then Rob sees me.

'Good God, Jill! What've you done?' Blood runs down my wrist. He marches me to the sink, thrusts my hand under cold water. 'You've got to stop doing things in such a hurry! Hang on, I'll get a plaster.'

'It's just a little cut.' A sea of blood swirls down the plughole. I watch my hubby of nearly ten years, in his white T-shirt that strains appealingly over his broad chest, open the junk cupboard above our fridge. There is an avalanche of odd shoes, empty gin bottles, Hoover bags, cookery books, panty liners, Christmas cards, you name it, to which he says 'Fuck.' He tries to stuff it all back in there, unsuccessfully, gives up and lets it tumble on to the floor again.

'That's why I never go in there,' I volunteer.

'Where do we keep the plasters, Jill?'

'I don't think we do keep plasters, Rob.'

'Well why not? We seem to keep everything else.' He picks up a panty liner in his fingertips and says, 'What in God's name is this doing here?'

Despite a throbbing finger, I smile.

'And how many times do I have to tell you that you need to leave this by the hob in case there's a fire?' He brandishes the miniature fire extinguisher he bought for me last Christmas, which I keep trying to throw out with the rubbish because I get tired of humouring his paranoia. But he always drags it back out again and plonks it by the cooker, which just gets in my way, so now I stuff it up there in the unmentionable cupboard.

'Stay there. Don't move.' He disappears down the narrow parquet passage that flanks our main living area, which is essentially three rooms knocked into one. Something builders liked to do in 1970s semis to give the illusion of space. I hear him climb the stairs, his work-boots imprinting manly thuds above me. He reappears with a roll of loo paper.

'While you were gone, my arm fell off. Look, it took my whole shoulder with it. I don't think toilet roll is going to cut it.'

'OK, funny pants,' he says. His warm hand holds up my wrist, and his other carefully winds loo roll around my wound, a slow and thorough process of mummification. 'You could have sliced your finger end off.'

'Pity, it's my middle one too. I use it so much.' I demonstrate.

He pretends to bite at the rude gesture. I watch my husband as he works away on me. His serious, fine-featured face, eyes of the darkest grey-blue, the knit of his brows under his tumble of chestnut hair, and his tight-drawn concentrating mouth. Suddenly I fill with an urge to kiss that concentration off his face, just to turn a shitty day into a good one. He must catch it in my expression because he looks at me for a moment in that briefly red-hot way that a man will look at a woman when she's not a blood relative. Our gazes hang there. My heart starts a wild ticking. His hand that was bandaging me slows. His thumb that was pinned to my wrist, strokes it now. My eyes savour his even-tempered mouth with its up-curled edges. And I almost forget my hunger, my headache, my shitty day and my sore finger. I close my eyes and drift in to him. My face is poised for his kiss; his breath makes little draughts on me.

Seconds pass. I open first one eye, then the other. Rob is studying me, just peaceably taking the measure of my face. His eyes have apology written all over them: the kind that would choke you if you tried to voice it. Somewhere far inside me, a cringe slowly unfurls. For a second he tenderly joins his forehead to mine, and we just stay like this in recognition of this thing we can't talk about. And then it's over. The moment gone like it was never there. Rob's attention returns to the dog. I turn back to my vegetables: onion, red pepper. I immerse myself in slicing them, my hand moving fast and furious with the knife. The dog play-growls as Rob roughhouses him. The words line up in me but I cannot speak them. The elephant in the room is sucking the air I need to breathe. I bang a can of coconut milk on the marble worktop, push cubes of chicken around my chopping board. The onions are making my eyes stream. 'You've not seen the green curry paste have you?' I peer into the fridge. My voice sounds fallen. What is lost between us will never come back.

'No,' he says. Then, 'Oh, you mean that green stuff in the jar? Yeah. I think I ate it.'

'What?'

'I had it on toast the other night when you were out with the girls.'

'You had it on toast? Green curry paste?'

'Yeah. Why? What's the big drama?'

I throw up my hands. 'Well how am I going to make curry now, then?'

'Sorry,' he says.

After we eat our curry-less curry in silence, I drag myself upstairs. A pile of clean laundry that I made him bring upstairs yesterday is dumped in the middle of the floor. Well, to give him credit, he did put it on the bed first, but moved it to the floor later so he could get into the bed. Rob will happily leave it there, just wearing things from it then taking them off again until the pile replaces itself like an exhibit for the clothing cycle of life. You'd never think he was a slob when you see him in his spanking white T-shirts, with his thing for Italian leather shoes. Nor when you see the fastidious pride he applies to his job as a self-employed carpenter who can build anything from a chair to the house it's going in. I'm not particularly tidy myself – kitchen junk cupboards will attest. But picking up my own mess after a long day is one thing; picking up his makes me want to kill him. Sometimes I'll chase him around the house, smacking him with a towel, shouting, 'I'm not your bloody mother!' Mostly, though, I just tend to do everything myself, because it's less tiring than arguing about it.

I pick his dirty work jeans off the newly washed white duvet cover I just put on – *scream!* – and experience the urge to wring his neck with them. Then I catch myself. I'm projecting my anger on to something else – on to dirty jeans and clean laundry – rather than dealing with what's really wrong. *Get over yourself, Jill. It's hardly the end of the world that he didn't ravish you on the chopping board. Just go downstairs and tell him it's time to talk.*

Downstairs, Rob is staring through the window watching Kiefer having a pee. 'I hate how he squats. I think somebody's going to have to show him how to do it like a man.' He looks at me now. 'How's your finger?'

'It fell off.'

He reaches for my hand, kisses it. 'A four-digit wife. I've always wanted one.'

There, once again, I have opened my mouth, but the words just evaporate.

CHAPTER THREE

Rhododendrons are abloom in gardens as I drive my mam and dad to the beach. It's one of the first really warm days of the year.

My dad has dressed her in a pink and lime-green sundress with a green cardigan. He's put too much blusher on her cheeks, though, and her lipstick is bleeding over her lip-line, making her look like a drag queen.

'How is David?' she asks. This has to be the tenth time she's said this in as many minutes.

'Rob, Mam. My husband's Rob.'

'David,' my mam says, with an infatuated sigh. 'David is a lovely boy.'

We park opposite a stretch of white Georgian town homes and the Seaburn Hotel, where my dad used to bring us for Dover sole and claret for my mam's birthday. My mam is carrying a bag – the lunch she said she'd packed us. I was very impressed until I saw it was actually a bag full of toilet rolls. 'Well, we're going to really enjoy those,' I said. Reflexively, I sometimes catch myself treating her like a child, and I know how much she would hate that. We truck over to a spot of sand in front of the white pavilion, and set up camp. My dad troops off to buy us ice cream from the van, but comes back empty-handed saying the driver was picking his nose. 'He was in it up to his elbow!' I roll my eyes. Our family clearly never got the couth gene.

We sit for maybe half an hour. Mam delves into the carrier and asks me, with the haughtiest disdain, why on earth have I brought toilet rolls, and where are the sandwiches?

'I'm going to go and get us a sandwich from Morrisons,' my dad says. But I tell him I'll go. I brought him here to try to relax, plus I feel like taking a walk. They've done wonders to the seafront since I was little. New pubs, Italian restaurants and designer fountains front on to cinder-toffee sand and swelling green-blue waves, like bolts of velvet in an upholstery store. I pass the amusement arcades and the fairground rides with the music blaring and the kids' high-pitched squeals. In the supermarket, I zip around filling a basket, and in the checkout queue I think of the conversation with Rob yesterday about how Michael Irving had stood over my desk pointedly fingering through my *Hello!* magazine that was on my in-tray. 'He was doing it to imply that I read magazines instead of getting on with my work.'

'He probably fancies you, so he's awkward around you and he hides it by being a bit of an arsehole. Men are like that; especially married ones because they feel guilty. So they want to act like it's your fault for being too much of a temptation.'

'Speaking from experience are you?'

'What else would I be speaking from?' He gave me his sly smile. Then he said I shouldn't have magazines on my desk though, so I had it coming. So then we got into a fight. He said if I was that sensitive about it, maybe it was because I knew he was right.

I pay, then I march briskly out of there.

I vaguely register that there's a lifeguard sitting on a lookout post by the shore. I get back to the beach where our chairs are and . . . oh no. 'Have you seen an older couple?' I ask some kids playing nearby. 'They were sitting right here.'

'No, missus,' the cute little one says.

I dump my shopping on the chair and hotfoot it across the sand to the toilets. I shout in the men's and then look in the women's, but nothing. The beach is vast and I can't see them anywhere I look. Then I remember the lifeguard. I hasten down the sand in pursuit of his yellow T-shirt.

'I wonder if you might have seen my parents.' I have to peer up at him because the sun is in my face. But I do happen to notice the pronounced muscles of his legs. He is wearing sporty-framed sunglasses, but he suddenly slides them down and his eyes meet mine over the top.

'I seem to have lost them.'

He's handsome. Surprisingly older, at least forty, with a yachtsman's weathered complexion, black hair that looks wet and raked back off his face, and intelligent, inquisitive eyes the colour of new pennies. Then he smiles, a demolishing testosterone smile.

What's so funny? 'It's not amusing,' I say.

'Forgive me. No. I am just . . . it is shock.'

He is looking at me in a way that I can't fathom. As though he knows me. He has an accent. I've never seen him before in my life.

He peels off his sunglasses properly now and climbs down from up high where he was sitting. And I can't help but notice the small everyday fact of his having a body like a god.

'My mother suffers from dementia and is prone to wandering off. I need to find them.'

'Of course,' he says, after a moment. 'I will help.'

We start walking back down the sand towards our chairs. More people have arrived – a couple of huge families – and it's hard for me to see past them. But then . . .

'There they are!' I am in disbelief. My mother is eating an ice cream as though she's never been anywhere else.

'She really wanted one!' my dad says. 'I decided what you don't know can't hurt you.'

My jaw drops, and then the lifeguard says, 'If you wanted the lifeguard to come talk to you, you could have just ask.' He grins diabolically again.

I am too busy looking at him like I don't quite know what to say, when my mother lights up, 'Oh, David!' A glowing beam of recognition comes over her face.

'Oh, darling!' The lifeguard spreads his arms for her, which makes my dad and I fold up laughing.

My mother launches into a chorus of 'You'll never miss your mother till she's GONE!' I do not know this extrovert person.

This man must think we're certifiably mad. 'Sorry,' I tell him. 'All this seems a little bit crazy, but it appears we don't need you any more.'

His eyes don't leave mine. 'That's a shame,' he says, boldly. 'I was just coming in useful.'

His face is strikingly gorgeous, though I am trying hard not to stare. A beautiful mouth. Lips like cut glass. The kind of breathtaking good looks you just don't see every day. So when you do, well, you have to let yourself appreciate it.

'Have a toilet roll.' My dad holds one out.

'What's your name?' this man asks me.

'Her married name's Benedict,' my dad says.

The lifeguard smiles again and I'm both impressed and embarrassed that he's taking it all in good humour. But he's still not leaving!

Go! I think, but tell him, 'Jill,' nonetheless.

'And I'm Andrey,' he says.

'Andrey,' I repeat, thinking, *Where have I heard that name before?*

He is watching me closely, his eyes sweeping my face like the second hand of a clock.

Something is wrong with this. Is he someone I could have met through work? 'Wait a minute . . .' I try to search my memory. 'Do I know you?'

He beams a smile now. 'You could have. But you never called.'

It takes a moment. And then I am knocked over by a feather. Andrey! Now I know where I've heard that name before! 'But – but . . . hang on.' I can barely get my words out. 'You can't be the person who left the note on my car!'

My dad coughs as though to remind us he's still there.

'Why not?' he says. 'Walk with me.' He pronounces it *valk*. 'Come on. I know you will die of curiosity now.'

I laugh. 'No! I actually won't!' This is faintly idiotic. 'But you're not the driver of a Mercedes SL 500!' For some odd reason, I start walking with him.

'Because I do this for a job?'

Before I am in the embarrassing position of having to say *well obviously!* he says, 'There is more to people than what they first might seem, you know. Surely I don't have to tell you this . . .' He looks me over. 'Disappointing!' But then he quickly adds, 'But as it happen, you are right. I don't drive expensive Mercedes. I drive car that was parking opposite Mercedes. I was witness to your terrible parking and I saw an opportunity.' His face launches into the craziest, most attractive, lascivious smile again.

'This cannot be! This is surreal.' I am shaking my head. He seems to find this amusing.

It's funny, though – I am aware of how buoyant life suddenly feels. I am thoroughly charmed. It's like I'm floating on another plane. *Get a grip!* I think to myself. I hear the distant echo of my mother's words. *Don't look too flattered or he'll think nobody has ever found you attractive before!*

'I was curious to see if you would call. Never can a woman resist man with nice car.'

'Hmm. Seems this one can!'

'You want to know rest of story?'

'There's more?'

He gestures for me to come closer, as though he wants to whisper in my ear. As if! 'The night of the car was not first time I see you. I see you before Christmas I think it was. In Afterglow bar. In red trouser suit. You were with friends. Women friends.'

Leigh, Wendy and I went there for our Christmas meal! He remembered the red suit! I spent a fortune on it and thought I looked fantastic in it, and all night Leigh kept calling me Mrs Claus, which was amusing until it became really annoying and I started to want to put the suit in a bin and set fire to it.

He stops walking and looks at me. I am paralysed there, in a form of friendly, playful suspense.

'I . . . I don't know what to say,' I tell him. 'You have a very quirky memory.'

'I think the credit is all yours.' And when he looks me over again I feel the effect of his eyes right to the soles of my feet.

We have walked back to his lookout post. I have so many questions. I want to ask him where he's from, why *is* he doing this job when he's older and seems – I don't want to judge, but – brighter than one would have guessed your average middle-aged lifeguard would be. 'I suppose working here you must see a lot of people you see around town,' is all I can manage.

'No.' He shakes his head. 'If you are asking if this happens before, then no. I can tell you honestly that it never has.'

'Hmm.' But believing him feels like I was born yesterday.

'The surprise is as great for me too,' he adds. 'I know you must return to parents, but will I see you again?'

I get the strong sense that he is hoping. 'Well, at this rate, I would say it's a sure bet.'

We smile at my attempt to turn an embarrassing situation humorous. The smile, the eye contact . . . they both linger for one or two moments more than they should. It strikes me that I'm flirting. I had forgotten how good it feels.

'Well, all I can really say is I hope you will come back. Life is short, you know.'

I am just wondering what he means by that when he adds, 'You know, if I hadn't seen a wedding ring that night I would have talk to you. But with friends there, and wedding rings . . . is not so easy.' He shrugs, then adds, 'Even for me,' in flat-out recognition of his being a bit of a Don Juan. 'When I saw you again with car . . . it was too miraculous, you know? I think, if she unhappy married, perhaps she call.'

He meets my eyes now, but something ever so slightly changes in the air. *Hmm! Because somebody puts a phone number on my car I'm going to ring them for a roll in the hay?*

The smile slides, not too inconspicuously, from my face, even though I recognise I'm having a massive overreaction. I'm sure he didn't mean it that way. Perhaps it's my guilt kicking in. Flirting with an obvious ladies' man on a beach when I am married – it's beneath me.

'But I'm not unhappily married,' I say, perhaps a trifle more priggish than I intended. 'So there we have it.'

So there we do. For a second I catch confusion and slight exasperation in his expression.

I don't want to look any more. Trying really hard not to appear any sillier than I already feel, I turn and make a bold effort at walking smartly back down the sand, aware that, for a moment or two, he continues to look at me.

Jill! I think. *You sad little attention-seeker.*

So that little dalliance lived and died a short, sharp death. Shame. It was nice while it lasted.

CHAPTER FOUR

Newcastle won. It was a good game, as matches go. Free tickets are one of the perks of my job and I'm almost certain that's the only reason Rob stays married to me. I grab his arm and dodge Michael Irving and his wife as they come out of the private box from which the manager's family and the other football elite view the game. 'With an arse on her like that, no wonder he's after you,' Rob says. We file out with the crowd that'll soon be stampeding down Northumberland Street like a herd of manic zebra chanting *Howay the Lads!* – the local anthem.

Rob's going away tomorrow to suss out a contract job for some show homes in Penrith, so we won't be late home. Besides, we can't leave the puppy for long. 'Don't want him getting depressed,' as Rob said.

'Or he might do something really terrible like phone the Samaritans and hang himself with his rope toy when they can't make sense of his bark.'

'You're a hard-hearted woman,' my husband playfully scolded me.

We walk around town looking in shops. Then we pop into the Italian ice-cream parlour run by two brothers that serves good coffee in the former Lloyd's Bank building. The young one openly flirts with me and barely gives Rob the time of day. 'Midgety little git,' Rob mutters under his breath as we take our coffee and amaretto cookie over to the last free window table. 'Another one of the flies, is he?' One of his crude running jokes. He says I am like dung. I attract all the flies.

'Jealousy becomes you!' I grin at him.

As we leave, the Italian shouts, 'Ciao, bella!'

'Why does he think you're called Bella?' Rob squeezes me, gives me his sly smile.

The sun brings people out in droves. We wander around, enjoying it, then decide to go to a Quayside restaurant for a meal. But first I go back and buy the pair of white jeans I tried on earlier. You could never call me an impulse shopper. 'Does my bum look big in these?' I model them for him again.

'That, and your thighs are rubbing together.'

'Perfect.' I hand over my forty pounds.

Walking down Grey Street, Rob stops to gaze at its subtly descending curve, and the ancient sepia-coloured buildings on either side that seem to stand on military parade. 'I've always loved this city,' he says. He seems a little flatter than usual, nostalgic.

'Come on.' I take hold of his hand and drag him, but then I conveniently forget to let go.

We disappear under the footbridge and come out at the Quayside. I'm just thinking how we haven't had a fun day like this in ages when we cross the Blinking Eye Bridge. A handsome young father barrels towards us with his kid in a pushchair, wheels rumbling across metal, the little lad squealing with the thrill. I happen to look up at Rob. And I see it. The quiet anguish.

When we were first married we didn't really talk much about having children. I think it was a case of us both assuming we were too young, and probably equally assuming that when we did try for a baby, one would come on command. You do, don't you? You never imagine that the most natural thing on earth is not going to come so naturally to you. Rob never seemed massively sentimental about having children. I've seen him actually grimace at babies and say things like, 'God, it's got a face like a worm-eaten sprout.' Or, 'Eat, sleep and shit, that's all they do. You can't have a conversation with them.' But then, about five years into our marriage, he started dropping hints. 'Should we paint the second bedroom neutral, until we know which sex we're having?' Then I caught him making a crib, a beautiful, sleek thing with soft edges made out of bone-coloured wood. 'Just testing my skill set,' was his explanation.

Then Wendy's little Nina was born severely premature, making the possibility of her living as fragile as a snowflake on the plume of a feather. There were so many problems, but she kept bouncing back. Then she had to have part of her liver removed. In some ways, because we were all so close, I felt so in step with every twist and turn in the agonising drama. I'd come to love the baby and was so invested in her living that I found myself developing a little silent claim on her. Arrogantly I would think to myself, if she makes it, it's because I willed it hard enough . . . But then she died. She died before our eyes and I just couldn't get over it. I am sure I reacted way more strongly than I probably should have done, considering I wasn't her mother. I felt I had to hide my grief from Wendy because I wasn't really entitled to it. But it made me certain of one thing. We had to try to have one of our own.

We tried for over a year. I got tested and was fine. Then Rob got tested and found out he had a problem. 'Total sperm count: zero,' he read to me from the piece of paper that came in the post. We trooped off to see two specialists. I couldn't get my head around the diagnosis. I thought that if Rob could ejaculate he had to have sperm. Some sperm. Enough to do the job. I kept thinking of the gynaecologist talking me through what I saw on my pelvic ultrasound, how mesmerised I was to see my body preparing to create life. How sad now that my little eggs would be like the French Lieutenant's Woman in that film, wandering the shores of my fallopian tubes, waiting for a lover who wasn't coming. It left me bereft to think I'd never have the sights, smells and tastes of being pregnant like other women. I didn't go potty and stalk maternity wards or steal babies at bus stops, but I'd take strange dislikes to food, my breasts would be tender and a strange brewing feeling took up tenancy in my stomach. 'I have to be pregnant,' I said to Rob. 'Why do I have morning sickness? Why is my period late?' Rob would get annoyed. 'Azoospermia! I have no sperm! You're not bloody pregnant!' And then my period would come and I'd plaster on a happy face for Rob, but inwardly I'd massively mourn that baby I'd been so sure I was having. I felt like they say amputees feel when they lose a limb – knowing it's gone but feeling it's still there. Then I'd say, *Jill, snap out of it; you can't miss what you've never had.* But you can. You can grieve without having lost.

But here's my secret. I never actually bared my soul to Rob about this. I could see how sad and guilty he felt and I didn't want to add to it by showing him the full scope of my devastation. But he must have guessed. 'You can leave me, you know,' Rob said one night when we were trying and failing to fall asleep. 'If you left me for somebody who could give you a baby, I wouldn't think badly of you one little bit.' I felt one of his tears roll into my hair. 'I'd still love you, but with the best will in the world, I'd let you go. And if I saw you walking down the street one day with your new husband and your child, a part of me would feel nothing but joy for you.'

'Of course I'm not going to leave you!' I told him. 'It doesn't mean that much to me. Honestly. You're my life. Not some baby that I've never consciously wanted until someone said I couldn't have it.' I planted protective kisses on him, trying to make that feeling go away, of catching myself in a lie. Because I did have my moments where I'd see my life in scenes with some other husband: leaving Rob today, meeting someone else tomorrow, marrying him Thursday and having his baby by the weekend. I'd just have to look at a man with his child and find him instantly more attractive, because he was virile. My old criteria for a partner – tall, dark, handsome, sense of humour, job, no beer belly – seemed a naive and distant second to that glorious F-word: fertile.

Infertile. Childless. Barren. We can't have children. At some point we'll have to get round to telling everybody. But Rob doesn't want to yet, so I have to respect that.

And I'm OK about it. Ish. I've stopped wanting what he can't give me. Almost. I suppose I'm like that. I can still feel like a woman without being a mother. And I still have a family because I have Rob. Besides, we could always adopt, which we've not talked about yet – because, well, we've not talked.

Because Rob has taken it badly. Rob has come to obsess about what he can't have. Rob feels a failure. Rob feels less than a man. Rob would never tell me this. But I know. After all these years with somebody, you know the things they cannot say. You feel the things they can't feel. Maybe that's why he's gone off sex. Maybe it reminds him of his failure – or *our* failure. I try not to focus on it. I keep thinking, *Give it time*. But then I just get impatient to have everything be good between us again. The few times we have made love since we found out, our inability to make a baby has lain there between us, like some third wheel on a date. I worry we will never get past this. That the time will come when he'll want to be in the arms of somebody who doesn't have this history with him, who doesn't sometimes burst into tears when they're in bed with him.

And I bleed for him. I bleed for us because we've fallen into this dark place. And I just want to make him all right again, see him happy again, but I don't know how.

Now, on this bridge, since seeing that dad and his kid, all the joy seems to have been wrung out of him, leaving only a sad and pensive shell. I take his warm hand as we arrive on the Gateshead side in front of the Baltic Centre. The sun has been dramatically exchanged for that thin quiet rain that soaks you in seconds. A girl is quickly packing a harp into a case as people scatter on to buses that are switching their lights on. We go inside to take cover, stand by the window and watch it coming down. We do this without speaking. When it eases off we leave. On our way back across the Blinking Eye, I can feel his sadness; it is palpable. All because of seeing a father with his son. I don't know what to say to him, so I just take his hand in mine again and give it a reassuring squeeze. 'Thank you,' he says, as though we have just undergone some sensitive thought transference. 'I love you, you know.' His thumb massages my knuckles.

We stop halfway over and listen to a Newcastle that seems to have grown louder in the rain. To the right of us is the floating nightclub boat. People often ask us how we met. You always feel pressured to have some wildly far-fetched or romantic answer. And we don't. Apparently, I was standing on the edge of the dance floor with a group of mates, in my buttoned-up blouse, with my poodle perm that was so trendy at the time, and Rob thought, *There's a rose among thorns.* And then when I smiled at him – because apparently I smiled and I don't even remember – he said to himself, *Please, God, let this work.*

It sounds like a non-story, yet everyone always coos when he gets to the part about asking God to make it work. So I feel bad giving my version after that. That I thought he was too introverted. Too proper. Too *Heathcliff*, with his tumbling dark hair, intense sapphire eyes, and his quiet, almost lurking, way of watching me. But then I found he had a sense of humour. I uncovered it, completely not expecting it to be there, and then he transformed before my eyes. And we just sort of clicked. Then he seemed to get cheekier, and we clicked more. And all my friends kept saying how good-looking he was, so I thought, *Well, I'd better cotton on to that soon, too, because I don't want them thinking I'm strange.* When he proposed, we were in a Chinese takeaway waiting for the one order they'd forgotten, so we opened a pile of fortune cookies. My first one said, 'If you learn from your mistakes, you will learn a lot today.' Rob threw it over his shoulder. 'Blargh! Life lessons! Next!'

The next one – his – said, 'Hidden in a valley beside an open stream, this will be the type of place where you will find your dream.'

'Right then. Don't like valleys.' He tossed that one too.

My next one said, 'A very attractive person has a message for you.'

'Clearly wrong.' I glanced around. 'I see no very attractive person here.'

His last one he read right as the food arrived. Then he promptly knelt on the floor.

'What on earth are you doing?' I asked.

He showed me the little piece of paper.

If you have something good in your life, don't let it go.

'I'm not letting you go,' he said.

An aeroplane passes noisily overhead, pulling me out of my memory. A train slides over the bridge on its way to Sunderland. Everybody moving, going somewhere, except, I sometimes think lately, us. I climb my free hand up his arm, feel the downy hairs. I married the love of my life, the first, the only. And when I fell for him, it wasn't because I was thinking I wanted to have his babies. I was thinking that I love him and I can't imagine ever letting him go or not seeing him again. I am so happy when I'm with him. I am this lit-up person.

The other day I asked him why he never dances with me in the supermarket any more – he would do silly stuff like that, pull me into him while I was loading the trolley with discount wine and boxes of fish fingers, dance me on the spot, while I laughed and pushed him away, and people passed and smiled. Not so long ago he'd have thought nothing of kissing me on this bridge in broad daylight.

'Rob . . . ?' I gently nuzzle up to him, my breasts press into his arm. He stiffens, pulls away slightly, but enough for me to notice, so that no part of his body is touching mine any more. Then he seems to register what he's just done and puts a friendly arm across my shoulders. We stand without speaking and stare at big ships.

We eat at a new Asian place that opened in a reinvented garage behind St Mary's Church. The food's good, but the atmosphere is decidedly too funky for our mood. I push chicken around my plate with a fork. The things we can't talk about speak in a voice so loud that it drowns out even our ability to chit-chat over dinner. All this – what? – because he saw a man and his son? Or was it because I snuggled up to him on the bridge? We sit here like two empty eggshells. I keep looking at him hoping he'll say something, but his eyes are fixed in a blank stare while he chews food he doesn't even taste.

There's a couple at the next table, a good-looking pair a little younger than us, drinking matching orange cocktails. She's got one of those elfin haircuts and is effortlessly sexy. They're not saying all that much either. But a cross-current runs between them, in their silences, their glances, their occasional knowing laughs. There is heat between them. And I can't keep my eyes off them. A lump rises in my throat that I can't swallow back down. I know they know I'm watching, but my fascination outweighs my manners. As we leave and I slip into my jacket, I glance over again. The girl is slowly climbing her bare toes up his trouser leg.

'Rob, I think it's time we talked,' I venture gently, when we get home and go and sit in our sunny front room. There, I've said it. The evening light is making it harder for me to see his face properly and easier therefore to confront him.

'Oh, Jill, don't go spoiling a nice day.' He tussles with Kiefer, as though trying to block me out.

'We *have* had a nice day, Rob. A lovely day. This is why we have to talk.'

He sighs. 'What about?'

My heart cracks. 'About why you don't want me.'

'Want you?' He looks genuinely surprised. 'What are you talking about? Of course I want you.'

'But you obviously don't want to be intimate with me any more. You don't fancy me.'

I can read all that pain backed up in his serious, kindly blue eyes. 'Where has this come from? Fancy you? Of course I fancy you. I've always fancied you. You know that.'

'Then why won't you make love to me? We never even kiss any more, and when I initiate it you always turn me down! Have you any idea how unfeminine it makes me feel when you keep rejecting me, Rob?' The words fall out sounding inevitably shallow and callous. I didn't mean for them to. Perhaps this is why I have avoided this conversation until now.

He suddenly looks shocked, tired, waxy-pale, completely done in. I've emasculated him. That was not my intent. 'Reject you? When have I rejected you? We've always had sex. I don't know what you're going on about.'

Does he really not? I am almost lost for where to take this next. He picks up Kiefer's rope toy and offers him it, catching his knuckles sharply on the coffee table, but he doesn't even flinch. The dog latches on and they play tug of war. I watch them in disbelief. I can tell he's upset, annoyed even, but I can't let it go now. 'Rob, it's been five months. You've not touched me in all that time. Do you honestly think that's normal? Is it normal that we've not even talked about it?'

The dog's growls grow louder with Rob's encouragement. 'I need to feel like I have a husband . . . How do we live together just tiptoeing around each other? Around *this*? How do I condition myself to be sexually unaware of the man I love? Tell me, because I don't know. I don't know how to act around you any more.' I rub my face hard with both hands and when I look up he is watching me, just holding the rope toy steadily as though he's not even aware of it any more. 'If you take the sex out of a marriage there has to be a whole new set of rules and codes of conduct. But I don't know what they are!'

'I don't know what you're babbling about! Rules and codes of conduct? What the . . . ?' He just shakes his head, looks at me as though he is genuinely mystified. But I see something in his expression. A lack of truthfulness with himself.

I try to calm down. 'Rob, you won't tell me what's wrong. I can't get a handle on you any more. I don't know what you're thinking. What's happening with us? You recoiled from me on that bridge. It was like you couldn't bear the feel of my body. Is it something I'm doing wrong? Tell me and I'll change. I'll do anything. Rob, look at me!'

He looks at me with sad hostility. 'I don't know what you're on about. Recoiled? On the bridge? When?'

'Are you playing a game with me now? What's this about?'

He looks away, vulnerably.

'You can't withdraw from me like this. It's cruel. And unfair. And you're not like that. This is what I don't get. It's like . . . it's like your heart's not in it any more. In this. In me. In our marriage . . . It's as though because we can't have a family, you don't want *me*. I'm not enough.'

'Oh, give over! My heart's not in our marriage? This is insanity! Maybe you've been spending too much time with Leigh.'

I happened to tell him the other day that she seems a bit down on her marriage.

'What?' This incites rage. Does he really think I'm influenced by Leigh, for God's sake?

I get up, go to the window, my heart hammering. I hear the beat of it in my ears, drowning out even the sound of the dog.

'Is there somebody else? Is that what it is?' I don't know why I am saying this.

He gets up abruptly. 'That's it! Now you're being ridiculous! This is ridiculous! I'm not listening to it any more.' He storms off through the arches into the kitchen.

I quickly pad after him, with Kiefer following. He snatches his car keys off the windowsill and walks down our passage to the front door. 'Where are you going?'

'Out!'

'I won't let you run away.' I kick my slippers off and waggle a foot into one of my trainers; Kiefer takes off with the other one, thinking we are playing a game.

'I'm not *running* away! I'm getting away. From you!'

'I'm coming with you!' I wrestle my shoe off the dog.

'No, you're not.' He throws a hand over his shoulder, dismissing me.

I try to snatch the keys off him and he sends me a look that's filled with frustration and despair. 'Grow up!' he says, taking my hand off his.

He goes to open the front door, but I try to block him. My heart is thumping. Part of me wants him to just shout and get really mad because at least it's some show of emotion, isn't it?

'Don't go,' I plead, when I know I'm not winning here. 'I swear, if you walk out now, don't come back.' I don't mean it.

'Don't be a drama queen,' he says. He grabs hold of my shoulders then gently slides me out of his way. I make a grab for his arm again, but he's already outside. I run after him, thinking about hurling myself on to the bonnet if I have to. I don't recognise myself. I've become a raving lunatic.

'Come back,' I beg. I don't want him getting in a car and driving when he's angry. Nosy Meghan Thomas from down the road passes with her pink-nosed bulldog and glares at me over our hedge. When she's moved along, I burst into tears. Rob backs out of the drive. I go inside and the house feels so empty now. I always recognise my deep love for Rob in these dark moments after we fight, where there's the possibility I might have lost him. I wait to see if he's going to come back. He'd do this after our petty little spats. Walk out. Drive off. Get to the end of the street and turn around. The second he'd walk back in that door, we'd both know all was forgiven.

But he doesn't come back. I sit on the bottom stair. Kiefer sits on the dusty parquet and growls at me because I've upset his lord and master. Then I realise something. For the first time I'm angry with Rob more than I feel sorry for myself or for us. And I'm helpless more than I'm optimistic. My bag is under the hall table. I dig in it for a hankie and come across a piece of paper.

Andrey and a phone number. I never did throw it in the bin.

CHAPTER FIVE

'They had a row yesterday, Leigh and Clifford.' Wendy polishes off her second glass of wine while I am barely down my first. Rob's worked late all this week. You could say he's avoiding me. 'Jill, I didn't know what to do. It was totally odd, perverse behaviour for two adults who work together.'

'What was it all about?' I must say, it's fascinating being given a view of Leigh's working world from an insider's perspective.

'Well, Leigh was telling me *Fatz* isn't a popular brand with size 16+. But he's quashed her idea to launch a "Thin's Not In" fashion show, saying you'll never sell any woman on the concept that fat is more acceptable than thin. Leigh said she wasn't trying to change people's perceptions about body image, she was only trying to find a fun way of selling fitness wear to "normal" people, i.e., those of us who don't look like catwalk models. I saw some of the models she had in to audition. They were Nigella Lawson types – which was supposed to say you don't have to be thin to wear the *Fatz* brand.'

'What's wrong with that?' I can't imagine caring about anything so trivial.

'Well the opposite of thin isn't "normal", is it? I mean, I'm a size fourteen, and I'm normal. By saying "Thin's Not In" and showing somebody like me, well, it's supposed to be liberating and legitimising me, but really it's just saying I'm somehow unacceptable. It just perpetuates the notion that if you're not a twig you're not good enough.'

The waiter slaps our pizzas down. I'm ravenous, but Wendy is far more interested in conversation than food.

'I would have thought if you're making a powerful statement like "Thin's Not In", you need to have some very real-looking people who are genuinely large and proud of it.' She taps her knife handle on the table. 'I hinted this to her, but she said there was no way *Fatz* clothing was going to be seen dead on a load of "heifers".'

'She didn't say that!'

'She did. But the very point of the show was to attract heavier people to the brand! So, see what I mean? Sometimes her thinking doesn't make sense.' She rotates her pizza plate between her hands, like it's a steering wheel. 'If it were me organising it, I'd have the fashion show, but I'd get rid of this "Thin's Not In" business. I'd put a wide range of body types up there to show that it's all about the clothes not the weight, and *Fatz* is for everybody. Then you're making it a positive thing rather than fixating on this tiring issue of thinness.'

'Makes sense. Seems like an awful lot of drama to sell exercise pants, Wend, if you ask me.'

She mops some of the oil off her pizza with her napkin in her endless battle to stay on the right side of 'voluptuous minus the big chest', as she puts it. I'm hoping this is a sign we're going to start eating.

'Well, poor Leigh's done months of work for the show that he was previously all for, and now he's calling it off. He got hysterical when she told him he was listening too much to his silly showbiz friends and not thinking for himself. He tends to zoom around the place in some battery-operated tizzy-fit, his face turning as pink as his velour tracksuit.' Wendy does an impersonation with her hands. 'Poor Leigh seemed embarrassed that I'd seen him belittle her. Because he did say some pretty horrid things.'

'Like?'

She picks a skin of mozzarella off her pizza. 'Oh, I hate telling tales out of school.'

'But you can this once.'

'He called her a bag.'

I frown. 'Maybe he was talking about her handbag?'

'No. That was actually the kindest thing he said about her! I pretended I wasn't listening. I picked up the phone and had a very long conversation with a dial tone. Acted like I was sure this sort of outrageous, juvenile behaviour is part of any office.'

'It's certainly not part of mine.' I drop an oily mushroom on my white jeans. *Damn!* 'So it hasn't put you off working there?'

'Mmm . . . No. As long as nobody is behaving like that with me, then, as Neil said, I've got nothing to worry about, have I? Besides, Leigh and I went for lunch right after. She told me how she used his private toilet the other day and saw what she thought was toothpaste by the hand basin. It was Preparation H. We had a good laugh.'

I grin. 'Have you ever thought about going back and finishing your degree?' Wendy was halfway through a degree in law when she fell pregnant with Nina.

She twists her mouth sideways, the way she will do when expressing frustration. 'I do think about it sometimes. But then again I think aspirations to be a lawyer were part of my distant past. And if I really, really wanted to be one, why haven't I tried before now?'

'You did try. You began your degree.'

'Oh, well. There's that. I started and I gave up.'

I've often sensed a bit of a mystery around this issue. As though there is more to it than she is telling. I often wonder if perhaps Neil is against the idea.

She asks about me now. I keep it fairly benign – the usual suspects: my parents, my boss, the neighbours, the puppy and how he would rather garrotte himself on his choke chain than just stop pulling me. How I'm almost regretting getting him – but how do you say that these days? That you wish you could give your animal back? And I do love him. But mainly when he's asleep. 'So, how's being a working woman fitting with your home life?' I ask her, to get off the topic of me. What I mean is, *How is Neil adjusting to not being the centre of your universe?*

There was a time, a while ago, when I started to resent showing more than a token interest in Neil. It's not as though he's massively sociable with us. In fact, in all the time we've known him, he's never once asked Rob or me a question about ourselves. And I can't believe it's because he's spent endless hours listening while Wendy talks about us, so he knows everything already. He's just one of these people who always seems to be just tolerating being with you.

'Well, I don't think he cares to hear Leigh and Clifford dramas. It's so small compared to what he's got on his mind every day. But things are good. I have to get all my housework done with less time, but we still manage to have a nice dinner with a good bottle of wine.'

That's about the closest Wendy gets to referencing a sex life. Wendy is a private girl. You never know if she gets constipated before her periods, nor do Leigh and I have any idea how many men she's slept with. I think it's a couple at most; Leigh thinks she might be hiding a whole sordid past from us.

'Neil's not sure why I felt the need to work,' she adds now. 'He thought I was doing fine teaching yoga, and it's not as though we're hard up. But he's very supportive in his way.'

Supportive. Yet when an admin job came up at Northumbria Police he didn't want her applying for it. She only ever said it once and it was never mentioned again: 'No one wants to work under the same roof as their partner, do they?'

She slumps back in the seat. 'And after all that talk about fat and thin, you'd better not even ask me if I want dessert.'

'Do you want dessert?'

'Yes.'

We order two tiramisus.

It crosses my mind to mention that Rob and I aren't getting on too well lately, without actually going into details. Perhaps if she'd share something very personal about Neil and her, I would open up. But she'd have to go first. I decide against it. When she opens her purse to pull out her credit card, handsome, supportive Neil is smiling at her from the plastic picture window.

Saturday morning. Our phone rings. I roll over, squint to see the clock. Rob's already gone to work, and it's not even nine a.m. I pat for the handset on the bedside table, dreading it being a mother emergency. Things have been ominously quiet since our day at the beach.

I hear a voice say, 'Help!'

'Good morning, Leigh.' I flop back on my pillow.

'We've got to talk. It's an emergency.'

'Let me guess. You just dreamt you had sex with Clifford. Or you've developed boozer's nose. Or you've bleached your top lip and it's gone blonde and wiry and you think you look like a walrus.' I've heard them all.

'Worse!' she says.

'Well, tell.'

'Can't. L about.'

I yawn loudly. Lately, for the life of me, I cannot sleep.

'I-need-to-see-you. Today. Desperately.'

Leigh loves being cryptic. 'Well, we could always go out for a drink tonight if you feel like it.' I'm suddenly annoyed that Rob has deserted me without any idea of when he'll be back. I'm tiring of the silent treatment – clearly my punishment for bringing up certain topics. In all our marriage, this is the first time we seem to be holding a grudge.

'Tonight? No! It can't wait that long.'

I get out of bed and pull the curtain aside. It's another lovely day. The garden is bathed in sunshine. An overgrown lilac tree gently knocks against our window. Across the fence, next door's bunny nibbles away safely in her hutch. 'Well, how about going through to Seaburn beach? We could go for a bite of lunch, have a walk, then later I can call in on my parents.'

'I love you!' she says.

'I'm going to have an affair.' Leigh's eyes are firing a new brand of devilishness, and are riveted on my face to gauge my reaction.

The glass that was on its way to my mouth almost slips out of my hand.

'I've met somebody, Jill. Somebody . . . Oh!' She makes this *hhh-aar! I'm withering!* noise, then slumps so far down on the bench that she practically slides on to the floor. She stays like that, playing dead.

I stare at her in disbelief. 'I'm not following. Met somebody? Who?'

'A red-hot, hot-blooded male, and he's actually interested in me! It's a miracle.' She wiggles her painted-on arches for eyebrows, fans her face, makes gargoyle expressions, and goes *Whoar!* and *Cor!* like a building-site worker. Then she sits up properly again. I've never seen anybody like this, except maybe Benny Hill.

'I bumped into him on Friday in the bank. He's, well, he's sort of a client of mine. On the retail side. His name is Nick. He's married, like I am, with kids . . . You know, we've met many times, but it was the way he looked at me, Jill, as though he hadn't really seen me until now.' Her face is wistful, mooning. 'It's the funniest thing – we talked more in that bank queue than in all the time I've known him. You know, when we've met in meetings, it's always so formal, obviously. You have to be a little bit careful . . . But oh, there was just such chemistry there!' She holds my eyes and I've never seen her look so fluttery and light. 'He asked me for a coffee. I was taken off guard and I said no. Then he said, "Well, maybe another time." So I'm not sure what to do . . .'

And she's spent the last week analysing whether it's up to her to make a move, or whether she should wait and see if he makes one.

For somebody who manages millions of pounds of sales for a hip company, it seems hard to believe she'd obsess over something that doesn't sound to me like it's worth her energy. 'Well he might have literally just meant go for coffee, and "maybe another time" might have just been his way of politely saying see you later.'

'Ah, but you weren't there, were you? There was intent in those eyes. I know how much he was hinting for it when he said how boring his marriage was.'

'He said how boring his marriage was? In the bank queue?'

She studies me as though she's trying to decide if I either disapprove or disbelieve her, and for a second I think she might turn on me. But then she says, 'I was thinking of getting a hotel room and just emailing him the time, the place and the room number.'

'Good Lord! You can't do that!'

'Why not? He either bites or he doesn't. Then you know. No more suspense.' She does a double take at my shocked face. 'Why? Have you any better suggestions?'

'Do nothing! Keep well away!'

'Nothing? Nothing isn't an option, Jill. All my self-induced orgasms have his face on them.'

I try not to let my jaw drop. 'But you said you'd never have an affair! That they were tacky!'

'I know. But that was before there was anybody to have an affair with.' She does a dirty chuckle, and I honestly do not know what to think or say. Who is this person?

'I tell you, Jill, the thought of sex with him . . . I can't think straight.'

53

'Because it's just happened and you're all flattered and on a high. But it'll pass. You'll forget about him.'

'I've told you, I don't want to forget about him; I want to fuck him.'

Her directness, and the distastefulness of this, slaps me hard. We are not playing around now. She is serious. 'I thought you never wanted to ruin your life? I thought you wanted your life to be so very different from your mother's?'

Her mother met most of Leigh's 'dads' by doing prison visiting. Then, two years ago, Leigh found out she had a twin sister – her mother had kept Leigh, but had given the other baby away. Leigh tracked her down, with Wendy's help, and after a bit of talking on the phone they decided to meet. We drove down with her to Leicester, like the three musketeers, and we all went to the coffee shop where Louise had suggested meeting. Wendy and I sat at one table, which was a very odd feeling indeed, and Leigh sat at another, waiting for Louise to show up. But, sadly and mysteriously, she never did. Leigh couldn't get over it. We drove home and she just kept saying, 'Why does nobody ever really, really want me? All my life I've been made to feel I'm either in the way of somebody's freedom, or I'm not good enough; I'm not really worth loving.' Wendy and I reminded her that Lawrence and Molly don't see her that way. By the time we got home, Leigh said we had to promise her that we would never bring up Louise's name again. And we haven't.

'"A trustworthy, loving family is the greatest gift you can be given," didn't you once say?' I remind her.

'I'm bloody miserable!' It comes out forcefully with more drama than she usually displays. I can tell she's miffed by my lack of support. 'It's not that I choose to be. I just am. I try to count my blessings; it doesn't work. I feel I'm on a precipice. I have to do something to help myself. I would have thought that was obvious to anyone who was really paying attention.'

Meaning me. I hate to say it, but no – it's not obvious. Because I've always just thought that's who Leigh is – high one minute, low the next

– but ultimately she's not about to destroy the one true thing she's got. Not when she's finally found a measure of peace. And I have believed this because she's told me it enough.

'You know I would never fuck up Molly's life like my mother did mine. The ice-cream man moves in on Monday, tells me to call him dad, that he's waited all his life to meet a woman like my mother, then by the weekend all that's left of him is an empty Magnum wrapper.' She chortles, mirthlessly, holding my eyes until I have to smile too, despite it not being funny. I always find it both admirable and bizarre that Leigh can actually laugh off so much of the shitty stuff that has happened to her. Though of course it's probably good that she can. 'I just have to do something purely for me. Not for Lawrence or Molly or Clifford, for me. My happiness counts just as much as theirs, doesn't it? And maybe I'm one of these people who just need more stimulation than life's providing. And maybe I'll get that by having a harmless fling. I just don't think I can shag only Lawrence until the day I die, Jill. I'm tired and I'm uninspired. I badly need a thrill. And it's just one affair. I'm not talking about going on some sexual rampage with every man alive until I'm ninety.'

She's saying it like I might say it's just one more glass of wine . . .

'Anyway, I'm probably more of a sexual person than you and Wendy. And you two are both very happy in your marriages, with your men. But I'm longing for a bit of rough. Lawrence's puniness used to be attractive after I'd been with all those dick-swinging, dick-head boyfriends. I liked him having legs like an eight-year-old Ethiopian. But you know last week he went for a blood test and kept the plaster on for four days! And he kept showing it to me like he'd had open-heart surgery. It's such a turn-off!'

This makes me smile. Normally she'd say something like this, or tell me he was on the Internet all weekend looking for holiday packages to Lapland, and we'd chuckle. But Lawrence's foibles don't feel like a laughing matter right now. I notice, too, that as we have been talking her sparkle has quickly disappeared and she looks almost catatonic with misery now. I actually feel a little sorry for her. This endless chasing of a fleeting self-esteem boost! Her upbringing really did mess her up. As she'll often say, 'You know my mam never once gave me a cuddle or told me I was beautiful.' And I think that's so sad. Because my mother was the opposite. My mother did that every day.

'I hear you, but I'm not sure an affair's the answer, Leigh. I mean, think of what you'll lose in your marriage. You'll reach your golden wedding anniversary knowing you were the Olympic gold-medallist who took steroids. You didn't win a fair game even if you have impressed the rest of the world.'

She just looks at me blankly and blinks. 'Maybe I don't put such a high value on loyalty as you do, Jill. Or maybe I think there are many other ways of being loyal. Ways that more than compensate for the one way that you aren't.'

'But this man's a client, Leigh. You could get fired over it.'

'Oh, nothing like that'd happen!' She swings curtains of black hair off her shoulders. 'I know what I'm doing. I'm going to give it an expiry date. Say, six weeks then it's over.'

I'm still reeling from how calculated all this is. 'But what if you fell in love?'

'You always romanticise everything, Jill. I'm not like that. It'd be strictly the business. We meet, we bang, see you tomorrow. Six weeks, then we both walk away. No harm done. Just something fantastic to look back on.' She takes a long drink, and the spark of excitement is back in her eyes again. 'I mean, don't you think it'd be great?'

I don't know why Leigh's prospect of hanky-panky should suddenly get me feeling all wriggly. 'Maybe. If it worked like that.'

'But I'd make it work like that. I have to, Jill. If I don't do something, I . . . I can't go on.'

'I don't know. Can't you just get a new job? Take a holiday?'

'New job? That job pays our mortgage and keeps Molly in private school and singing lessons and Lawrence at home so he doesn't stress himself into an early grave. And a holiday, well, having to look at Lawrence in a pair of Speedos for a week just makes you die a slow, silent death behind your sunglasses.'

I shake my head at her, fondly.

After a long pause, she says, 'Don't tell Wendy, though, huh, please? I mean, I love her, but you know what she's like. She'd never understand cheating. And that's fine, but I don't need someone's judgement. You know me, I just can't adore like she does. My daughter, yes. But not men. It requires a suspension of disbelief that I'm not capable of. Besides, I wouldn't want it getting out. At work.'

'Of course I won't tell her. It's not my place.' We hold eyes. I can't think of anything the three of us have not shared. Perhaps only in the beginning, when I first introduced Leigh to Wendy, who had been my yoga instructor, initially. Wendy wasn't sure she liked her – until Leigh proved what a good person she was when Wendy lost Nina. But we've been through so much as friends since then that it will be hard to start excluding one of us now.

'I know what you mean about needing something to happen that makes you feel better,' I tell her, with bleak enthusiasm, while we're on a secrets-sharing roll. I tell her about Rob and the infertility. The lack of communication. The lack of sex.

She barely blinks, listens through, without interruption. It's only when I'm done that she says, 'Well, I'm shocked, Jill. I really am . . . Gosh! You're so attractive I'd have said you would have to fight him off every night.' Then she adds, 'Are you sure he's not having an affair?'

'What? Of course not!'

'Well, like you've said, he's always working late. He's gone off sex. Aren't those the two major signs? I mean, I wouldn't think he would be either, because he always seems so besotted with you. But that's the point, isn't it? People aren't always what they seem. And men, even the happiest of them, if they get an opportunity elsewhere . . .'

'Not Rob!' I shake my head, vehemently. I wish I'd never told her. 'You have to understand, since he's taken on corporate clients the whole nature of his business has changed. He doesn't just make furniture any more. Now he spends more time managing subcontractors, doing paperwork, quoting on new business. He's got a lot on his mind. In addition to the infertility.'

'I'm sure you're right,' she says. 'And having no sperm is a big deal for a bloke. I'm sure he feels less of a man. So that's probably why he's gone into a shell.'

'Well, it's not like he's the only man on the face of the earth with that problem!' *Less of a man.* I won't have anybody think that about Rob!

'No, but you know how men are about their penises. It affects them badly, doesn't it? They aren't less masculine because of it, but they feel they are.'

I am shocked to see, though, that her eyes have filled with tears. 'I feel for you both. That's a big cross he's got to bear. And he doesn't deserve it. And neither do you – especially you. None of this is your fault.'

Her pity touches me. I feel bad for feeling annoyed at her. But she has hit on something: this is not my fault. Then she tells me Lawrence once donated his sperm when he was in art college. There could be a million little Lawrences obsessively trying to find themselves and sending daily letters to Father Christmas. We have a good laugh.

Then, out of nowhere, I tell her about my bizarre encounter with the lifeguard.

'So that's why you wanted to come here! You devious devil!'

'No! It's not! Not at all! I told you, I want to see my parents after . . .'

'Right!'

'No! I'm being serious! I mean, it was flattering and everything. To have been remembered like that. He's very handsome. And quite charming. But he's a randy middle-aged lifeguard. What am I going to do with someone like that?'

'I know what I'd do with that!'

'Funny how just talking about him is bringing him alive again.'

'It's definitely a bit of an unusual story. The note. How he saw you twice before in Newcastle, and he remembered your Santa suit . . .' A devious glint of envy appears in her eyes. 'You see, I get someone who just wants to have sex with me. You get the full romance.' She looks sad, briefly. 'Anyway, from what you've said about him it sounds to me like he's got a bit more about him than perhaps his job would suggest. I'd be tempted to find out.'

'We could at least take a walk that way and then I could point him out to you from a distance, if he's there, that is.' I am taking ridiculous delight at the idea of her seeing him – and of seeing him again myself. It's so disloyal to Rob, but then again it's only a bit of fun. 'I mean, if you'd like. I'm not going to crumble if we don't.'

'Don't you think it could be fantastic?' she asks, as we trot out of there, back to being our mischievous teenage selves.

'What?'

She sends me conspiratorial eyes. 'Simultaneous affairs.'

CHAPTER SIX

I'm looking through Leanne's *Cosmo* in my lunch break. 'One Hundred Ways to Turn Your Man On'. I think I read the same article twenty years ago. Apparently I still haven't learned. 'Have you tried any of these?' I ask her.

She squints from her desk across the room. There's a cheese plant behind her chair that looks like it's growing out of her head. 'You wha'?'

I wag the page.

'Turn him on? Got no problems in that department, Jill my dear.'

'Want this pile of rubbish back then?' I'm just about to boomerang it when, as luck would have it, Michael Irving walks in and catches me.

'Jill's a great reader,' he says.

'*Sieg Heil*,' I salute him when he's gone back into his office, and the girls chortle.

I'm just putting my jacket on to go home via the supermarket when my phone rings. It's Leigh, summoning me to Au Bar. 'It's of the utmost urgency,' she tells me.

'Oh,' says Rob, when I ring him and tell him that I'm in Au Bar and I've just ordered a glass of Pinot Grigio and I'm probably going to be eating here too. 'I thought we could have gone out for a meal tonight, as a treat.' It's been ten days since our big fight. It's felt more like ten months.

'Well, you might have mentioned that earlier.' It did cross my mind this afternoon to go home and make a nice meal and try to make up with him when he came home. But it just felt like too much work with no guarantee of me not being left standing there with egg on my face. 'Look, Leigh needs to talk. Something important. I can't get out of it now.' *I didn't think to check with you first,* I'm about to add. *To be honest, given the way you've been acting lately, I didn't think you'd be bothered.* But I don't. Because that'll only hurt us, not heal us. Having the last word is overrated.

'Well, you've made your plans. You can't go back on them,' he says, like the ever understanding person he is, but I can tell he's disappointed. 'I'll just see you later, then.'

There's an awkward pause and then he says, 'I love you. And . . .' A bit more awkwardness . . . 'I'm sorry, Jill. I know things are strained between us—'

Leigh whips in the door. I tell him I must go. I experience an ominous feeling that I'll regret misplacing my priorities. She looks beautiful. Different. Elegant, in a loosely pleated, knee-length little dove-grey skirt with a cream, cowl-neck blouse. The skirt flirts with her legs as she walks, in fifties-style sling-back sandals. 'My God, you look fabulous!'

'We're fucking,' she says, and flops into an armchair, claps both hands over her mouth. When she sees my face, she says, 'Oh, stop looking at me like that!'

'You're joking, right? Surely?'

'Why would I joke? We've been emailing. I sent him one, saying it was nice chatting with you last week, et cetera. He wrote back, said we must do lunch sometime—'

'*Do* lunch? Is that how he talks?' I hate him already.

'He emailed me at eleven o'clock this morning, picked me up at twelve, drove me straight to his house.'

'His house?'

'We didn't exchange a word in the car.' She runs her hand down her throat. Her neck is unusually flushed and blotchy. 'I was barely in his front door when he got me up against the wall and then he was lifting my skirt and sinking to his knees.'

My eyes drop to her skirt hem. 'Good God.' She clutches her bottom lip with her top teeth, and I don't know if she's going to laugh or cry; she is just this strange, unreadable concoction of emotion. Then she starts giddying her feet and doing the Benny Hill thing again, complete with construction-worker noises. We're attracting attention.

'Where's his wife in all this?'

'Oh, she works all hours. Apparently they don't have much sex.'

'And his kids?'

'School. Obviously.'

Her tongue slides out and she play-pants. 'I tell you, Jill, he's wild in bed.'

'Is he?' I try to sound chirpy, like she looks, like she feels, like I want to feel for her, but I thought all that business about this Nick person was a joke.

I accidentally put my wine glass down so hard it nearly cracks. My eyes keep going to the hem of her skirt. I am torn between wanting details and being embarrassed to listen to them. I'm fascinated by the topic of people being good lovers. Having only ever had one, you do sometimes wonder how they compare. 'Why, what's so great about him?' I casually pick up my drink again.

She crosses one leg over the other and I glimpse her white panties. 'Well, for starters we just connect. You know what it's like when there's that instant heat and you just collide in passion?'

Have Rob and I ever collided in passion? Right now, I feel like colliding my brains with a high-speed train.

'The fact that we both have partners, that we're doing something wrong, it just seems to turn the temperature up seven hundred degrees. Phew!' She whistles. 'And Jill, he's got so much stamina. In the space of an hour we did it three times! I've been with men who are purely animal in the sack, but with him . . .' Her normally disenchanted green eyes softly twinkle. 'He's got a tender side. He's lovely. I don't ever remember enjoying the feeling of a man's sexual, urgent body like this. Something as simple and basic as pure lust. His sweat. The scent of him. He's just this big hunk of incredible, undeniable male flesh.'

I stare at my wine glass. I should have just gone home to Rob.

When I look up, she is studying me. 'You think it's bad of me.' Some invisible truth is erected between us.

I shake my head. 'No. I just didn't think you'd do it.' I feel awful for Lawrence and Molly. Did our giggly afternoon put her up to this? Part of me wishes she hadn't told me, yet my heart is still pounding from what she said he did behind that door.

'Well, d'you want to hear the rest or not?' she asks, with friendly blackmail.

'Just don't tell me you did it in his wife's bed.'

She huddles in the corner of the comfy chair, looking self-satisfied, even gloating. 'No, I made him take me into the spare room. Funny though,' she smiles. 'He wanted to.'

Yuck. I hate him. I feel personally offended. As though it were my bed it happened in.

'We did it on the stairs first. I've still got carpet burn.'

The stairs? That film springs to mind, *The Thomas Crown Affair*, with the ever sensual Rene Russo: her and Pierce Brosnan tumbling nakedly all over the house, to that raw, erotic music. It was on TV again two nights ago.

'He took me into the bathroom. Got me on the worktop—' She shudders like she's having an orgasm in the chair. 'Jill it was as though my life and my marriage and everything didn't exist. All the stresses just left me and I was young again. Only, it was better than years ago. Because this time I was there for the right reasons. I was doing it because I wanted to, not because they did.' She becomes distant, lost in reliving it again, and I find myself being fascinated by the sight of her. 'Then it was really weird. He . . . well he did this thing. Over the bath.' She meets my eyes, squarely. 'Maybe this is too much detail for you.'

'I can handle it.'

'Well, he made me straddle the side of the tub so my lower body was, well, you know . . .'

'Not really.' My heart hammers while we hold gazes.

'Well . . . you know how cold the side of the bath is when you sit on it. And you know what that does. The contrast of hot and cold . . .'

I give her my best encouraging blank face.

'We had one foot in the bath and it was the way he . . . rocked me there, then entered me from behind.' She looks at me then does a double take. 'My God, look at your face! You look like your head caught fire!'

I touch my cheek. I am burning up. 'It's the drink.' I try to act casual, bored even, like I've been there and done that a million times before. 'Go on. You were saying.' I pretend to look around the room, as though I am only half interested.

'What you having then?' a busy waitress in a thigh-high split skirt interrupts. *Something I'm not,* I feel like saying, suddenly aware that this story has turned me on. Leigh grabs the drinks list off the table, scans it distractedly while I gobble her up with my gaze. Now I know how eunuchs feel. Nobody is pulling me into the bath for a bit of straddled ecstasy. Nobody is causing all my blood vessels to dilate. I look around this bar: the fit young men and women and all the throbbing sexuality. I feel old, and staid, and like I've massively missed out. Leigh orders a crantini. I feel like so many degrees of separation.

'You won't believe it, Jill.' A gloating grin sets on her face again. 'He's big too.'

Kill me, go on. 'But they say size doesn't matter. It's what you do with it that counts.' Rob always says he's eight inches. But then again, Rob claims he's six feet two. I reach for my wine glass, but can't pick it up because my hand is shaking. I tell her I have to go to the toilet. I bolt into a stall, plant myself against the door. My heart thrashes like the propeller of a helicopter. I stand like this for ages, as this ungodly energy courses through my body threatening to send me off the deep end. When I come out I have to hold my wrists under cold water to cool myself down.

When I go back outside I can't find anything to say. It's like sitting here with a different person, one I'm not sure I have much in common with any more. 'You did use protection . . . ?' I'd hate to think where he's been.

She grimaces. 'It happened so fast. But he says he's clean. He's always been faithful.'

Oh yeah, right. Mr Gymnast of the Bath who took her to his house! Panic for my friend flies in me. I can't believe how naive she's being! But neither can I bring myself to say the famous last words: *Well, he would say that, wouldn't he?* Because if I felt like this, I wouldn't want somebody spoiling it for me either.

'Another thing you're going to hit me for.' She grimaces again. 'I came off the pill, remember? Because of all the headaches I was having. But I think that was just all the stress, when Cliff and I weren't getting on, before Lawrence left his job when his OCD was really bad. So I'm going back on it.' She sees my look of horror. 'Look, Jill, don't be my mother. I know what I'm doing. Besides, now's a safe time. So stop worrying for me.'

'Well, sorry.' She's going to get pregnant. I just know it.

She titters then turns quite serious and wistful again. 'He's nice, Jill. We just click on so many levels.'

'What? Stair levels?' I try not to roll my eyes.

Normally she would have a go at me for this. But now she's got better things to think about. 'You measure yourself by who you're fucking, you know. That's why men always want the pretty young things. Besides, he's alive and charismatic, and he's masculine and he's daring, and he doesn't give a shit. That's why he does so well in his job. And there's something very sexy about that.'

There is, admittedly. I stretch a smile. He sounds horrible. I'm eaten with envy. I look at her knobbly knees and I wonder if she'd have showered before she went back to the office. 'You're going to fall in love. I just feel it in my water.'

'Get out! I told you, this is a fling. I've given it an expiry date. End of the summer, that's it.'

It was six weeks before. It's grown by a month.

'Besides, he's cheating on his wife, isn't he? You know me; I could never be with a man I couldn't trust. I'm far too much of a psychological screw-up for that. Why d'you think I married Lawrence?'

'I thought it was because you were done with the boyfriends, the break-ups, the one-night stands. You wanted steadiness and something real.'

'And he'd never cheat and he'd never leave me.'

'And you loved him.'

'Yes. And I do. But I've always known Lawrence felt lucky to get down my knickers. And at first you sort of get off on feeling like you're doing them a big honour. Then you just think maybe he doesn't deserve to be there.'

God, she sounds so mean! Has she always been this nasty, and I'm just seeing it now? Have I allowed the fact that I can have a really great time with her to blind me to the fact that very often that good time is built at the expense of others? Or has this affair given her confidence to reveal her true self? I wonder if she ever did love Lawrence. Or did she just marry him thinking it would relieve her of all her psychological baggage?

'You know, I'd forgotten what I was capable of with a man until I saw how I was with him today.' She does that dazed stare again. 'It's so different, sex without love, without arguments, without shared history. Just a carefree bonk with somebody you really fancy.'

She stares at my glum face. 'You don't understand me, do you?'

'I do. I understand wanting. I just don't understand doing.'

'Well, maybe I'm just different. I can't take things too cosy or too much the same for too long. What I'm doing with him is just vital to who I am. And I don't have to be proud of it. But I can't deny it either. And I'm certainly not going to be ashamed. I've not murdered anybody.'

It feels like we're brewing to have words. But as though she senses it too, she says a light, 'Roll on tomorrow lunch!'

'At his house again? You can't keep doing that, Leigh! You'll get caught. His wife'll come home. His kids . . .'

'I told you, she works.' She takes the second martini glass off the waitress, unsettling her drinks tray. And as she doesn't offer to get out her money (an occasional bad habit of hers that Wendy and I frequently bellyache about), I pay our bill.

'Although I have to say, the chance that she might . . . it certainly adds to the excitement. Danger is the best aphrodisiac.'

'It wouldn't be for me,' I say. I'm not built that way. I've never known anybody who's had an affair. I just want to sit and stare at her. 'You're all flushed again. I hope that's gone before you see Lawrence!'

She runs a hand exotically down her throat. 'It's been so long since Lawrence gave me a flush, he'd probably think I've got rosacea or the measles. He'll read the doctor's book until he puts holes in the pages.' She flings one leg over the other and I catch another glimpse of her underwear; the underwear that I imagine this Nick peeling off with his teeth. 'I don't know if Rob has ever made me flush.'

She wiggles her eyebrows. 'Well, I bet I know someone who would.'

Walking in through my door, into my faithful marriage, feels like coming into a snug harbour after all that. Kiefer comes running. I stroke him and he pees and I mop it up with a hankie without feeling one ounce of impatience. The TV is on loud. 'Hiya, treasure,' Rob says from the sitting room. *Treasure.* All's forgiven and forgotten about now. He's not even put out that I went out with Leigh. Suddenly I brim with a fresh desire to salvage us. Rob's not having any affair; I don't care what Leigh said. He's suffering, and I regret every wrong word we've ever had. I stand in the doorway looking at him lying on the settee watching the telly. Slobbed out, but handsomely so.

Then I think, does he look all that excited or keen to see me? If it were a choice between me and someone on *Grey's Anatomy*, whose life would he save?

I tell him I'm going upstairs to get changed. My voice sounds strained. I walk into our bedroom, then flop down on the white duvet and just lie there staring at the ceiling. Leigh's having an affair. Part of me still can't believe it. I wonder if a promiscuous past makes it easier to cheat in your marriage. Funny though, it was nice believing that a person's wild and wanton ways could be tamed with the right love. It seemed to make anything possible. Now it all just feels like a big charade.

I strip off, get into my dressing gown, go into the bathroom, stand there and gaze at the side of the bath. I still can't picture what the hell they did. I'm feeling the need for pictures. Would I even want those acrobatics? No. Slow and sensual is more my style.

The adverts are blaring when I go back downstairs, after having applied a tiny bit of perfume. Rob turns the volume down. 'Did you have a good night? What was Leigh's big news?'

'Oh, nothing much.' It's strange lying to Rob. Yet I can't tell him. Leigh told me, not Rob and me. Besides, Rob would be furious if he knew what she was doing or that I was in any way involved. Even though he'd probably think Lawrence had it coming by wearing flowery shirts and believing that in his past life he was a reindeer. 'Room for me?' I squeeze beside him on the couch.

'Something reeks like a tart's boudoir.'

The no-frills side to my husband makes me smile. *Jill*, I think, *this is real. Rob is real. Your marriage is real.* I gingerly cuddle into him, waiting to see what will happen next. The dog drags his cushion to the middle of the floor and starts humping it. 'So is *Grey's Anatomy* good tonight?' I ask, trying to blank out a picture of Leigh and some man with a lovely body and a large never-mind going at it on the stairs.

'Oh, this is an old one I taped. I've seen it before.'

There we go. Me, or a rerun. It's a hard choice.

He tickles my ear and down my neck, and a slow sigh comes out of me as I lose myself to his touch. We stay like this, while I blankly stare at moving pictures. The programme ends after about twenty minutes. 'What are you thinking?' Rob asks.

I'm thinking, *Please just tickle me. Keep your hands there.* 'Oh, nothing really.'

'So what did the two of you talk about? It must have been something, for all these hours.'

'Nothing major.' I uncover a bare shoulder. Rob's hand goes there, instinctively. 'I love it when you touch me like that,' I tell him. His fingers stop moving. I sneak my dressing gown down a bit more, inch up a tad so his stilled hand now finds itself by my breast. The cold air makes my nipple stand out. Not so long ago he'd have got an instant hard-on and we'd have done it doggy-style over the settee. I will him to make a move. Even just a token acknowledgement of my near nakedness. It doesn't have to lead to anything. I just want something to remind me that he's my husband not my brother. He seems to mind-read. His big hand cups my breast. I look down at his bashed-up, working man's knuckles, gridlocked with tension as I wait to see what he's going to do. But he does nothing.

'So was the town very busy tonight?' he asks. He pushes me up and slides out from under me. I freeze there, half sat up, with my breast hanging out, while he goes through to the kitchen and opens the fridge door.

I can't even chirp a 'Not really,' like I might have done in the past to save face. *Jesus, Rob. Jesus!* Kiefer is now in manic humping mode. Even the dog has got a better sex life than me.

I get up, and go upstairs to the bathroom, smarting from the shame of his rejection. I can hear him flicking through TV channels again. If I go back down there and say anything, he'll say, 'Oh, well you can't just expect me to get horny, just like that . . .' And I can't argue with that. Because somewhere in our past I've said similar lines myself. But part of me lives in this dream world where marriage is for lovers, and married sex shouldn't need a schedule – at least once in a while. And I should be able to want intimacy from him without feeling like he must take me for some mad sex pest.

Perhaps my ego is too fragile, or I'm too obsessed with sexually keeping up with the Joneses. If he'd just say, *Look, Jill, this is just a spell. We're going to be OK.* But I don't sense a silver lining; I don't see any hope. I take off my glasses and wipe tears away. I run the bath, turn the lights off, feeling like I'm setting the scene for some very intimate encounter with . . . myself. In the water, I prop my feet on the green tiles above the taps, gaze down my shapely curves to my newly varnished toenails. This body that I try so hard to keep nice for him. Why do other men fancy it and the one man I want to fancy it doesn't? Then my mind goes back to Leigh. Uncharacteristic envy barges in, rattles through me, leaving me stunned from its force. My friend is a good person, yet she can hang her conscience on a coat hanger in a strange man's house.

Maybe I can too.

CHAPTER SEVEN

'Ta-da!' Leigh materialises from the lingerie changing room in Fenwick's, her lithe, boyish body clad in a lacy red bra and pants set. She twirls for Wendy and me and then disappears again, casting me a sly smile over her shoulder. Mistress Discretion she's not.

Wendy whispers, 'What's come over her? Why does she think we care what her underwear looks like?' Through the gap under the door I watch her bare feet step in and out of an array of lovely knickers. Wendy fingers a lacy thong. 'And they're not even on sale.' We both know Leigh will never buy anything if it isn't on sale. We've witnessed her pull buttons off things to get the assistant to reduce it by ten per cent. Yet last year she got a pay rise and spent three thousand pounds on a Rolex. 'The damned thing! Leave it off for two days and you've got to wind it up!' she moaned some time later.

Out she comes again, in a purple and black set this time, sending me looks that say I know something about her. Leigh is normally not a flaunter. Leigh is the type to stare in a mirror and say, *My bags are so big they're becoming my bottom lip.* Or, *I could get skin grafts off a sun-dried tomato and you'd never be able to tell.* But since she's been seeing this

Nick she hasn't made comments like that. She just seems so high on her own fantasticness. It's almost irritating.

'I think you look good in all of them,' Wendy says, then adds under her breath, 'So does the rest of Newcastle.'

Leigh totters back into the fitting room. Wendy and I wander over to another section and Wendy whispers, 'She's been like this at work. So jaunty and happy. And we never go for our fun lunches any more because she's out at "meetings". She keeps asking me to tell Clifford that she's with a client. Anybody would think she was having an affair.'

If I told Wendy, I don't know who she'd think less of – Leigh for doing it, or me for letting her secret out of the bag.

'The other day she mentioned she was off out to see Nick. So I think it might be our client Nicholas Barnes . . . She keeps looking at me enigmatically, like she wants me to ask her something.'

'So ask her. She'd ask you.'

'She already did. The other day she asked me if I've ever had an affair.'

She is clearly itching to tell Wendy. 'What did you say?'

'I said "Who with?" and she seemed to find that funny.'

Leigh reappears and troops off to the till with a hundred pounds worth of new smalls! After that we go to Marks & Spencer for a cappuccino in Café Revive. Not like we need reviving.

The following week it's belly dance class. Venus, our instructor, shimmies and pirouettes, making Egyptian 'pretty hands' in the air, the coins in her hip scarf jingling like I can never get mine to do.

'Now girls, belly dance was traditionally a fertility ritual performed to an exclusively female audience,' she tells us. 'But you might want to imagine you're doing it for your special man.'

I feel like telling her that, actually, I don't have to imagine. I recently spent two days sewing tassels on a bra, and making see-through

Harem pants, then I sat my special man down, lit candles and put on my special 'Awedony' song. Then with my back inches from his face I started shimmying with everything I had in me. When I turned around, he'd gone. I was doing it to an empty chair.

'I don't have the knack,' I tell the girls. 'Belly dance, or St Vitus Dance. It would be a tough call.' They chuckle.

Despite being more of a sporty-girl than a girlie-girl, Wendy is actually great at this. Something to do with her radiating pheromones that come from having curves that her husband appreciates on a very regular basis, I am guessing.

'Clench those Kegels,' Venus instructs. 'Imagine clamping down on a very large penis.' 'Oooooh!' say all us women, and I think, *Yes, chance would be a fine thing.*

'I wish she'd not say things like that,' Wendy scowls.

'I know.' Leigh winks at me. 'It makes me envious for what I don't have.'

'What's that?' Wendy asks her.

'A very large penis.'

Wendy looks Leigh over, deadpan. 'Well that's something you want to be pleased about. You wouldn't look half as good in those exercise pants.'

'Hip drops!' Venus shouts at us. 'Up-thrusts!'

'Hey!' Leigh demonstrates. 'A movement I can do.' She winks at me again.

'Lawrence's going to like those,' I tell her. She sends me a dirty grin.

As we leave the building, four handsome firemen are on their way in and stand aside to let us pass. 'Cor,' Leigh gawps after them. 'If there's a fire in there I think I'll run back inside.' We head to the juice bar for our green smoothies.

'Wend, we really have to think of an exciting PR stunt to open the new Metro Centre store,' Leigh says, apropos of nothing.

'Oh, don't ask me about PR stunts. I'm not very creative,' Wendy's face glows from the exercise and the fun. 'That's your territory.'

'We'll work on something together,' Leigh says. 'But speaking of being *creative*. Jill and I were just having a chat the other day about how to put the spark back into your sex life.'

Were we? I scowl at her. Where is this coming from? I'm getting tired of this cryptic business in front of Wendy.

Wendy stops chewing on a granola bar.

'I personally don't think you can once it's gone,' Leigh motors on. 'Do you?'

'I've never really thought about it,' Wendy says.

'Sometimes you have to just accept your marriage is how it's evolved and get your pleasure in other departments.'

Here it comes, I think. *She's going to tell her.* I hope she doesn't. Telling one friend is a sanity saver. Telling two is a day at the circus.

Wendy checks her phone.

'As you get older, you just get a different set of men problems, I think. Young women all just want to be married to a good man, and they've no idea how fast the novelty of that wears off. And those of us who are married to good men all want to be married to somebody else's good man. It's odd how the world works.'

'Speak for yourself,' I tell her, and Wendy looks up from her text messaging and gives me one of those looks that says, *What's come over her?* 'I don't want somebody else's man, Leigh. And neither do you.'

'Neither does Wendy,' Leigh adds. 'Wendy just wants to be married to Neil.' It sounds more like an insult rather than admiration.

'How do you know what I do and don't want, Leigh?' Wendy holds Leigh's eyes now. It's the first time I've ever seen her look a little miffed by anything Leigh's said.

Leigh's jaw drops. 'Well, don't you . . . just want to be married to Neil, I mean?'

74

Wendy licks the rim of her plastic glass before pelting it at the bin. 'Not always.'

Leigh sends me a glance. 'Eeks! Ask an honest question, get an honest answer!'

To lighten this up I tell them how Denise at work told me her husband is addicted to Internet porn. 'That's disgusting!' Leigh says, but I sense she's a little disappointed that she's not holding court any more. 'I'd murder Lawrence if I caught him looking at porn!'

'Why?' Wendy says. 'It's not like he can actually have sex with any of them.'

Leigh looks slightly annoyed as Wendy is somehow getting the upper hand here. 'Oh, come on! What if that were Neil? I mean, could you even see Neil doing that?'

'Well I certainly wouldn't want to see him doing it. But could I *believe* he'd do it? Probably.'

Leigh's expression is priceless. 'Rubbish! I think Neil probably has a bit more class than that.'

'Anyway!' Wendy chirps. 'Time for me to get home.'

When Wendy has gone, Leigh says, 'I've seen him every day this week, and a few evenings!'

'You're not still going to his house?'

'Well, we can't at his office, too many people around. But sometimes we can't make it there. We have to pull over and do it in the car. Look,' she drags the neck of her T-shirt down. Beside her nipple is a love bite.

'My God! What if Lawrence sees?'

'Oh, he won't! I haven't let Lawrence near me in ages.'

We walk to our respective cars. I am conspicuously silent. When I get to mine, all I can manage to say is, 'See you later, then.'

Saturday of the long bank holiday weekend, Rob is working again. Leigh is at Lawrence's parents' caravan. Wendy and Neil are having an anniversary getaway to Ireland. I am so restless, I don't know what's wrong with me. I walk the dog, try to do chores around the house. Nothing helps.

The beach is busy. And, unlike that day I came here with Leigh, he is here this time. He sees me, I know he does. I am lying on my red beach towel trying hard to look like I'm engrossed in a novel. He keeps turning his head. It seems the sight of me has suddenly made it impossible for him to get on with what he is doing.

Two minutes later, his yellow T-shirt is blocking my sun.

'Hello again,' he says.

I am wearing green shorts, and my white T-shirt is rolled up and slightly tucked under the bottom of my bra to reveal my pale stomach. I feel his eyes like electricity on my skin.

'I didn't think I'd ever see you again,' he says. 'Not with mother and dad today?'

'No,' I tell him. 'Not today.'

He squats just inches away from me, the sun backlighting him, illuminating the attractive, wolfish, weather-beaten aura around him. I am drawn to him like a meteor on a collision course for earth.

'You know, I think last time I say something and I upset you.'

I pretend to look puzzled. 'No. I don't think so.'

He studies me, trying to read me. 'Well, if I did, I am sorry.'

I close my book. 'It's fine.'

'Where is your husband today?' he asks, inoffensively. 'It is holiday, no?'

I prop myself up on my elbows. 'He had to work.'

'No one should have to work on holiday day in summer.'

'I agree.'

'No children, then?'

I have come to dread this question. 'Nope.' People never usually settle for just 'No'.

His eyes are more amber than brown and they hold mine steadily. 'There is no law.'

I cock my head. 'Law?'

'That says you can't come to beach alone while husband works if you don't have children.'

I smile. 'True. And that's a good thing. For me, anyway.'

I sit up fully now and reposition the bookmark to the page I was reading to give myself something to do. 'What is your accent? I was meaning to ask.'

'Russian.'

'Have you been in England a long time?'

'Some years.'

I sense he's about as fond of prying questions as I am. 'No going back?'

He hesitates for a moment. 'No, Jill. I don't believe in ever going back once choices are made. You look ahead only. If you don't, you live life very divided in your mind.'

He has remembered my name. 'I only meant for a holiday,' I say.

'Ah,' he smiles. 'I see. Then no. No to that too.'

I dig in my bag for my bottle of water. He watches. He watches my every move. When I tip my head back I feel his eyes on my throat as I swallow. 'This must just be seasonal work, though?'

'If you ask how I survive, I run methamphetamine empire on side. That accounts for the calibre of car I drive.'

I laugh. 'You're joking, of course. I mean, I hope!' We hold eyes through our smiles.

'Of course,' he says. 'Nothing as wild as that. In summer I like outdoors so this is what I do to enjoy life, and rest of year I am personal fitness trainer in expensive private member club, and then I am coach to kids in swimming club, which means the most to me.' His eyes run the length of my arm. 'What sort of exercise do you do to keep in shape, Jill?'

'Oh, well, yoga, the gym sometimes, and belly dancing.' *And if only you could see what a pretty sight that is!*

He looks at my stomach again. 'Belly dance, eh?'

I take another drink of my water. 'So what is Russia like? What was it like living there?'

'Russia? Argh!' Those amber eyes fill with nostalgia for a moment. 'Russia is fantastic country, but it is changed. Growing up I had good life, of course. Good family. Yes, there was hardship. But when it is all you know, you just get on living. You find joy because we all do. But when you get older you feel impatience with things.' He changes position so that he is now sitting beside me, then Andrey talks about Russia in a way I wish my history teachers had. All the while, his attention roams around the beach, clearly mindful of his job. He is very expressive and well spoken and I feel bad for thinking it's a pity he's a forty-something lifeguard. I tell myself I'm a bit of a jumped-up snob, and I should lap him up for five more minutes then get on my way home.

Then he says, 'I was a lawyer back home. A lawyer of commerce in St Petersburg.'

'You were a what?' My incredulity is out before I can stop it. 'A lawyer and now you're a lifeguard? And a fitness trainer and a coach?' This cannot be.

He squints at me in the milky sunlight, charming crinkles etching around his eyes. 'Well, is not so strange as is sounding. To explain why I coach, before I was lawyer I was actually swimmer. I was on the Russian Olympic team when Soviet Union boycotted the 1984 Los Angeles Olympics.'

'You were an Olympic swimmer?' I lay a hand on my chest in shock. Though this part is actually quite believable.

'I would have been, if my country had allowed for me to go. Twelve weeks before Olympics, Soviet Union pull out.'

'Oh no!' I scour his face, his hair, his very credible big swimmer's shoulders. 'That's just awful! You must have been devastated. You must have trained so hard.'

'All my life!' His left foot is resting on my towel.

'How old were you at the time of the Olympics?'

'I was eighteen. I am forty-nine now.'

He knew I was fishing for his age. He looks younger. 'My father, you know, he saw how much swimming was my goal, but he is one of these people . . .' He wiggles his fingers in the air, as though summoning the word. 'Is not true believer in things he not understand?'

'A sceptic.'

He clicks his fingers. 'Yes. My father, he was lawyer and a sceptic. His father was lawyer. His father before that . . . Even my mother family. They all lawyer too. For him it was unthinkable that I not become lawyer like everybody else.' He shrugs. 'And so I did. But it was always hatred for me. In my blood, in my veins, it was hatred to practise the work.'

'You hated it,' I correct him, and we hold eyes and he's clearly not making this up. I wonder what it must feel like to be judged the wrong way by what you do. I feel a certain admiration for him.

'Then I come to England, where, of course, I cannot be lawyer unless more training and qualify – so why? When I don't like? So now I coach swimmers. Kids. Hopefully next Olympic gold-medal winners. And to get by, there is my personal training. Being competitive, in sport, in career, is not always a healthy path to happiness. Besides, Jill, life is not all about where you were and how far you have fallen. It is simply about where you just are. It's about joy you find in having some inner satisfaction in yourself, and this often come from having nothing to prove.'

'Wow,' I say. 'That's quite a journey.'

He runs his eyes over my face, my throat again. 'I live in my means and am happy to do so. Only problem I talk too much.' He smiles now. 'What dreams did you have, Jill?'

The question takes me aback. When did anybody ever ask me that? I don't want to tell him I don't think I ever had any. Or that I've only just realised that now. Or that I wouldn't have thought he'd have had any either. 'I don't know. I danced as a teenager. Ballet and tap. I was good, but not the best in the class. I passed my GCSEs, but I had no interest in attempting to go to university. I suppose I never really had one thing I was burning to do. For me it was more about earning a wage, having a life outside my job, meeting a good man.'

'Which you did.'

'Which I did.' I skirt around that one. 'So how on earth did you wind up in the North East?'

He smiles. 'It getting long time for me to talk now, must go soon, but it was a woman. A journalist from Yorkshire who was writing book on former Soviet Union. We met in St Petersburg; she needed lawyer. We became involve. Then she come back to England, so I come. But it did not work out in long term. So I come here.'

'Oh, I'm sorry.'

'Don't be,' he says, and then with a twinkle in his eye, 'She was nightmare. I am not sorry.'

'Have you ever been married?'

'Almost. But I am not so sure I believe that two people are meant to pledge themselves to each other, take vows that at the time of taking them they can't possibly know if they will keep.' He looks at his hands, at his fingernails. 'I have seen many marriages where the couples haven't grow together, where after so many years they aren't the people that either would choose again.'

My guess is he'd have no problem having an affair with a married woman. Because he doesn't view people as possessions. 'I must go,' he says suddenly, and gets up. 'Sadly.'

It seems to come quickly. The ending. He flourishes a hand around the beach as a wave breaks noisily near the shoreline and giggly kids scamper over it and dogs bark at it. 'Enjoy this time to be just Jill . . . Every day I come here I remember how lucky I am to have choice to be here and to appreciate. Whereas at the age I am now, my father had embolism and died. He loved law, yes. But in end, law killed him.'

'Sometimes just enjoying is a guilty pleasure,' I say.

He looks at me again, shrugs, and I can tell he's a person with a lot to say and he doesn't do small talk and he isn't finding this easy. 'Don't ever feel guilty,' he says. 'About anything.'

He holds my eyes, says it candidly, squarely, and I feel it in my stomach.

'Come back,' he says, backing up, his eyes very much still on me, his intent still very much alive.

I can't quite rally a reply. He holds my gaze until he's forced to turn, and the moment to do so is gone.

He wasn't expecting me to answer him anyway.

CHAPTER EIGHT

I lie in bed and pretend to read my novel, ablaze with thoughts of him, playing over his every word. A dishevelled, hair-uncombed Rob is sorting through the No Go Zone that is his top drawer, where he keeps a life's work of receipts, old Visa cards, the odd smelly sports sock, empty condom packets from eons ago, old anniversary cards, etc. He's looking for the receipt for an automatic shut-off iron he bought me that he now claims doesn't work.

A sobering incident met me when I came in through the door, high, almost floating, from the afternoon. Rob was holding a wad of nasty-looking kitchen roll. Kiefer was sitting, obedient and rather curious, at his feet. 'I found this on the carpet.' He brandished the wet handful at me. 'I don't know if it's vomit or the other. You'd think it'd be obvious, but it's completely got me beat. Do you want to smell it and give me your opinion?'

'What?' I glared at him as though he had two heads.

'If it's vomit, that's fine. If it's the other, then we're one step forward and two back.'

'Rob,' I said. 'You know something? I'm a bit puzzled.'

He was still gazing at the paper. 'It's one of life's mysteries this . . .'

'Stop it!' I shouted. 'What I'm puzzled about is . . . why is there sand all over the floor?'

'Sand?' he looked up. 'Ah. Because I got home a bit early and we went to the beach.'

I just had to hear the word beach to turn nauseous.

'We went for a little drive after work, didn't we, lad?' he said to the dog. 'And guess who we saw there, getting into trouble?'

I lost the ability to breathe.

'We saw Bill from across the street, didn't we? He seemed to be chatting up a couple of young girls.' He laughed, slightly.

'Bill,' I repeated, thinking, *Thank you, Bill.*

'We had an ice cream, didn't we, Kiefer?' He glanced sideways at me.

'What flavour did he have?' I asked when my pulse started up again.

'No. I had the ice cream. He just ate somebody's snotty paper hankie off the ground.'

I mussed the dog's head. Then I mussed Rob's too. 'Glad you had so much fun without me.'

Because I had plenty without you . . .

'Can you pack in doing that, please?' he asked, ducking from my hand.

'Sorry,' I said, and went to put the kettle on, breathing out a long breath of tight air.

'You sure you don't have the receipt, Jill?' he asks me now as I sit here in a daze. His tone implies that the mess of his drawer is somehow my doing.

I do an inner eye-roll. 'You paid for the thing. You'll have it.' I go back to my book and reread the same sentence I've begun thirty times. I can't believe he was a lawyer. And an Olympic swimmer. *S-vimmer.*

'It might have been in the carrier bag,' he says.

'I wouldn't know. I didn't even open it.'

Get a life.

He turns around and looks at me, exasperated. 'Don't you think there's something a bit strange about that, Jill? Why d'you think I bought you an automatic shut-off iron if I didn't want you to use it? Or is the opportunity to one day burn our house down so tantalising for you, eh?'

Rob is always on at me about forgetting to turn the iron off. But I'll say, 'Well, that's what happens when you try to do seventeen things at once.' But he seems to think his failure to do more than one thing at a time is a lovable handicap all men were born with, whereas mine is a genetic disorder. I give him that face. 'Maybe I was leaving it for you. You know, to acquire the ironing skill before you die.'

He narrows his eyes at me, goes back to raking through the drawer.

I watch him in his unclean T-shirt and think, *Rob, you're scintillating aren't you? For a Saturday night, this is real Rock Your World stuff, isn't it? The iron receipt.* 'I think Frank Sinatra bought one of them for Ava Gardner as an anniversary present, you know?' I tell him.

He freezes in that I-know-you're-being-sarcastic posture. 'One what?'

'A shut-off iron.'

He looks at me over his shoulder. 'I bet his bloody worked though.'

I try to get on with reading my book, but my mind is racing off to what he would be like in bed. I can't stop seeing his eyes. The fit but not overly gym-honed body. The nostalgia in his face when he talked about Russia. Then I hear Rob say, 'Argh!'

Oh, come on! What next?

He has stopped stock-still. He is holding something. His entire body is poised in quiet fascination. 'Remember this?' He shows me and his face is a picture of warmth and tenderness.

I take the little laminated card off him. 'It's my old gym membership!' I haven't seen this in years! 'God, I look so young. And that perm!' I chuckle. 'I didn't know you kept this!'

His face lights up with nostalgia. 'I've always loved it. Your hair like somebody rolled you in the clippings bin at the Poodle Grooming Parlour.' He smiles. Then he does something that steals my heart. He pops a kiss on it – on my little laminated face – his love for me seeping like some quiet reminder into the air.

I feel like the worst cad.

I put my book face down on the bedside table. I could never do it, despite the nice fantasy. Cheating might not be wrong for everybody, but it's wrong for me. 'You sure the iron's broken, Rob?' I ask my big soft-hearted hubby of nearly ten years. I clamber over the top of the duvet and go to dig it out of its box, a sudden chastened participant in the trivia of our life. 'It's not a loose wire in the plug?'

He scowls. 'No, it's not a loose wire,' he says, in that tone that says, do-you-think-I'm-a- monkey?

I go over to the socket and plug it in. The little red light comes on.

'It's working!' he says, mystified.

'You just had to switch it on.'

Buried, but not dead. Despite my best efforts, I spend the week with little else but Andrey on my mind. I am not myself. I am in a permanent, twenty-four-hour-a-day heat. I somehow manage to bake chicken in cling film, almost take the lead for a walk without the puppy, and nearly tone my face with nail polish remover.

It's been over six months since Rob and I have had sex. I'm trying very hard not to count.

I still have his phone number. I dial it once, listen to his voice in his message, hang up. A couple of times I drive over to the beach, camp out in a strategically inconspicuous spot, and stare at him while he does enthralling things like scratch the back of his head, or kick his sandal against a rock to dislodge the sand. You'd think he'd chat up all the girls, but he doesn't, I'm pleased to see. I stop short of following him when he goes off shift because that's got mentally unhinged written all over it. At work the girls comment that I seem unusually distracted. Then I make two nasty accounting mistakes, either one of which could have landed me the sack had I not noticed in the nick of time. In bed, I try, but fail, to fall asleep. I seem to wait all day until I can lie down and just think about him without distraction. The thought of his wide, tanned hand. That hand on my tummy – the tummy he kept looking at. His kiss. That astonishingly sexy, cut-glass upper lip, on my neck. Andrey's hands and kisses. Not Rob's. Lately I'm not imagining anything physical to do with Rob.

By Wednesday, I'm exhausted. Wendy rings me at work. She sounds flat. 'I'm not coming to work out with you tonight. I'm a little tired. I had a bit of a bad argument with Neil last night so I didn't get much sleep.'

I have never heard her say she's had an argument with Neil. 'Is everything all right, Wend? What was it about?'

'Oh, it was nothing. Trivial really.'

Trivial, but a bad argument? Sometimes I wonder why she bothers telling me anything at all. 'Well, why don't you come out anyway? Exercise makes you feel better. Aren't you always telling me that?' I realise I want her there for my own selfish reasons – to change the track of my thoughts, and the mood and inevitable conversation between Leigh and me.

'Erm. No. I think I'll give it a miss. Leigh was getting on my nerves a bit today at work. I think I need a spell off.'

She doesn't sound herself. But, honestly, if she's not going to tell me then I'm not going to drag it out of her.

In the gym changing room, Leigh stands there in scarlet bra and panties, swinging her new raven hairdo, jangling her gold double-hoop earrings. She looks exotic, like a flamenco dancer. We claim treadmills beside each other and start pounding them. She's still seeing him every lunchtime. The other day he came to her office. Wendy was at a doctor's appointment and Clifford was out. They did a frenzied grind against a wall by an open window, with Northern Goldsmiths' clock chiming in the distance. 'The sex is only getting better, if that's possible, Jill,' she pants. 'It's true that women are at their prime in their thirties; I've never had such powerful orgasms, or so many. It's fantastic. I don't want it ever to end.'

'Aren't you horrified Lawrence's going to notice how different you've become?' I mean, I can see it! Even Wendy can. I pound hard, trying to exorcise something as I do it. The need for a hot, sweaty tangle with human flesh runs loose in me, faster than my legs.

'Look, I do what I do with him then I go home. I don't sneak out at night. My life goes on as normal. So my mind might be somewhere else. Lawrence doesn't know that. We always assume other people are mind-readers, Jill, but they're not. It's hard enough being in your own head sometimes, without trying to be in somebody else's.' She's panting heavily. A bead of sweat disappears down the V of her top. 'Actually,' she says, 'affairs are a lot easier to have than you'd think.'

In the sauna, we lie on opposite benches in our towels, our heads turned to one another. 'Tell me something bad about it,' I say to her. 'Tell me a downside.'

She seems to try hard. 'I can't. There isn't one. Doing this just makes me wonder why I was faithful all these years. And the funny thing is, Jill,' she sits up, her towel falling from her small breasts. 'You know, since I've had a lover, I pick on Lawrence so much less. And you can tell that he's more relaxed because of it. Even his OCD is better.' She wipes her running mascara. 'In a peculiar way this affair is saving my marriage. Fucking another man is actually doing Lawrence a favour.' The door opens and somebody comes in. Our gazes slide apart. In the changing room we dry off. 'Are you still thinking of going for it with the Russian?'

she asks me, given that the other day – madly – I told her I'd gone back to the beach. 'I mean, now that your marriage is back on track.'

I also lied the other day because I felt bad for telling her I'd gone back to the beach. If this thing that Rob and I are going through turns out to be just a blip on an otherwise happy landscape, I don't want my marriage remembered for the bad things I've said about it because they have a way of obliterating the good.

'Well, I'm not sure it's one hundred per cent back on track,' I say, knowing the only reason I can't tell her how un-back on track it is, is that she'll then know I lied. Then she'll think things are worse than they even are. 'Besides, he's not exactly said "come on let's do it". He knows I'm married.'

'Boring!'

'No, actually, I like that. If he were all over me it'd put me off. At least he's got class.'

'A classy lifeguard.'

'Don't mock!'

'Well, you initiate it then!'

'I can't.' My eyes suddenly brim with tears. 'Oh God, Leigh, I don't know what I'm coming to.' I plonk down on the bench. She stops drying her legs, looks at me, shocked.

Right this minute I am so damned sad. But I'm sad for all the wrong reasons. I'm sad because I'm married, and I like this man and it's wrong. And I hate myself for feeling like this. And I hate that my marriage has fallen to this. But what I hate most is that I'll never be wooed again, I'll never fall in love again, all that's ahead for me is fixing what's broken. I give a sad, thin, grief-stricken little laugh.

'I thought all I wanted was to fix my marriage. But now I'm not so sure. Maybe there will be a second chapter for me. Maybe Rob and I have come as far as we are going to go.' I look at her frankly, through a veil of tears. 'Maybe I should have lived more before I settled down.

I'm scared that I'm starting to doubt not just my future with Rob, but my past too.'

'Look, Jill.' She sits down beside me. 'I know you love Rob. And I'm certainly not going to encourage you to be unfaithful. But you're my friend. You're the one I care most about. And you've not judged me. So I'm certainly not judging you. And I can tell you're unhappy. You're starting to wear it all over your face. So if there's something you badly need to do, do it. Do it, and to hell with guilt. Guilt is only something invented by people who are too scared to do what they really want.' She looks at me directly and I think of what Andrey said about guilt. 'You're not going to get your life back once it's over. I'm convinced you don't have some burning desire to shag around and make up for lost time – because believe me that's not the fun it sounds. But maybe you were destined to meet this man for a bit of fun to get you through a difficult time in your marriage. Maybe he's come along to somehow save you.' She stands up, starts putting things in her bag. 'But if you're not going to go for it, then forget about him or you're just tormenting yourself. Basically' – she rolls up her leggings – 'piss or get off the pot.'

My very ladylike mother used to use that expression all the time.

At home, I lie in the bath and contemplate my menstruating body. My breasts, which always seem bigger this time of the month, spread and float on the water. Little pieces of my endometrium unfurl in the water like sea anemones, which reminds me what the root cause of all this is. Why couldn't we have been able to have a baby? Maybe I should have wanted it more from day one. Perhaps I had no right to change my mind. But is this some sort of divine punishment – our marriage biting the dust? I will not let it happen.

So why am I swinging? Why does Leigh's 'Elastoplast' solution sound a little appealing? Why do I wrack my brains to make a mental list of all Rob's flaws and try to make them add up to enough reason for me to cheat? Why does part of me wish I could find out that he were having an affair so I could have my own in revenge? If only I were like Wendy: generally content and still somewhat in love. Or Leigh: devoid of a conscience, but still fundamentally a good person?

In bed I lie awake next to a mound of snoring husband, thinking about marriage and fidelity, temptation and honest friends. But what was it Leigh said? That being with Nick makes her realise she'll never enjoy sex with Lawrence again. So she did answer my question. The one bad thing about her affair: when the party's over she'll feel like she's going home with the consolation prize.

I smile to myself in some sort of smug satisfaction about my righteous commitment to my failing marriage. I glance across at Rob's back, his heaving barrier of shoulders. Then I shut my eyes, slip my hand under my nightie and take the only course of action I'm left with.

CHAPTER NINE

'Something very odd's happened.' Wendy's voice is missing its bubble. I am putting my socks on while I sit on the end of the bed. Rob has just come out of the shower with a bath towel around his waist, and for the first time in my life I can't bear to look at him. 'You know how Leigh wanted ideas for opening the flagship store at the Metro Centre? Well, she's decided she wants to give away five hundred pounds' worth of merchandise to the first person who comes in the door naked. She thinks half of Newcastle is going to be lined up outside in the buff.'

'She's probably right.'

'Well, she wants to invite the national media. She thinks it's brilliant publicity for the brand. And a couple of days ago Clifford happened to ask me my opinion of it.' She takes a deep breath. 'So I said, well, I can certainly see it attracting attention. But I actually have a problem with that on two levels. One: it's wrong to ridicule people even if they do very stupid things. But two: if this gets on the telly, well, I just don't think it sends the right signal to the rest of the country about the North East. It's just reviving all the old stereotypes, and why would you want to do that with your modern brand? Having a load of silly girls embarrass themselves for a bag of free clothing . . . I don't know. I think it's wrong. And if it were my company, my brand, I'd want to associate it with something with a bit more class than that.'

'And you told him this?'

'Well, I was a bit less vehement, but yes.'

'And?'

'He completely agreed. He really latched on to the point about class.'

'Well, that's great!'

'No, it's not. Because five minutes before that, he thought Leigh's idea was the best one since sliced bread. In fact he thought it was so good that he actually thought it was his idea. And now that he loathes it, he's coming down very hard on Leigh for "leading the brand astray". And she seems to think it's all my fault.'

Tits up. I tell you, I predicted it. Never mix business and friendship. 'Well, what did she say?'

'She said, "Well, just because one person has no sense of humour . . ." So I suppose that meant me. Then they had this massive fight. And I had to listen to the blow by blow.' She takes another deep breath. 'Jill, what do I do?' ·

'Nothing. I'm sure it's over with now. Leigh doesn't hold grudges.'

'Doesn't she? Yesterday morning when I went in, there was a note on my desk. It said, "Please phone the Metro Centre and find out the fire hazard policy for crowds outside of stores. FOR MY IDEA YOU TRIED TO SABOTAGE."'

'Sabotage? She used that word?'

'She did. She didn't spell it right but she did. She even put it in block capitals.'

'Well, go and tell her that was completely uncalled for!' As I say this, Rob gives me a curious scowl.

'I can't. There's going to be a very strange atmosphere if we end up having a big row. I mean, she's my friend; I can't just switch her off at five o'clock. And I don't want her thinking that just because I haven't worked all these years that I'm too sensitive . . .' There's a pause. 'Jill, I did something really cowardly. I just thought, *Oh, I can't face this.* So I went in to see Clifford clutching my cheek saying how I had a really bad toothache and I'd just got an emergency appointment at the dentist. So now I'm sat at home nursing a toothache I don't have, trying to work out how I'm going to go back to a job I'm not even sure I want any more, and all this feels . . . beyond childish and ridiculous to say the least.'

'It is childish. She's being childish.'

'I thought about telling her I'd changed my mind, that the more I think about it, it's actually a good idea. But why should I do that? Why should I pander like that and take back what I believe in?'

'I don't know, Wend. Maybe for an easy life! But what's Neil say about all this?'

'Oh, he thinks I'm overanalysing. Mind you, I didn't tell him the toothache part. But he did say I should be on my guard about her – she's obviously not the person I thought she was.'

'Well, I think you should go back in, say your tooth's fine now, and act like none of this has ever happened. And if it ever happens again, you'll take her to task then.'

There's silence for a moment. 'Lately, Jill, I just wonder what I'm doing. Marketing exercise pants. I don't know . . . all my life I've fantasised about standing for something. Just . . . if I could get into a company where the work is a bit more relevant to something I'm interested in or has some bigger meaning . . . I wouldn't mind just being the receptionist. I'd gladly do it.'

'Finish your damned degree!' I can't count the number of times we've had this conversation.

She pauses. 'Leigh keeps saying that. And she's right. You both are. I just . . . Well, Neil doesn't think it's a great idea. But then again, Neil has no respect for education as he did OK without it . . . I just don't know what it is with me. I seem to have this mental block where this topic is concerned. I mean, I am able to finish it. I want to. Yet, for some reason, I'm not doing it. There's always been Neil or the lads stopping me. Way back it was my A-level grades that prevented me going to read law; I could have just resat them, but didn't. Then I took a job and it was the job that stopped me going back to study. Then it was my parents dying, then Nina dying. And now that nothing's stopping me . . . *I'm* stopping me. I know I'm not afraid of failing, but maybe I'm afraid of succeeding.'

'Well, personally, I'm very glad I was a complete ambitionless no-hoper because this career angst just seems like more trouble than it's worth.'

She laughs, finally.

Sunday is Lawrence's fortieth birthday. We're all invited to a barbecue at Leigh's. 'Oh Christ, do we have to?' Rob groans. It's funny how after all these years our husbands have nothing to say to each other. Neil is too hard to read and awkward with conversation. Lawrence is too artsy and talks too much about his feelings.

'I've got this really bad toothache . . .' Wendy says, when I ring to make sure she's coming.

I laugh. 'Oh, come on, now you're playing silly beggars.'

'She said she put it in capitals for a joke!'

'Oh,' I say. 'You talked to her about it?'

'I did. I couldn't let it drop. She treated me to a nice lunch. In fact, she was over-the-top nice with me. But I didn't get the wrong end of the stick, Jill. She was annoyed. The face doesn't lie, even if the block capitals do.'

Leigh and Lawrence have a lovely home, a four-storey Edwardian terrace that they bought for next to nothing, fixed up, adding dashes of Leigh's great taste, and now it's worth twice as much. The rooms are tiny and unusually shaped, with uneven floors and high ceilings. And before you can climb the steep, narrow stairs you have to duck your head under a sort of hanging ceiling. It's cute. It has loads of character. But it's a patient person's house. As Wendy once remarked, perfect for some rather with-it dwarf.

Lawrence is standing at the barbecue, repetitively turning and prodding the hamburgers. His shoulder-length, dirty blonde hair is pulled back into its trademark ponytail, and he wears what we've come to think of as his uniform – a Paisley cotton shirt with the sleeves rolled back and faded, ripped jeans.

'Leave them! They'll disintegrate!' Leigh says, in despair. 'Come grate some Parmesan instead for the salad. We'll put Neil in charge of the burgers.'

Rob slaps Lawrence's back as he walks past him. 'No worries, mate. I can't barbecue to save my life either.'

Lawrence sends Rob a look of quiet appreciation. I have always liked Lawrence. I know his entire body weight is probably on par with mine, but I've always thought he has a placid, rather magnificent face with its razor-sharp cheekbones, and the far-apart blue eyes. It oozes peace and goodness. Perhaps he's not the next James Bond, but when he looks at his wife, it's with a certain quiet manliness that issues forth from him in the same way that his thinness exudes strength. 'Marriage is the process of finding out the kind of husband your wife would have preferred,' he says, and Rob laughs. 'I read that in a book and it sounded so apt.' Lawrence sends me a look of sheepish pleasure. 'In fact, I think it was written for Leigh.'

Neil, who's been quietly leaning against the fence with a beer in his hand, as though in a contemplative world of his own, saunters over to the barbecue. 'You good at it?' Leigh quips over her shoulder as she sets olive oil and balsamic on the picnic table.

'Me? Good? The best,' Neil says, and Leigh gives Wendy and me a playful look that says, *God! Doesn't he love himself?*

Maybe it's just me, but whenever we get together there's something a little bit painful in Neil's attempt to appear at ease. And I have always marvelled at how the moment he says anything that is even vaguely humorous, we all seem so grateful for it, that we celebrate it far more than it deserves. 'Policemen. They don't trust us ordinary folk,' Rob will say, semi-seriously. And I think he actually has a point there. 'I bet if you stole a chocolate bar when you were twelve, Neil would look at you and somehow know,' Lawrence once said to us, obviously when neither Wendy nor Neil was present. For a moment there, I was watching him standing nursing his bottle of Stella. The muscles in his forearms were flexing as though even they feel the strain of our forced encounters. I bet he hates them. To give him the benefit of the doubt, maybe it's all part of being an important detective; he can't relax. As though Wendy notices it, she walks over to the barbecue, stands right beside him and says something that feels private. Being a good foot shorter, she has to look up at him when she talks which appears sweetly idolising. At one point his free hand drops and settles briefly near her bottom, and I stare at it. And for a brief second I picture being here with the Russian. Having him touch me like that. I walk back inside and perch on the stool by the open patio door.

'Here,' Leigh thrusts the block of Parmesan at Lawrence. 'Do about half, please.' Lawrence says something to her – something I can't hear – and she chortles. So he still has the ability to make her laugh. I watch them for a moment or two. You would never know.

Molly follows her mam to the fridge, singing and making scissor movements with Barbie's legs. Wendy's lads sit on the patio steps, hunched over in mutual desire to send a signal that being here with their parents is too uncool. 'Wend, give the lads a beer,' Leigh tells her.

'I think they're OK with lemonade.'

Paul, the cheeky one, shouts, 'No we're not! Speak for yourself!'

'You're not, son?' Wendy rubs Paul's shaved head with its zigzag lines that match the ones in his eyebrows. 'No, you're really badly done by, aren't you? I'm just a really horrible parent, aren't I?' Paul bats her off and chuckles. Wendy looks over to Neil, but I see that Neil is watching Leigh walk out from the house holding two bottles. Rob is watching her too. I sense both men are probably noting the denim miniskirt and the unusual aura of confidence that radiates from her. Rob has already told her she looks great, although later he'll probably tell me she looked like mutton dressed as lamb in that skirt. That's Rob: master of insincere compliments when he's got nothing else to say.

'Here,' Leigh thrusts the beer at the boys. 'I can't have you thinking we're a bunch of geeks now, can I?'

The lads' faces light up. 'Right on there, Leigh! You're the best,' says Paul.

Leigh's studying gaze moves between the two boys who look almost identical, and so much like their dad. I wonder, reading her suddenly wistful expression, if she's thinking of her own twin. If she's thinking that somewhere out there is another woman who looks just like her, maybe even thinks just like her, only this woman wants nothing to do with her for reasons she will never know. I remember Wendy saying, 'Phone her. She may have just got cold feet.' But Leigh said no.

Ben looks up and grins with triumph at his mam.

'There you go,' Wendy says, deadpan. 'My lads now think my best friend is cooler than their mam. It'll never do.' Her hands lock around one of Neil's forearms and she says something to him again, secretively, and I wonder what it is. I wonder what this topic is that's between them tonight. Perhaps, *Don't worry, we'll eat and this will soon be over.*

Leigh takes her eyes off the lads and looks at me with that expression that says I can read her thoughts. Then she turns and sees Lawrence grating Parmesan for England. 'Ah!' She grabs the wedge off him. 'Stop!'

'What else would you like me to do?' he says, as she chortles at him and shakes her head. Then he winks at Rob. 'Hopefully I've proven myself useless.'

'Ah!' Rob says. 'My trick too. Great minds think alike.'

'Book yourself in for a lobotomy,' Leigh mutters to Wendy and me. And then she tells him, 'You could top our glasses up. But first see if Rob and Neil want another beer.'

'Great idea.' Lawrence looks quietly pleased with life, then gets right on to the task.

How does she act so normal? I watch her sail around her kitchen assembling food. She's got it down to an art. It's almost pathological. From time to time she catches me watching her, sends me that secretive, defiant, this-is-all-bearable-because-of-HIM smile. Call me old-fashioned, but it seems hypocritical putting on a big 'do' for your husband while you're having it off with somebody else's. I said to her the other day, 'You're not really going to have a big knees-up for his birthday, are you?' She looked at me like I was quite mad. 'Why not? He's not dead, is he?'

I go back to watching Rob now, without him knowing I'm doing it. Something about this party is unhinging me. Yes, he's lovely, and yes, if I met him for the first time today, I'd be attracted to him. But if the Russian were here I am not sure he'd stand a chance.

But no, I don't want to be like Leigh and Lawrence – with a secret running parallel to everything they say and do. I get the urge to relieve Lawrence of a bottle of beer and take it outside and plant a kiss on my husband. So I do. 'Thanks, treasure,' he says, as I give him the new drink, and he chinks the bottle to my wine glass.

'So what did you buy him then, Leigh?' Wendy joins me back in the kitchen. She looks curvy in white Capri pants, white runners, and a black cap-sleeved T-shirt that shows off the lovely toned V of her bicep. 'I mean, other than the underwear.'

Leigh looks confused. 'Underwear?' Then her eyes meet mine. 'Oh! That! Yes. Well, I bought him Botox.'

'Botox!' Wendy looks at me. 'But he hasn't got any wrinkles! He has fantastic skin.'

Leigh tuts. 'It's not for his face! It's for his feet. You can use it to stop sweating. Didn't you know?'

'No!' we both chorus, and she gives us a look that says we have to get with the times.

Lawrence comes into the kitchen, smiling benignly, and Leigh says, 'Shush! I'm giving him his gift later.'

'Later?' Lawrence glances from his wife to us. 'What do I get later?' By his face, it's obvious what he's hoping for.

'The burgers are about ready. I take it we want them well done. No salmonella.' Neil cocks his boyish face and platinum hair around the door, and smiles at his wife.

No salmonella, I think. Wow. That's hilarious. We must all fall on the floor.

The sleeves of his gunmetal grey shirt are rolled up and his stainless steel watch beams from a suntanned arm. He looks almost funny doing something domestic. I must admit, his out-of-placeness makes him look effortlessly fanciable. If only he had a personality.

'I love samon-ella!' Molly chirps, going over and hugging her mam's backside.

'No, sweet pea. You love salmon. That's a bit different.' She grins at Neil.

'I may have to have a little procedure,' Wendy says, as she watches Neil go back outside.

Leigh stops stirring risotto and we both look at her. 'On your tooth?' Leigh quips.

Wendy glances at me. 'No. Not on the tooth.' She tops up her wine glass. 'It's nothing really. I had my smear and they've found abnormal cells.'

My heart sinks. 'Abnormal?'

'You've not got cancer!' Leigh and her sledgehammer tact!

'No, I don't think it's that. But they have to get a better look at the cells.' Her gaze shifts out of the window, to where Neil is tending to the burgers.

'My God,' Leigh and I say in unison. All that fuss she made of this silly SABOTAGE business, when she knew she had far bigger things to worry about!

'It's most likely nothing,' Leigh says, trying to make up for her gaffe. 'Lots of women have abnormal smears, don't they?'

'Of course. That's what I mean. It's nothing to really worry about.'

But beneath the bravado there is something vague and unconvincing about her.

'Well, how do you feel?' I ask her.

She shrugs. 'Fine. But I've been having a bit of breakthrough bleeding. That's why I went for a check-up.' Her mam died in her forties from some sort of female thing, I forget exactly what. My heart flutters with dread.

'Don't you have regular smears?' Leigh asks, looking genuinely worried now.

She shakes her head. 'I hate people messing down there.'

'But you always said you went!'

'That's because you two do, so I lied.'

Leigh looks at me in exasperation. 'That's insane, Wendy! You've got to start taking better care of yourself! Start putting yourself first!'

I sink into the chair at the kitchen table. 'Does Neil know?'

'I'm not saying anything until I've seen the specialist. What's the point of worrying him?'

'I don't know, because he's your husband, Wendy,' Leigh says. And Wendy looks at me, as though to say *precisely.*

We eat at the picnic table under a mulberry tree. Leigh and Lawrence's back garden is full of climbing wisteria and hidden paths and birdbaths, thanks to Lawrence's eye for design. Wendy's news has put me off my food, and Leigh doesn't eat much either, although I suspect for different reasons. I happen to look over and catch her off in a daydream, and I think, *Jesus, can't you think about anything but yourself just for two minutes?* The conversation inevitably comes round to the murder at the university that Neil was interviewed on the North East News about, then Leigh comes alive and starts quizzing him in a way that none of us dares. I watch Wendy watching him as he talks, how her eyes comb over him, but with an air of detachment. 'Well, as I see it, Neil, there seems to be two truths,' Wendy interrupts his explanation of things. 'What the police are saying, and what the media are reporting.'

'I think you've had too much wine.' His response comes off like a put-down, and I wish I had better followed what they were talking about because now you could cut the atmosphere around the table with a knife.

'Sorry,' Leigh says. 'Maybe we should change the topic.'

It's a very lovely meal. Some time later, Leigh materialises from the kitchen, carrying a two-tiered iced cake, a bewitching smile on her face. 'Ta-da!' she and Molly chant. 'Happy fortieth, Lawrence!' Leigh pipes. And Molly bursts into a soprano chorus of 'Happy Birthday to You'.

Afterwards, as I am helping Leigh take plates into the kitchen, she says in my ear, 'I smell trouble in paradise.'

CHAPTER TEN

It's here. July the twenty-second. Our tenth wedding anniversary weekend. Rob will get me a card. Hopefully not the same one he sent me last year that he dug out of the top drawer. I will hope for a small and thoughtful gift, but that will be conspicuously absent. When they don't make much effort, you start matching their behaviour with your expectations, thinking things like: *If he came in with a big bouquet of red roses, I'd come down to breakfast in a garter and suspender belt.* But it never happens. And it's far easier to blame Rob for not taking the initiative than to actually take it myself. My nagging must have penetrated, though, because for my birthday he got me the dog. I'm certain it was to ensure I'd never ask him for anything again. But this year is different. I'm giving it my all. Our marriage deserves nothing less. I keep thinking of him kissing my little picture.

I have it all planned. I am whisking him away to Bamburgh to stay in the very lodge where we spent our honeymoon; I even booked us the same room. I've splurged on an expensive bottle of champagne, a new dress for a posh dinner, and a sexy nurse's outfit because he once said that he wished I'd surprise him with one sometime. I was trying it on in The Sex Store, and the fire alarm went off in the mall. There was me, running outside in fishnets, white vinyl mini-skirt and a skimpy red cross for a top. Got some very strange looks from people, and the firemen had a field day. Anyway, I'm doing it. I'm trying my hardest not to think the words Last Ditch Attempt.

'I thought we'd go have a look around the shops for a new bedroom carpet,' I tell Rob when I've got him in the car. He doesn't know I've dropped the dog off at the kennels, and that our luggage is stashed in the boot.

His face falls. 'Carpet? Shopping? On a Friday night?'

I try not to smile. It's raining hard, sadly, but hopefully it will be better tomorrow. The wipers are going like the clappers and I can barely see.

'Why have you just turned on to the motorway then?' he asks, after a grudging silence.

'You'll find out.' I try not to smile.

Traffic is heavy up ahead, and I'm aware of not getting too close to the car in front.

'You're driving like a senior citizen,' my husband says.

'It's not me,' I tell him. When I accelerate the car seems to be resisting me. I barely get the words 'I think there's something wrong with the car' out of my mouth when my battery warning light comes on. 'Oh, shit! The battery's going flat.'

'It's not. Those lights have come on before. Just ignore it. Where on earth is this shop, anyway?'

I am forced to reveal my surprise to put him out of his misery.

'Ah!' His face brightens. 'You planned this? A romantic weekend away for us?' His first question is who is taking care of the dog.

'I did. And I think we should call the AA. The car isn't driving right.'

'Well you know how long we'll wait if we call them. In this weather. Let's just get there. We can ring them while we eat dinner.'

I do my you-win sigh. Rob gives my hand his I-know-best squeeze. We turn off the motorway and follow a trunk road as it seems like it might be faster than sitting in traffic. Rob thinks we're going the wrong way and directs us on to another road, but there is progressively less civilisation around us and I think we're best off going back to the motorway. 'I think it's this way,' he says. 'Just keep going for a bit.'

But after about ten minutes it looks suspiciously like we've arrived in a field of sheep.

'I think you've cocked this up somehow,' he says in that gah-you're-useless tone.

'I don't think I did!' I peer through the splashing rain hoping to find the main road again. I don't get far when our car seizes, the dash lights up, and then everything dies.

'Right,' I say, in that tone.

Rob sends me a sly glance. 'I feel an *I told you so* coming on.'

I want to kill him. I always listen to him and he's always wrong! 'What do we bloody do now, clever clogs?'

'Call the AA?'

'How do we explain where we are when we've got no signal on our phones?'

He looks around him. 'Good question.'

The rain pelts a broken tune on our roof. We have some stupid argument now about who's going to go walking to find someone who can tell us where we are, so we can let the AA know where to find us.

'You are because I'm not wearing a coat!' he says.

'You are because I'm the girl and I did all the donkey work for this weekend to start with because you couldn't get a romantic idea in your head if your life depended on it! And you're the one who got us into this, or did you forget that Mr I've-Seen-the-Bloody-Lights-Come-on-Before?'

'All right, all right!' he says. 'I think I got the point!' He climbs out of the car, swearing and pulling up his shirt collar, and I watch the navy blur of him disappear down the road and I swallow a small chuckle.

An hour later. Where did he go? Canada? Then I see the blur of him return. 'The tow truck's on its way and it'll tow us to the hotel and then take the car to the closest garage. Fuck,' he says, water dripping off his nose end. I start to laugh.

'It's not funny!'

A sheep comes up to our window and goes '*Mehhhh!*', and I have a fit of the giggles.

Rob sits there dripping wet with his teeth chattering. I peep at him out the corner of my eye and am suddenly filled with love for him again. Rob, I wish you'd just take me right here in the car!

Look! I see a pig flying.

Another hour later a walking tattoo with a central nervous system ties us up at his big back end and then we hop in his truck and off we go. By the time we get to the hotel it's after eleven p.m.

They've let the room. The new person on the desk assumed we were a no-show.

Despite a painful argument, the upshot is they are fully booked – they've become really popular since they got written up in the *Mail on Sunday*'s Best Romantic Getaways – so we have to find somewhere else.

The only place that can take us gets two stars on TripAdvisor. Rob goes to take a shower. 'Did we happen to bring our own toilet paper?' I hear him shout. The shower barely works. Rob comes out of it with soap stuck to his chest hair. 'Smell something funny?' he asks when he hops into bed beside me.

'Like?'

'Death. Formaldehyde.'

I'll save the nurse's outfit for tomorrow. Rob lifts an arm for me to settle under. 'Happy anniversary, treasure,' he says. 'Nice idea. Shame about the execution.'

The next day the rain doesn't let up. We mosey around the town anyway, wander up to Bamburgh Castle, stop to stare across its walls to a very foggy and deserted Northumberland beach. I suddenly recall a photo of me, aged about six, posing in a pale-green and cream sundress, on a blanket on the sand with my father – the castle in the background. In my childish mind, it felt like we were so very far away from home, and the whole business of being there was so very adventurous. My dad hated having his picture taken, but made an exception for the ones I was in with him. This memory makes me say something brave. 'I was thinking the other day that maybe we should adopt a baby.'

Some seagulls do a shocking scream overhead. Rob doesn't even look up. I look at his profile, his long, slim-bridged nose with its perfectly rounded tip, his right eye that's not blinking, the dark blue of its iris and the fringe of long, black, curly lashes. 'I thought you said you weren't bothered about having a kid.'

'I'm not really.' The lie is starting to turn on me. My inclination to keep it up is failing me. 'But sometimes . . . Well, like the other day at the barbecue, I just thought how I could see myself having a daughter like Molly, who I could be close to like I'm close to my own mother. I think that would be very nice.'

'You can't always guarantee you'll have a great relationship with your children. Many don't.'

'True. But I think *we* would . . .' I am aware of a clutch of anxiety as I try to make a point that is so easily defeated. 'I also sometimes think, gosh, we'll have no one's wedding to go to, nobody's house to spend Christmas at . . . When we're much, much older we'll have nobody dropping in to make sure we're all right.'

Still his faraway gaze doesn't budge. 'I can't live my life worrying about when I get old, Jill.'

'I know. Neither can I. And I'm not. It's just, well, in some ways I think it'd be good for us to have a little person to raise and love. Good for you. To be a dad. You'd make a lovely dad.'

I force myself to continue even though an inner voice is telling me it's useless. 'I was even thinking I could get an appointment and find out about sperm donors.'

He looks at me now, in horror. 'Sperm donors? You want some strange man's semen in you? Someone who you've never even seen? You've just picked him off some list?'

My heart's thumping now. I clutch the cold castle wall. 'I don't think it works quite that way.'

'What if you got HIV?'

'Oh, Rob, it's pretty regulated. I'm sure—'

'You won't know the first thing about him! His family history! What he was passing on!'

'I think they have to declare stuff like that.'

'Oh yeah. Some bloke who sells his sperm. He's probably really honest.'

I want to tell him Lawrence did it. But then he'll know Leigh and I have talked about this and then he'll be even more disappointed in me. 'Rob, let's not end up fighting. It was just a thought. I should be able to speak about it without being trodden into the ground.'

'Well, from all this thinking you've obviously been doing, Jill, I'd say you've made your mind up.'

'I've what? How do you draw such conclusions? I punched in "sperm donors" on the Internet, read about three pages, now you're making it sound like I'm giving you some ultimatum.' I want to throttle him and say I just want to talk about it! Like normal people. How are we ever going to get past it if it just sits there? 'Look, admittedly I used to be ambivalent about wanting kids. Now I am less so. I've tried not to make it a focus, but I'm not going to lie and say it's not there. I would like to adopt a baby.' There. I've said it.

He stuffs his hands in his pockets, leans against the wall with his back to the beach, looks at his shoes that are impacted with sand. The wind blows his hair around his face. 'I don't know, Jill. If I can't have one of my own . . . How do I know I could love somebody else's?'

'Oh, please! Look how much you love Kiefer, and he's a dog!' He gives me a penetrating, querying, washed-out look. 'I know you, Rob. If somebody put a little baby in your arms and said it's yours, you would love it instantly and madly with your entire being. Because you'd know it was a little baby that somebody gave away, that somehow found its way to you. And because you're a loving person.'

He doesn't look convinced. 'I understand you wanting one. And you shouldn't have to adopt. You should be able to have one naturally. It's not you with the problem. And I told you before, if you have to leave me . . .'

He looks up, scours my face, looking more handsome and more pained than I've ever seen him. 'If I could give you a baby, Jill – if there was a pill I could take or an operation I could have – I'd do it gladly. It would make me the proudest person in the world.' He moves his hand towards my face, but takes it back quickly. 'But I can't. And there's not a damned thing I can do about that.' He moves hair off his eye, puts his hands in his jeans pockets, looks back to his feet again. 'But you can do something about it. As I've said before, you could go find somebody else and be a mother. But I hope to God you'll do it before it's too late.' He turns and looks across the water, and the mist seems to blow in a close, cold circle around his head. 'What would hurt me the most is if I thought you stuck around another ten years and then realised that staying with me was the biggest mistake you made, and then you'd live the rest of your life bitter because of it. I don't want a bitter wife. I don't want to have to carry around your regrets as well as my guilt for the rest of my days.'

It sounds like he wants rid of me.

I press the corners of my eyes. I mustn't cry. Tears will break us. 'I don't have regrets and I'm not bitter, and I never will be. I just thought that if we decided we still wanted a family, adoption would be one way for us to have it.'

'Well . . .' he says, still not blinking. 'I don't think so.'

He turns and starts walking away from me. The seagulls squeal again, and he looks up at them, and his feet make a lonely leaving sound that reverberates through the castle walls.

For the rest of the day our mood hangs damper on us than the rain. I don't know how much more of this I can take. It occurs to me to tell him some bullshit about how it's fine and I am OK with his decision because my instinct is always to make him feel better, to put my needs second to his. But no. I can't do it. What, exactly, is he doing for me?

Rob drives us home on Sunday. I sit there quietly staring out the window. Instead of a celebration of ten years married, where we might muse on the next ten to come, this weekend has been the last straw and feels more like the end of my world. The dark-green Northumberland landscape slides by and I see it in flashes between bleak thoughts. Am I to give up on Rob ever being anything other than a rather withdrawn but abiding partner to me? I'm too young to settle for that. And none of this is my fault. Try as I might not to see them, the words *we are over* just keep writing themselves on my mind.

When we pull up at our front door, my eyes latch on to something on our 'Welcome' mat. 'What's this?' I say after we get out of the car. The first words I have spoken in two hours.

Lying in plastic wrapping on our doorstep – a very rained-on plastic wrapping, I might add – is a bouquet of two dozen long-stemmed red roses.

A pain builds up on the bridge of my nose. 'Where did these come from?' I scoop them up in my arms, their dewy fragrance punching me.

I turn and look at my husband of ten years leaning on the open car door, head cocked, watching me. His desperately sad face bears a quietly-pleased-with-himself look, all of a sudden. 'I had a man deliver them yesterday. I didn't know we wouldn't be here, did I? They were supposed to be a surprise. One that doesn't bark and do its business on the carpet.'

CHAPTER ELEVEN

'I'm dying to give you the updates on the shag of the century, but first, how was your anniversary?' It's Leigh on the phone. I'm in Boots filling a basket.

I can tell she has zilch interest in my anniversary so I just say, 'It was nice, Leigh. Very nice.' I find myself, coincidentally, in front of the condom shelf, my eyes going over colours, textures, sizes. I walk further up the aisle to get away from them and find myself staring at men's deodorant. Old Spice. A sea of it.

'Was he impressed with the nurse's outfit and the bubbly?' She's giddy, giggly and annoying.

I wish I'd never told her. 'Somewhat.'

'Did nursey-nurse and her medicine chest mend things in the old penis department?'

'There's nothing wrong with his penis, Leigh. His penis has never been the problem.' I say it a bit too loudly. A fellow shopper looks at me with startled fascination.

'So I can assume you did it then?'

What is she? A teenager? 'I have to go,' I tell her.

I drop my basket on the spot and hurry out of there, pushing rudely past people. I hurry until I'm halfway down an unpopulated side street, where I have to bend over in a painful pant.

I can't go home, so I walk around the town, full of the ailing state of my marriage, wondering if I'm blowing us out of perspective, if there's a bright, light side I'm not seeing because I've convinced myself I can't. It's a sunny evening. Shops are closing, metal shutters clanging to the ground. Somebody is picking expensive watches out of a jeweller's window, and the barrow boys are loading their things-unsold into vans. Suddenly, the sky goes very dark. In about three seconds my white T-shirt looks like it's been lifted out of a pail of water. I pelt past Grey's Monument as people who've been sitting there, soaking up the sunshine, run into Eldon Square for cover. Under the awning of a pie shop, I stand and watch it coming down in one long spectacular sheet, bouncing noisily off the ground like grey lightning. Behind me, people disappear down the slippery steps of the Metro. Everybody going home. To their families. Why don't I want to go home to mine?

My phone rings. I want it to be Rob telling me that he's suffering like I am, but it's Wendy. 'I have a new phone,' she tells me. 'And a new number. I got one like Neil's. With all the fancy bells and whistles.' She asks how my anniversary was.

'Not great. We had a fight.'

There's a pause. 'I thought you sounded flat. Is it anything you want to tell me about?'

'No. It's fine. How did your appointment at the hospital go?'

'All right, although I find that whole business of people looking down there so unpleasant. You'd never think I've had three kids.' There's a pause highlighting the obvious reference to baby Nina. 'But they were very nice at the clinic.'

'When will you find out?'

'Not for a few weeks. They did a colposcopy and they biopsied some tissue.'

'A biopsy?'

'I'm sure it's nothing . . . They didn't seem overly concerned. By the way, the naked scramble for a bag of free clothing at the Metro Centre is back on again. Leigh has convinced Clifford it'll make him a national name like Antony Gormley. Because Gormley did it in *Domain Field* – had people of all shapes and sizes strip naked before wrapping them in cling film and covering them in plaster. That was art. This is exercise pants. Clifford doesn't see a difference. Leigh's busy writing the press release.' There's a pause. 'Oh, Jill, it's a silly little place to work.' Then she adds, 'But the positive is, since I told you both about my minor health scare, Leigh has been so fabulous to me!' I can hear the amusement in her voice. 'She keeps saying, if there's anything I need . . . Asking if I'm too stressed. She says she wants to come with me to my next appointment.'

'That's nice,' I say. I should have suggested that too. 'Will you let her?'

'Good heavens, no! You know me. That's a lot like turning a drama into a crisis.'

We ring off. I feel a soupçon happier.

'Don't go,' I say to Rob on Saturday, when he announces he's off to York to do a job for a few days. 'Send somebody else.'

'You know I can't do that, Jill.'

'Can't or don't want to?'

He's honest enough to shrug.

As our front door shuts I think, *That's it. You desert me and whatever I do from now on is your fault.* I even go as far as to tack *you bastard* on to the end, but it doesn't fit.

In my car I have every intention of going to see my mam and dad. Only at the Board Inn, instead of turning right, I keep going straight on.

I sit on the wall, hugging my knees, partly mortified to be here, a part of me still seeing those roses on my doormat. With my dark sunglasses on, I can pretend I'm just looking around. But my eyes keep sliding over to him, up there on his lookout post. He has seen me. He keeps glancing back over his shoulder at me. He hasn't made any effort to come over. It's rapidly feeling like the end of my world.

The beach is busy; kids and dogs and an advancing tide – plenty for him to keep his eyes on. And he's doing just that. The longer I sit, the more embarrassing this feels. I watch a young family, the dad play-boxing with his little boy who is wearing an emerald-green floppy sun hat and funky yellow-framed sunglasses.

I should go. If he doesn't come over in ten minutes, I'm gone.

Is he making a point? The point that he isn't interested any more?

Ten minutes turns into another half hour. 'Oh God,' I mutter under my breath. My eyes are sore from looking in one direction, at him, while I've got my head turned in the other. 'Please come over. Please, please . . .' I need his attention like I need a drug.

He's snubbing me. I'm certain. But if I just get up and leave it's going to look like I'm bothered by it. So I make the quick decision that I might as well be adult about this, just go over there, say a casual hello, and then leave. And then never, ever, show my face here again.

'Never again' makes me barely able to breathe. I'm right on the verge of getting up, but then . . . he's climbing down from his steps. My chest tightens. He walks on a direct course for me. My heart crashes in my eardrums. I quickly pretend I don't notice him coming, to hide my rabid delirium. But he's smiling. That smile I only have to think of lately to get nothing done with my day. It registers in me with the quick, stomach-lifting thrill of being on a small boat bumping over a large wave. I give up the act, smile back with pleasurable painful relief.

'Hi,' he says, looking me over quickly and plonking down beside me on the wall. His leg touches mine. His eyes go straight to my green cork-heeled sandals with the spaghetti straps.

'Nice,' he says, in that charming way of his. 'Can you walk in them?'

Walk. *Valk.* 'Not really. But I give it my best try.'

He smells of sunscreen, has a white trace of it that's not properly rubbed in on his neck. 'I have looked for you every day, you know,' he tells me, while he gazes out at the waves and I make a quick study of his profile, engraving it in my mind. 'I have want to see you again.'

'I bet you say that to all the girls.'

He meets my eyes. 'No. Actually, I don't. I have not felt that for a girl in such a long time.'

My heart lifts. I look out to sea and I feel him study my face now. 'Do you want to go have cup of coffee, my shift is nearly finished?'

I don't answer and he says, 'Maybe you'd like to think about it. For an hour. Maybe two weeks. How about I go away, give you some time, and you come back in three years . . .'

I grin and his eyes smile back at me. 'I wouldn't mind an ice cream.'

'I did not think you would come back,' he tells me as we stand in line at the van. 'You are too nice a girl.'

I've missed the lilt of his sentences. 'So my coming back makes me not a nice girl?'

His eyes look at my mouth like a man does before he kisses you. 'An exciting girl, I think.'

We get our ice creams – he orders and pays. We claim a bench on a jetty of rock that overlooks the sand, and there we sit and make small talk. He asks me how I've been.

'You know, Jill, I have what I think you would call a dilemma,' he says after a while.

I can feel the soft hairs of his leg next to mine. 'Being?'

'In life and in love, I take my lead from the woman. If she give me sign . . .' His eyes meet mine. 'But then sometime, you know, you just think, to hell with sign.'

'You're a "to hell with it" guy, aren't you?' I feel utterly nauseated with bravery.

He looks at me, surprised. 'No. I am not.' He shoves the end of his cone in his mouth, licks the tips of his fingers. 'But it's the old competitive swimmer's instinct. It will appear when it needs to win.'

'I am not sure I follow.' I believe I follow perfectly fine.

'What I mean is, with you . . .' He meets me fully in the eyes. 'You give me very little sign. And I don't want to be improper.'

My mouth goes dry. And then I say it. I will never know where I got the nerve, but I do. 'I've never had an affair before. I wouldn't know where to start, what to do.'

He doesn't even flinch. Just looks at me long and truthfully, while my heart pounds. 'You don't have to do anything. I would do everything.' His eyes roam over my mouth. 'All you would have to do is be present.'

And without a second's warning, he leans in and kisses me.

CHAPTER TWELVE

Now I am in his car. I am sitting in a beaten-up white VW Golf outside a block of flats. Mortified. Terrified. Electrified.

He drove with one hand on the steering wheel and the other holding mine. I sense he's treading carefully. We are sitting here as the engine turns, his foot doing a discreet rapid tapping. I'm sure he knows that one clumsy move will scare me off. His gentlemanly consideration for me helps.

In a moment of bravery I hear myself say, 'Let's go inside then.' A part of me is saying, you are disgraceful. Another part is saying, it's just a fling. People have them all the time. Leigh's having one. For a lot less reason than I'm doing this.

My heart hammers up three flights of stairs, leaving me wheezing like a windy radiator, which he jokes about. I notice how he keeps behind me; I feel his eyes on my legs and bottom. It does terrible things to my nerves. We reach the top floor and walk the threadbare carpet of a dim corridor that smells of stale cigarette smoke. The crackled reception of a radio filters under somebody's door: Oasis. That song; something about Sally waiting. He stops at a brown door with the number six nailed on wonky. *A number for my sins.* He wiggles a key in the lock and the door squeals open. He gestures for me to go inside. I do so, cringing slightly at this place.

It's funny when you see a person's home for the first time. His is no palace. But what can I expect? He won't make great money. The living area is no bigger than our spare bedroom. The blinds are dipped and the place smells unventilated, of sleep. I take in the sparse furniture. A sofa. A portable TV with a crane-shaped aerial that looks like it was left behind from the 1970s. A coffee table bearing a crushed can of Stella Artois. An armchair with his laundry dumped on it. The spare living of a single man. It's very much him: pared down, nothing fancy. But empty, so empty compared to my own home.

He sees me having a good look. 'Would you like drink? You know. I am meaning tea, of course.' He's awkward at this too. I feel strangely comforted.

I start babbling, 'Do they like tea in Russia? Isn't there a place called The Russian Tea Room?'

'Ah yes.' He nods overenthusiastically. 'Yes, in America. In New York. I have been,' he says, keenly.

'Oh,' I say, keenly back.

That dies on the vine. I don't know what else to say. Neither, apparently, does he. A sense of imminent conquest fills the air. A fridge clicks, making me jump, and he sees. And I'm pleased. Because, insane as this sounds, it makes me feel more respectable. There's about six feet between us. He is standing in front of a scratched sofa that belongs in a charity shop window, covered in loose tartan covers that don't fit at the corners. I am standing on a clawed-up doormat. I am barely inside the door. As though only part of me wants to be. My eyes tick around in circles, like the second hand of a stopwatch.

'You look like girl who is going to run.'

His telepathy makes me smile. I look at his face and experience a fresh reminder of how handsome he is, and how nice he is, and how much I've thought about being with him. 'I'm not. I promise.'

He smiles warmly, his eyes make a slow sweep of me in a universal language, and I feel it in my gut. My heart starts clashing around, right and wrong in a big face-off inside of me. The note on my car, the meeting on the beach; all this had to be. He's not just anybody. He's the man who saw me around Newcastle and remembered me from the hundreds of women he must see as he goes about his life. I take a few steps towards him and feel the wood floorboards give slightly under my feet, unsteadying me, as though I am balancing barefoot on swelling waves. I stop close enough to feel the heat of his body, and look up into his eyes, which are focused on my mouth. As I reach up on my tiptoes, his arms go around me, sweeping me an inch off my feet. And then he is kissing me again. Easier this time. Like he is pushing on an open door. Amazing how instinctively we fall into a rhythm, how we fit. I make small moaning sounds. Kissing a new man after all these years is a delicious shock. He kisses my smile, backing me up carefully towards what I imagine is the bedroom. I brim with this incomparable feeling of being sexy, sexual and wanted. My eyes flutter open and closed, like I'm fading in and out of consciousness, noticing the open pores under his eye, a few wrinkles, dashing imperfections. 'You saw me in my red suit,' I whisper into his skin that smells of sunscreen, salt and ice cream.

'Hmn. It did very nice things for your ass.' His hands go there, on top of my skirt. He makes a small moaning sound.

For a moment our pupils bounce and bob with each other. We collide now, with doors and walls, stumbling over shoes, sending a small table scraping along the floor, and making it, somehow, into the bedroom.

'I think I've fallen for you,' I tell him. It comes out in a husky whisper. Strands of my hair stick on his lips, and I peel them away between kisses.

'You're such a sexy girl,' he replies.

He's well versed in this. Without any preamble, his hands find the skin he's yet to lay eyes on; underneath my panties, the bare cheeks of my bum. He swiftly hoicks me up, so that my legs are around his waist. As he pins me up against a wall I say 'Oops!' because a framed print slides to the ground. In the soft of my back, the pointing finger of a light switch. Then his thumb is thrust inside me.

I gasp at how fast it's moving. I register the sting from a sharp fingernail. *Slower, slower,* I think. But it all happens so quickly. We fall on to a bed, which is hard on my back. He tugs at my shirt, grabs my breasts out of my black balcony bra. And then his mouth clamps on my nipple somewhat painfully and I exclaim, 'Ah!' He is oblivious to this. His moans have a new momentum. This was not what I was expecting.

And then I see them in my mind. Those red roses on my doormat.

I look up at him and don't recognise the strange face I see there. A face that is suddenly not even attractive to me. I am aware of my body shutting down, turning off all electricity. He hovers above me, fumbling with his belt, drunk passion on his face. 'Baby,' he says.

Baby?

My eyes home in on a damp patch on the ceiling. Several cracks. 'Baby,' he says again, turning me off more and more each time he says it. For moments I am mesmerised by that stain. And then it's as though I am up there, floating, looking down at myself. And I see this person – me – near-naked, breasts out, skirt hoicked up, knickers askew, not much poetry to it at all.

This is a let-down. It sounds in me like a hard shock. I catch sight of his penis and think *Oh hell, no!* But he pulls my underwear aside and is in me so fast. I feel him now, chafing, because I've turned so dry. I shove his shoulders.

No! – I want to cry. I want to cry, *No!* But nothing comes out.

I push with the heel of my hands, and his fingers dig into the cheeks of my bum, but he clearly thinks it's all part of our passion, and he says 'Oh, baby!' again, in that accent, and I want to yell *NO!* But I can't. It's all choked somewhere far inside me. Heartache and regret blaze within me, stopping my words.

His breath is thick all over me, coming in grunts. Mine is barely coming at all. 'Stop,' I say. 'For God's sake, stop.'

Or do I say it? I don't even know. Only, perhaps, in my head?

Sadness is raging in me. All I can see is Rob's face. And then he comes.

The tears pour out of me. He sinks on top of me like a spent athlete. And I want to throw up at the warm injection of a strange man's fluid inside me. I shove him. He moves in to nuzzle me, but ends up smacking his face in a pillow because somehow I've struggled out from under him and am scrambling to stand up, seeing stars. I'm seeing Rob. My marriage sits there like a burnt-out fire in some warm place in my mind. I suddenly recover my voice and the sob that was strangled somewhere inside me comes out now.

'What is wrong?' he asks, clearly oblivious that this has been anything other than a great time for me. 'Where you go? Why you cry?' He moves to get up.

'Stop,' I say. 'Don't come near me!'

I can barely get the words out for my sobbing. The tears are rolling down my cheeks. His semen is trickling down my thigh.

The lonely music is still wafting under a door when I escape into the passageway, which is a fog of cigarette smoke. I hurry towards the 'Exit' sign, my feet slipping out of these stupid sandals. I can barely make the stairs out through my tears. I take my shoes off and clip down them. Outside, it hits me.

I've left my bag up there.

My bag with my purse, credit cards, keys . . . I pat my pockets. Oh, thank God, not my keys.

But where is my car? He drove us here. I don't know where I am. I wasn't paying attention. I'm like some prostitute thrown back on the kerb. My shirt is not even done up properly. I rub hard at my eyes and squint in the sunlight both ways up a street. A man is walking towards me; an elderly man in a Hawaiian shirt and bifocals. He is walking an obese sausage dog that has its head in one of those lampshade things. He looks at me then does a double take on my face.

'Nice day for it,' he says.

CHAPTER THIRTEEN

I run upstairs to our toilet and throw up. It cascades from me, nearly taking my eyeballs along for the ride. Then I sink to the floor by the bowl, hug my legs and shiver. The dog sits straight-backed and alert in the doorway, watching me.

I manage to run a bath, cock a leg over the side into the too hot water, almost numb to the scorch that slides up my body. I let the water run, slide down into it, draw my knees up and rock on my bum, feeling it soothe me down there where I feel so sore. I stay like this, with my chin floating, until the water goes cold. Then I crawl out, shiver, and throw up again before I reach the bowl. The phone rings repeatedly. I hear it from the floor of our walk-in wardrobe where I somehow find myself, sitting wrapped in a wet bath towel. Even as a kid, I loved to cry in cupboards.

I should have told him to stop. Or did I? Why can't I remember? If I did say it, why didn't I say it sooner? Why is it all such a blur when it only happened hours ago? All I really remember is mumbling something about how I had fallen for him. Did I really say that? Then there was that grubby ceiling, and he was calling me *baby*.

I screw up my face and press the heels of my hands into my eye sockets, praying for it to undo itself, for it all to have been a bad dream.

I don't sleep Friday night at all, but by Saturday I'm so worn out I sleep half the day. When I wake up sometime in the early evening with a fuzzy headache, it hits me – strangely only now – that we didn't use a condom. My mind rattles through dates. I have to grab a pen and paper, write it down. I think I'm safe. Thank God. I can't believe I have something to actually be happy about.

Sunday is a blur. Monday morning, I wake up in a whole other panic. I'm at the doctor's as the doors open, convinced I'm riddled with diseases. When you think how old he is, all those years of bachelorhood, he must have had lots of women. And he clearly doesn't care about condoms. What if he's one of those blokes who take the attitude of *Well, somebody gave it to me so I don't care who I give it to . . .*

I don't know him, do I?

I never did.

What if I give Rob something? I think of his gorgeous clean body. How would I live with myself?

Diane Wilson, my doctor, doesn't work Mondays, the receptionist informs me. So I'm forced to tell a sheltered-looking young male locum that I've had extramarital sex and I'm going to need testing for STIs. He asks me, dispassionately, if my partner and I used a condom. I feel like I'm back in school. I can't tell him why we didn't because I'm not even clear myself. I want to say, look, I've been married for ten years. My husband was my only lover. I don't just carry a box of them around in my bag on the off-chance. I'm not that sort of person. But I don't tell him anything. I just sit there cringing. Some time later, clutching my prescription for the morning-after pill, I skulk out of there, convinced he's watching me like a disappointed parent.

I can't drive. I just sit there in my hot car gripping the steering wheel. A burly traffic warden taps on my window, saying I have to either move or feed the meter. I tell her I've no change, hoping she'll see the state I'm in and take pity. 'Then move it, will you,' she orders. So I do. It's a miracle I get home alive, or that I don't kill somebody.

Rob calls on Monday night from some hotel in Yorkshire, and I am feeling violently ill, probably from that damned pill. He says he's been ringing and ringing and when he tried my mobile some man with an accent answered. I'd completely forgotten my phone was in my bag! So now I have to make up some story about how I was mugged, to account for this, and for why I had to cancel our credit cards, and our bank debit card. We got a new PIN recently and I could never remember it, so I've been carrying it around in my wallet. Rob would kill me if he knew.

I babble out my pack of lies. The agony he clearly feels for a trauma I've not been through shames me almost more than the trauma I have. I have never lied to Rob beyond your average white one.

'Well, I can't believe you didn't call the police!' he says after he's asked me to describe in precise detail every last cut or scrape I'm tired of telling him I don't have. He can't seem to believe the bloke could have mugged me without at least leaving a bruise.

'It was a bag grab,' I keep telling him. 'He pushed me. I fell, but I just went down on one hand.'

'Please tell me you went to see the doctor, Jill.'

'Like I've said sixty times, Rob, I don't need a doctor. I'm fine.' Oh no. What if the surgery calls when Rob is home and leaves a message for me to ring them? How will I explain that?

There's another exasperated pause. 'For Christ's sake, Jill, just do me one favour: call the police. Just call them. Right this minute.'

I break a cold sweat. 'But they never go after muggers—'

'That's not the point! You can't go around not reporting crimes because you think the police won't do anything. What kind of society would we be living in if everybody did that?' He sighs again. For a brief and shining second I think he's giving up, then he says, 'Look, I'll phone them for you. In fact, I'm going to hang up and ring them right now.'

'No!' I blare.

'What do you mean no? Why can't I call, if you won't?'

'Because . . . because I don't want you to!' I'm practically shrieking. 'This is my business! I'm the one that was hurt!'

'I thought you said you weren't hurt.'

I pause. 'I'm not. I mean . . . I'm not.'

I can hear his frustrated breathing. 'Jill, you're acting very weird. What's wrong with you? You've got me very worried.'

I start to bawl. 'Don't you understand? I want to try to put this behind me.' I am incoherent. I am over the top.

He pauses. His voice softens. 'Don't cry like that. Please don't cry. When you're there and I'm here and there's nothing I can do to comfort you.' He breathes deeply through his nose and I hang on to that phone thinking, my God, Rob, please don't ever stop caring about me like this. But I've got some awful sixth sense that my days are numbered. 'Look,' he says, 'why don't you call Neil. He'll tell you what to do. I'll even call him if you—'

'Rob, please, please stop wanting to call people. Just drop it.'

He's silent for a moment or two. Then he says, 'Hang on a minute. I've just realised something . . . Your mobile got stolen. So when I rang you – that must have been your mugger! The bastard answered your damn phone!'

My heart stops.

'Right then. I'm calling him back. The fucker. This'll shock him—'

'No!' I scream.

'Yeah! Never mind no!' He sounds excited, like he's relishing putting the boot in.

'No! Just leave it. Please, please, leave it.'

I can tell by the heavy sigh, and his even heavier silence, that he's throwing his hands in the air. 'I tell you, Jill, I really don't understand you sometimes. All I want to do is call the bastard and give him a piece of my mind. Or maybe I'll call the police and give them the number . . .' He's thinking aloud.

'No! How many more times do I have to say it?'

'Christ,' he says, clearly shocked by me. 'OK. OK. Keep your hair on. I won't if you don't want me to.'

My hysteria comes down a peg or two. 'D'you promise?'

'I don't know why it matters to you, but . . . look, all right, if you insist.' Then, after a moment or two, he says, brightly, 'Look, I have an idea. Why don't you come down here? Take the train in the morning. Put the dog in the kennels. We'll check into a hotel in York. A nice one. Nicer than the one I'm in. It'll take your mind off this. Or you're going to sit and dwell on it.'

'No,' I snivel. I ache at his concern for me. 'I just want to be alone for a bit. Can't you leave me alone?'

I can tell he's lost for words. 'I don't know why you're acting this way, Jill. I mean, you said it yourself, you just got your bag nicked. They didn't hurt you . . .'

If I don't get my act together, my behaviour's going to give me away. 'You're right. I'm being stupid. I'm fine. I'm just tired and I don't really feel like travelling to York, that's all.'

He sighs. 'Well, if there's no persuading you, I'll see you sometime tomorrow.' There's a pause and then he adds, 'I love you, you know.'

'I love you too,' I cringe.

We hang up. I immediately ring up and report the loss of my mobile, then rack my fuddled head to see if there's anything else I've overlooked. Eventually, I crawl on to the bed and hug Rob's pillow and tell it the one thing I can't tell him: how sorry I am for what I've done, what a disgusting disgrace of a human being I am.

That corridor. The wonky number six nailed on to that door. Why didn't I run when I saw that hovel? The thin bedsheets. His penis inside me, and however many others he's been with. I look at Rob's pillow. This pillow used to belong to my one and only lover, on my sanitised bed, in my fragrant life. And what staggers me is the overbearing reality of how we can never go back.

I run another bath, dumping some salt in it to act as a disinfectant. Then I dig out a turkey baster from our kitchen drawer. Then, crouched in the water, I fill the baster and inject the warm salty water up inside myself. It feels melodramatic, like something I've seen in a Mike Leigh film. But with every squirt I imagine I'm cleansing every bit of his disgustingness out of me, ridding myself of him thoroughly.

Sometime on Tuesday – or is it Wednesday now? – I remember I have an animal and I take him around the block. He charges down the street, scanning the scene for entertainment and mischief. So when he finds it, in people and their dogs, I have to stand and pass the time of day, and act normal, which is a massive strain. As I come back in the door, the phone rings. It's Leigh. 'Wendy and I have been ringing you at work, but they said you've been off, they think you're sick but they're not sure. Your mobile's dead. We're worried. What's the matter?' So I tell her the mugging story and how I had to cancel my phone.

'Jesus, are you all right?'

'Yes.' It's an unconvincing yes. I cannot, I must not, tell Leigh. Nobody, for that matter. Ever.

'Well, in that case, given that you're OK, can we go out tonight? There's something I'm bursting to tell you and it won't wait.' She has that irritating glee in her voice.

'Look, I'm not well enough. I think it's a bug – on top of the mugging. I really can't go to any bar.'

'Do you want me to come over?'

She wants to for her own reasons, I can tell. I just want her off the line. 'Look, no. I'll ring you when I'm feeling a bit better.'

'Well, don't take too long because we have to talk. You're going to be amazed when I tell you my news.'

A bit later on I hear my doorbell – the impatient ding-a-ling-a-ling. The dog barks up a storm. I hold my breath until I'm convinced they've gone away. Then the phone rings. It's Wendy. I don't answer, but hear her message: 'Where are you?' The concerned voice of a friend seems to reverberate off the sad walls of my heart. 'Leigh was insisting on coming round so I thought I'd come with her to see how you are. We're worried about you. But you're not there. We thought you were sick . . . well, maybe you went to the doctor's. Anyway, we brought you something. It's on your doorstep.' Then I hear Leigh chime in, 'Along with your belated anniversary present. I researched high and low on the Internet for this company, so you'd better use it. Anyway. I hope you get better. I'll try you later.'

I go downstairs when I'm convinced the coast is clear, and peek out of the window. On my doormat is a big carton of 'home-made' soup from that lovely new place that just opened in the town centre. And under it is an envelope. I open it and it's some sort of registration papers . . . to Canine Obedience School. Leigh has attached a Post-it note that says, 'They're the best in the area. Trust me, I am now an authority!!! I've got you eight lessons. If the little effer doesn't pass with flying colours I want my money back!!!'

I go back in the house, look in the mirror. I'm a weird shade of grey and I've still got burst blood vessels all over my cheeks from how hard I threw up. I have good friends. For some reason this makes me sadder, especially given that I can't confide in either one of them. I crawl back into the wardrobe and cuddle one of Rob's cardigans. Kiefer sits sentry outside, champing through a shoe.

Next thing I know, I hear my name. I open my puffy eyes, not knowing if it's day or night, except that I am still sitting there, and

Rob is crouched in front of me with the dog curled in a cinnamon-bun shape at my feet. 'What the . . . ?' He touches my face. 'Jill?' His thumb strokes my cheek. 'What're you doing sitting in here, for God's sake?'

Slowly coming around, I shake my head.

He pulls me into his chest, circles me in his arms. 'This is all because of the mugging?' He sounds sceptical.

I lay my head on him. 'I don't know. I'm not feeling very good.' I wasn't planning on being like this when he got in. I was planning on being washed and made-up and ready to do a very good impression of the old Jill. But he has come home early. My sweet, worried husband. Of course he would.

He kisses the top of my head, plucks me up. 'The bastard, I'd like to kill him,' he says, of the phantom mugger, and I bury my face in his shoulder. He carries me over to our bed, where he cradles me and tells me, 'If he comes near you again, I'll tie his feet in a knot and ram them so far up his backside they'll come down his nose.' He kisses my head again, as though his life depends on healing me. And I bumble something about how it's not just the mugging, but I think I've got a bug too.

We lie there for ages until he has comforted my tears away, and I've picked up the pattern of his breathing and I'm breathing in step with it.

Later on I tell him I want to go out by myself for some fresh air. 'Well, just take my phone and call me at some point and let me know you're OK. And for goodness' sake don't carry a handbag,' he tells me.

I am pitiably aware that I don't deserve this man. An odd change for a girl who, not so long ago, was so sure that she deserved better.

I walk down the Quayside, umbrella-less in the lashing rain, and stand on the Millennium Bridge overlooking the floating nightclub.

Then I drag myself up Grey Street, the street that today looks like its name. A drama is going on outside a clothing boutique between a young security guard and a pensioner who has a shirt dangling from a coat hanger that's somehow got itself attached to the back of her mac. I disappear down another street and come out at Fenwick's, where I order a cappuccino and am overcome with the urge to throw up again. I try to will the feeling away by being very, very still. Other than the odd crust of bread, I don't think I've eaten in days. My lips are chapped, my mouth parched, and I've got an ache in my pelvic region.

I walk back to the Monument Metro station and get on a train. I go to the end of the line and back with my head resting on the window, staring, as we pass through tunnels, at the alternating light and dark. And then I go home, not having reached any sort of clarity that I had hoped coming out would give me. As I walk in through our front door, I register how different everything feels now, once something's done that there's no taking back, since I let a third person into our marriage. Rob is on the sofa, in a room with no light. He hasn't put the telly on, and the dog is beside him chomping through a bone. The air is filled with loss.

I will win him back again, I think. Even though he doesn't know I've lost him. I get an odd comfort from this.

'Something terrible happened while you were out,' he says. His face is pure end-of-the-world misery.

I take steps backwards until my knees meet the armchair.

'It's too awful to put into words.'

He looks at me with that face, and I am frozen. I cannot speak or breathe.

Then he holds up one of his best leather loafers. 'The fucker half ate it. Look. Two hundred quid shoes and it's got a tongue now.' He shakes the shoe so that the sole flaps against the upper like the mouth of a leather puppet.

I'm so relieved I could practically kiss the dog.

'I'll never get a pair as comfortable as these again,' he says. 'I know it's nearly dinner time but it's almost put me off my food.'

We eat fish fingers and oven chips, which he makes for us. I watch him secretly as he lines up three chips on a bun, rolls it up and stuffs the end into his mouth. Poor naive Rob. What a higher price I should have put on his love. But if only he had talked to me! It wouldn't have got this far. I stare at his fingers, the upward-turning tips, his jaw, his ears, the expression of concentration as he eats. And I cannot, cannot believe that I've had another man inside my body; that I told another man I might have fallen in love with him.

'I don't want to push it, but are you sure you're feeling better? You seem . . .' He looks at me across the table. 'Still not yourself.'

I nod. 'I'm fine. I keep telling you.'

'And it's not very convincing, obviously.'

I fake great interest in a fish finger. Thank God he doesn't know. And as long as only I do, he never will.

He tells me about his weekend away. As he talks, I get a sinking thought. Shit. My mobile has my entire telephone address book on it, including Rob's, and there's no lock on it. What if the Russian copied numbers down before the phone got disconnected? If he rings Rob to tell him?

Tell him what? Why would he ring my husband? He'd have to be off his head. But what if he wants to return my bag? He might ring a friend. Or my work. I told him where I worked. What if he comes looking for me? What if he is waiting for me outside work? *No, Jill,* I think. *Calm down. He's not going to ring your husband or your friend or your work. He's not going to come looking for you. You were nothing to him.*

I tune back in to Rob, who is looking at me strangely. I flounder, not sure what expression I am supposed to pull because I've not heard a word he's said. 'You know, Jill,' he says. 'I sense this is about more than the mugging.'

I focus on my food. But my eyes burn from holding the tears back. Then I look up. His eyes, his whole face is filled with despair. 'Please tell me. Whatever it is. You can always tell me.'

I can't chew. Why does he have to be so nice? So damned there for me? The chips I swallowed won't go down.

'Oh God, why are you crying again?' he asks me.

I just shake my head.

I'm going to have to tell him, aren't I?

No. I can't. I mustn't. What kind of cruel person tells someone something that can only hurt them, just to make themselves feel better?

He starts to say something, but stops. A frustrated sigh comes out instead. 'I'm sorry,' he says finally, and his voice sounds choked and he clangs the cutlery down. 'I feel like you're about to tell me you're leaving me for somebody else.'

I glare at him, in disbelief of his words. 'Why on earth would you say that?'

He shrugs. 'Don't know. I suppose . . . I'm sorry, I don't think that. It's just . . . I'm obviously making you so unhappy. Because it's me, isn't it? I know I'm the root cause of this.'

Sometimes I think I don't give Rob enough credit. He gets up out of his chair, shaking his head, walks out of the room rubbing a hand over his face, doing a sharp intake of breath. He has his shoes on. The one the dog chewed. It makes a strange slapping sound on the wood. I hear him clump upstairs.

I get up and put the greasy pan in the sink and start washing it. I stare out of our window at the lilac tree that droops in blooms on the other side of the glass. I drop a glass on the floor and it shatters. I slap a hand over my mouth, suppressing a scream. This scares the dog, who trots off with his tail between his legs into the dining room.

I listen to Rob's feet up there on the ceiling. Then it all goes quiet. He has obviously gone to bed. Rob will sleep a lot when he's sad. When we first found out he couldn't have kids, he'd sleep half his day away. And I'd do anything to make him get up, throw the sheets off him and yank him back from the brink of whatever it was he was teetering on. Because I didn't want him sliding over there, being lost to me. Now, I think, at least if he's up there in that bed he's still mine. Just knowing he's there makes my life feel full and safe again.

I sit down and stare at the chair that Rob vacated. The few abandoned chips on his plate. The piece of fish finger on the end of his fork.

It's no use. I can't carry this alone. I'm going to have to tell him.

CHAPTER FOURTEEN

I lie awake all night analysing the pros and cons of clearing my conscience versus taking the bliss out of Rob's ignorance. By the weekend I'm in full-throttle panic. Oddly enough, Leigh keeps ringing and asking what's the matter, like she's on a mission to prise it out of me. And it's on the tip of my tongue to tell her. But all my instincts say don't. So I don't. Neither do I tell Wendy, who rings and exercises her more subtle approach. In my 'up' moments I'm glad I'm keeping it to myself. Other times, I sit there pondering about how ironic it is that I am a good friend to everybody, yet when I need a friend I don't have one. I mean, I do. But I have one who wouldn't understand me, and another who would understand me too much. I don't feel like opening up either can of worms. A problem shared is a problem doubled.

On Monday I call in sick again at work. Jan from HR wants a doctor's note. But I can't face the doctor again, so I tell her I'll see what I can do. And then I don't do anything.

But I do put on an act for Rob. I make dinner, I smile, I chatter, I deceive not easily, but at least with a degree of accomplishment. There's a part of me that needs to pour my soul out to him in his role as my best friend. But Rob's also my husband, and this time there's no separating the two. Then one night, over pork pies and chips, he lays his knife and fork down and looks at me. 'Jill, there's something that I have to tell you that you're not going to want to hear, but I feel I have to.' He has that face that says he's about to drop a large bomb.

'I've done something that I'm not proud of. I'm sorry.' He shakes his head piteously. 'I've thought about not telling you, but it feels like a bigger crime to keep it from you. So while you're already disappointed in me, I might as well just be out with it.'

The pork pie sticks in my throat. My heart sounds an awful, ominous, warning beat.

He rubs the back of his head, looks at me while I hang in agony. 'I've betrayed you,' he says.

I am waiting for him to confess that he has cheated on me – in an insane way, hoping for it – when he says, 'I rang the police, didn't I. About your phone. Right after I promised you I wouldn't. I hung up and I rang them right away. Told them that the bastard probably has your mobile and all they have to do is ring it and they'll have him.'

It takes me a minute to process this. 'You rang them?' I am astonished. 'Why?'

'Because he had the balls to answer your phone after he just ripped off your bag! That really pissed me off.'

'Oh no!' I clutch my head between both hands. When I rang to cancel my phone I was held in a queue for ages. What if Rob got through to the police before I got the phone disconnected? 'What did they say?'

'Not a lot. If you don't report it yourself there's not much they'll do. So it's sort of gone away.'

Relief escapes from me so hard it almost whistles.

We don't say much after that. He just seems to look at me like I'm a raving lunatic. Next morning, Rob goes off to work again and I am in a flap again. Wendy rings and I'm relieved it's her because I still keep thinking it's the Russian. 'Leigh's gone out and I was going to take my lunch break and wondered if you'd like to come.'

If I told her, at the very least she'd have advice for me that I don't have for myself. But I don't want to put Wendy in the same position that Leigh put me in: having to carry the burden of somebody's secret, whether they want to or not. 'Oh, I'm actually just about to go to see my mam and dad. I've not checked in on them in a while,' I tell her. She seems disappointed; she has no idea what I've just spared her.

Come to think of it, the thought of seeing my mam feels like a good one right now. Instead of driving I take the train through to Sunderland. I send my dad out for a pint. Then I curl up on the sofa with my mother and rest my head on her warm stomach, as she watches an afternoon soap with the volume turned down. She strokes my head, which feels like therapy to me, and I find myself looking at the photo on the mantelpiece, the one of me in my PE kit when I was about thirteen, with my face full of spots. I feel an awful clench of nostalgia and loss inside of me. I want to be that girl again. I want to live in that house we lived in, in that bedroom I slept in, with my mam and dad there with all the answers. My mother must sense something in me because all of a sudden she takes hold of my hand. 'How old are you again, flower? I always forget.' She has these moments of near-clarity, and you can see they frustrate her.

'I'm thirty-five, Mam.'

From my upside-down position on her lap, I look up at her face. I can see her brain ticking over. 'Thirty-five,' she repeats and squeezes my hand in her hot, clammy one. 'I have a thirty-five-year-old daughter.' She says it with such pride, and searches my face as though I am a foreign language she is desperate to understand. Then her hand smoothes the hair away from my brow in a repetitive, cherishing rhythm, like you'd stroke your dog or cat. 'Live your life, my darling,' she says. 'Because it passes all too quickly, you know.'

Her eyes go back to the telly. I squeeze mine tightly shut and suppress the urge to bawl.

'There's something the matter with me, isn't there?' she says after a few minutes of silent staring at the telly. A deep frown forms between her eyes. Then she looks at me, the frown disappears before I have a chance to answer her, and she seems to brighten. 'What's important though is are you all right, love?' And I don't know if we're for real now, or if we're in this other world that has taken her.

'I'm not especially all right, no,' I say. Then, without taking my eyes off her face I tell her that I had an affair. Just hearing myself say it is both agonisingly unreal and a massive relief. She picks tendrils of my hair, pulls them through her fingers like thread. My mother, who was always my best friend, who always took my part, even at times when she shouldn't have. I wait to hear what she's going to say.

She keeps on doing the hair thing, as though it's just enthralling her. Then her eyes wander back to the telly and the fingering motion stops. She points to some very good-looking blonde man with a white rose in his buttonhole. 'Chase is getting married,' she says, and then she smiles, as though she's so happy for him.

The following Saturday – the two-week anniversary of my infidelity – Rob and I have a wedding to go to. An old school friend who Rob has a bit of a love-hate relationship with. I want to get out of it, badly, but I am out of excuses. I'm going to have to come up with new and better ones to account for my 'off' behaviour. Besides, there's so much atmosphere between Rob and me lately that if I bail on his friend's wedding it just might be the last nail in my coffin.

The weather stays ideal for the day. The church is pretty; the bride, a picture. Fortunately, the bit I'm most dreading – the vows – I needn't have. The bride and groom have written their own, the vicar tells us. Rob mutters, 'Oh, God help us.'

And so the serious, cherub-faced, well-fed groom clears his throat.

'Diane, I stand here before you in pursuit of a lifelong commitment. You are my best friend, my soulmate, my everything. You complete me and have made me a better man.'

The words are like bullets, hitting then bouncing off me. I feel Rob's little finger loop itself around mine and my tears start to fall, even though the words are somewhat ridiculous. Rob looks at me, and I try to sit there stoic-faced.

'Diane, what is marriage if not a beautiful balance between two people who love each other? You and I, we complement each other beautifully. I wear the trousers and you are the belt that holds them up. Together we will face the world knowing that—'

Rob leans in to me and whispers, 'Our trousers will never fall down.'

A laugh bursts out of me. Rob digs me in the ribs to stop me making an inappropriate ripple in this sea of transfixed, obviously far less cynical faces. 'Shut up,' my husband tells me off with a small laugh. 'You'll get us thrown out.'

'Belts and trousers. The daft bugger,' Rob says as we walk around Whitley Bay market some time later, killing time between photos and reception. 'Where d'you reckon he got that piece of poetic brilliance from?'

'Byron? Keats?'

Rob chuckles.

'It was the blatant sexism that got me, though. If he'd said that she wore the trousers and he was the belt, then I almost could have stood it.'

Rob's thumb strokes my palm, and I can't help but wonder if we are bashing the idea of their marriage because we've made such a royal mess of our own.

'He always had everything ass-backwards, even in school,' Rob says. 'What happened to the classic vows? The ones that don't need dressing up in belts and trousers? Like the ones we said?' He brings my hand to his mouth and drops a big kiss on my knuckles. 'Those are the ones I will happily live and die by.'

I don't know where to put my face so he can't see it.

Later, in the function room of a large pub, we mill around a big buffet, filling our plates and topping up our glasses. Then it's speeches, and I marvel at the endless faith that's placed by everyone present in these two lovebirds to defy the odds; it's as bright as the noonday sun. And the cynic in me says enjoy your moment, and the forgotten romantic in me envies them for it, longs for some fickle finger of fate that could make Rob and me swap places with them.

And then it's the first dance.

Rob and I never had 'our song' on our big day, mainly because we thought it cheesy, but it was also because we didn't have the same taste in music. The bride and groom's song is Rod Stewart's 'Have I Told You Lately', though Rob is quick to tell me he prefers the Van Morrison version. The next tune, the DJ tells us, is Bonnie Tyler's 'If I Sing You a Love Song'. I've never heard of it and neither has Rob. But the DJ prefaces it by saying it's probably THE most romantic song of all time, in that gigolo voice that says he either fancies himself on the radio one day, or he just fancies himself, full stop. It's a nice tune, touching from the word go. Rob gets me up to dance, despite my saying I don't want to. As Bonnie says that if she sings her man a love song, it will always be with him to remember her by, Rob lays his forehead on mine and we inch without skill, but with honesty, around the floor. Just me, and this sentimental man I call husband, who'll always pretend he's not really crying at sad movies. Then Bonnie gets to her last line. As she sings to her man about how love songs don't leave you like lovers often do, and she's afraid that's what's going to happen to them, I feel something that makes me look up – Rob's heartbeat quickening under the palm of my hand, the sudden pressure of his fingers on my back. And through the changing red-amber-green haze of lights, his quiet blue gaze plunders mine. By his expression, you'd think I was a rare white diamond gathering and refracting light. One that, unfortunately, he's not going to get to keep. I scrutinise his face. His eyes are full of tears.

CHAPTER FIFTEEN

'You still haven't heard anything about your tests?' I ask Wendy as Leigh and I sit with her in Café d'Espagne. I can't keep avoiding them forever.

'Probably not for another week.' She seems so completely unconcerned. Leigh seems agitated, in a distant sort of way, if you can be distantly agitated. Her attention is far across the room, inhabiting another body, another life. I will say one thing: you definitely get tired of other people's affairs faster than they do. When we arrived, I thought she was a bit 'off' with me – perhaps because I haven't rung her back to find out what her big, exciting news was.

When Leigh goes to the toilet, Wendy says, 'I have to leave that job, Jill! I can't stand it any more. All the petty fights. A twenty-hour argument over whether the sequins on the new hot pants should be gold or baby blue. They're a couple of dizzy, deranged prima donnas. They're completely dysfunctional. I've never seen or heard of anything like it. I have to get out. Urrrrrhhh!'

I've never heard Wendy this desperate before.

'Jill, I have a brain. I don't need some massively important career, but I can't do this any more – act interested in things I don't give a damn about. I need to get out of bed every morning and feel like something

I do helps improve one person's life, or even just . . . helps improve my own. That would be a start.' She glances in the direction of the toilets, hurriedly whispers, 'She's so changeable. Especially lately. It's not really directed at me, I don't think; I honestly think she's having some sort of breakdown . . . One minute she's telling me I'm an asset to her, and the next she's saying I didn't do enough media calls because none of the journalists across the country are coming to the event. Clifford overheard me mutter to myself, "Well maybe that's a reflection on the event . . .", and then he told her the whole reason why nobody's coming is because the idea stank from the start.' She shakes her head again. 'It's so silly. It's overpriced exercise pants that, let's face it, despite all the claims to the contrary, go bobbly after you've washed them six times.' Leigh comes back from the toilets. Wendy shuts up.

Then Wendy goes to the toilet, and Leigh says, 'I have to talk to you! I know you've got your own stuff to deal with, but this is really important.' And I feel like an elastic band being pulled at both ends, and it's about to snap, and it's not going to be pretty.

'I've fallen in love,' she declares a few hours later, in a turquoise tea-light-illuminated bar in Gosforth when Wendy has long since gone home and it's just her and me.

'I love him, Jill. I don't know how it happened. But it did.' She positively glows.

I stare at her through a fug of exhaustion and uninterest, trying to make sense of what she's said. 'You're in love? With Nick?' My God, I knew this was going to happen!

She looks momentarily hesitant, then says, 'Like I've never been before.'

'But, wait a minute. What about Molly and Lawrence?' The magnitude of this hits me now. 'My God, Leigh! What about your family? What about Nick's? Is he in love with you too?'

There's a guarded look in her eyes now. 'Which do you want me to answer first?'

When I don't respond, she says, 'He's not one of these men who uses the love word easily, Jill. A part of him is afraid to be vulnerable. But he says he's crazy about me, which is the same thing.' Her tone is chirpy, over-convincing. She looks thin, like you could snap her in two, in her skinny leopard-print pants and a black, ribbed V-neck top. On the surface, confident – yet nervy and fragile, somehow. I think Wendy is right. She *is* having a breakdown.

'You've got to end it, Leigh. You said it was just going to be a fling, that you'd pull the plug after a few weeks. What happened to giving it an expiry date?'

She looks at me as though the reminder is in bad taste. 'I can't end it! I have to leave Lawrence.' Her eyes fill up.

'What about Molly?'

'Obviously, it'd just be until we got ourselves sorted. Then she'd come live with us.'

'You can't leave your own daughter!' What is she? Mad?

The glass she's holding tips slightly, spilling vodka on to her trousers. She sets it down and I notice how badly her hand is shaking. 'I said I'm NOT leaving her! What do you think I am? I said this would be temporary, to cause her as little upheaval as possible.'

'And what about his family? His wife? What about his poor kids? Where does that leave them when he ups and walks out on them?'

She stares at me through the thin darkness of this near-empty room, looking like a balloon that's suddenly losing air. 'His wife! His wife! You're taking everybody's side but mine.' Then there's a heavy silence. She puts a hand over her mouth, as though the magnitude of all this is dawning on her in waves.

'Leigh! The only side I'm taking is the side of sense.' I lean over the table because the waitress is standing by the bar watching us with a bit too much interest. 'You're going to leave your family for a married man with kids who can't even tell you he loves you? Has he asked you to do it?'

She shakes her head. Tears are rolling down her face now. 'Not in as many words. But I know it's what he wants. I think he's waiting for me to initiate it because he doesn't want to be the bad guy in all this.' Her voice is a valiant tremor. 'Oh, Jill, I feel so bad for Lawrence. It's going to be awful. It's going to kill him. I feel so terrible for everybody. What am I going to do?'

'End it and forget about it. You don't have any other option.'

She wipes under her eyes where her mascara runs. There's something desperate and pleading in the way she looks at me and I don't know whether I'm more angry or sorry for her.

'I can't,' she says. 'I just told you! I love him like I've never loved anyone. Ever! I'm a different person when I'm with him. He's everything I've ever wanted.'

'Oh, come on. You love the fact that he's charming and he's into you. You love the sex and how he makes you feel.'

'Isn't that enough?'

'If you were both single, maybe! But this isn't long-haul stuff, Leigh. It was a fling, and you've got all carried away. God, he'll probably have a fit if you go telling him you're leaving your family for him!'

She is vehemently shaking her head, her double-hooped gold earrings tinkle like wind chimes, but it's the headshake of denial not indignation. 'You don't know how unhappy he is in his marriage. It's all been an act. He's only stuck it out for the kids. She doesn't know what he needs. She's never known. But I know.' She's stabbing her chest with a red-painted fingernail.

Smart, cynical, worldly Leigh. Has she really fallen for the 'my wife doesn't understand me' line?

Her eyes are imploring me. Then she narrows them. 'I might have known you'd never understand.'

'Oh, come on! If I wouldn't understand why are you telling me?' My bluntness stuns her. But I'm on a roll. 'Leigh, you've always said you could never fall for a cheat. You said trust and fidelity were everything. Remember that?'

'But he's only cheated with me because I'm special. That doesn't make him a bad person. If anything it's a clear sign we're meant for one another. And despite what you think, he doesn't take it lightly. He's got a conscience about what he's doing.'

'He took you to his wife's home after you'd exchanged two and a half emails. He wanted to screw you in his wife's bed! That's having a conscience?'

She shakes her head, wordless. I glance across at the bar and the waitress is staring at us goggle-eyed. So is the barman.

'If nothing else, think how much your life is going to change if you leave Lawrence. Who's going to do all your laundry? Have your favourite muffins toasted in the morning? Put you at the centre of his universe because he loves you even more than he loves himself? Will he do that? Mr Big Bloody Position in the Retail Industry who walks out on his wife and kids? I somehow don't think so.'

She watches the flame bounce in the turquoise tea light. 'It's not like that.' She shakes her head, unsurely. 'Why are you not on my side? How do I leave him when I'm in love with him? For the first time in my life I actually know what it's like to be in love!'

'Just don't go back! Don't see him again! You said it yourself. It wouldn't matter who you were married to. You need risk and adventure. How long before you go off Nick? Then when does it stop?'

'It would stop with him. I wouldn't want anybody else after him. I . . . I don't!' She looks at me now. 'You think I'm messed-up?'

How do I answer that?

'I'm not like you, Jill. Men don't do double takes when I walk past them. I'm very realistic about the level I attract. And I never imagined a man of his calibre would be interested in me.' She looks at me hard.

'You know, all my life men have made me feel like crap. I've never been with somebody who makes me feel so good about myself.'

'Lawrence doesn't make you feel like crap,' I remind her. We have had this conversation before, when Wendy and I had to comfort her over her no-show sister. 'Leigh, you can't want to be with a man because he makes you feel good about yourself. You've got to feel good about you, regardless of men.'

She twists a paper napkin into a sausage. Her mother really has a lot to answer for. 'You don't understand,' she just keeps saying.

'Well, you're right. I don't. Maybe I can't. But you're making a massive mistake. I do know that.'

It hits me how ugly all this is. Hits me like a tidal wave. How ugly we are. I had standards for how I lived my life. And the gulf between them and what I've done is more than I can bridge. My head has started to tremble. I'm trying to stop it but I can't.

I'm aware of her studying me, of the easy shift in the air from her crisis to mine. 'What's wrong?' she asks quietly, her green eyes flooding with concern. 'Look at you, Jill. What's the matter?'

I try to breathe, but even my breath is shaking. Inside of me, there is such unspeakable rage and regret. She will not wangle this out of me. As tempted as I am, I must never, ever, tell her.

So I tell her.

I tell her the whole thing.

And as I do, I rue it. Because when I get to the part about how I fled from his room practically pulling my underwear up in the hall, I see something in her eyes. Glee.

'Well,' she says, after a moment in which I can tell this is going to go one of two ways. 'This is a bit of a shocker, isn't it? I mean . . . I think it's a case of the pot calling the kettle black.'

'What?' It takes me seconds to register this slap. 'I am nothing like you! I never was!'

She crosses her arms at her chest in some sort of shocking physical standoff with me. 'Oh, because you've only ever had one man? Give it a rest.' She rolls her eyes. 'I've always known you've judged me. You and Wendy took some pleasure in being the good girls who never felt they missed out and who ended up with their perfect men. I've always been different, haven't I? Somebody you both liked to have around for entertainment, but whom you couldn't quite approve of.'

'But that couldn't be farther from the truth!' Surely I didn't do that? Laud my virtue over her? I never thought that having only one man was a virtue in the first place! It just was what it was: my story.

'Yes, Jill, all along you sit there and you listen to my secrets and you want all the details, but in the back of your mind, I've known you've looked down on me.'

'What? I've envied you! A part of me has thought that maybe I should have lived it up more in my twenties. It's not normal to just be with one man. We all have our demons, Leigh. We all do.'

She contemplates me as though she doesn't give two stuffs about my demons. And I register something – that I am losing a friend. And with her she takes my biggest secret. In my mid-thirties I catch myself learning one of life's tough lessons – that there's no such thing as friends you tell everything to: only on *Sex and the City.*

'I'm sorry,' she says after a long silence. 'I suppose I'm just pissed off you never told me about the Russian, after everything I've told you. I sometimes feel like my personal business is everybody's business. But yours and Wendy's . . . You're both so guarded. Especially her. I sometimes think you must tell each other things, but you keep everything from me.'

It seems so childish. Yet what did my mother always say? When it comes to friends, two is company, three's a crowd.

She holds my eyes for moments, and I can tell something's coming . . .

'What?' I say.

'There's more.' Then she adds, 'You've not been honest with me. Well, I've not exactly been honest with you either.'

Something in her face, a quiet gloating, is frightening me. 'I don't like this,' I say.

'Promise we won't fall out over this.'

'Hmm . . . you're frightening me.'

'You have to promise.'

'Look, stop it. You're going to tell me anyway, whether I promise or not.'

'You're right. I am,' she says.

She sits back now and primly weaves her fingers in her lap, staring at her red-painted thumbs. 'Jill, you've been a good pal to me, but it seemed easier at the time to not tell the whole truth. Back when I thought this thing was going to be very short-lived.'

The waitress comes and asks if we want another drink. We both hurl a 'No!' at her, and she says, 'Gawd! All right!' and walks away, glaring at us.

Leigh suddenly looks quaky and unsure of herself again. 'It's not good. You'd better brace yourself.' She holds my eyes. I hold my breath.

'See,' she says, 'the thing is, I've not been having an affair with any client at work. There never was any Nick. It's Neil I'm in love with.'

CHAPTER SIXTEEN

I sit on our chocolate corduroy sofa nursing a glass of wine. And, in the twilight of our room, with the dog snoring on the cushion beside me, I tell Rob everything.

Well, not *everything*. Everything as it pertains to Leigh.

'Keep out of it, Jill,' he says.

'But she's going to do something terrible. She's got this mad idea they've been harbouring feelings for each other for years!'

'No they haven't! He's never looked twice in her direction.'

'I didn't think so either.' I mean, I know she's always thought him gorgeous. But Wendy's having a drop-dead gorgeous husband has always just been a bit of a giggle, something to pep up the conversation. As though if he didn't exist we'd have had to invent him.

'She must have put herself on a plate for him.'

'And he couldn't say no? Oh, come on!'

'I'm not taking sides,' Rob says. 'I just would never have predicted it.'

With more than a bit of irony I wonder who would have ever predicted me.

The dog stretches, yawns, pushes me with his back paws as though he'd rather have the sofa all to himself.

'Her poor little girl,' he says. 'Poor Molly. No kid wants to grow up knowing they were a product of some crap, failed relationship. Frankly I would never wish that on a kid, having been there myself,' Rob says.

I sometimes forget that Rob's dad absconded before he was born. The story is he went out for a haircut and never came back. Rob's mother tried to love him even more to compensate, but, as Rob once told me, 'You don't want that. You don't want a mam who tries to be a dad too. You want two proper parents. And you just want to be a little boy.'

'Well, there's Wendy's lads too! What happens to her and them when he runs off into the moonlight with Leigh? What am I going to do, Rob? I can't sit by and watch Leigh take Neil away from his family.'

He leans forward in the chair, resting his elbows on his spread knees. 'Yeah you can. It's not your business.'

'It is my business in some ways. She's made it my business! She says she was besotted with him from the word go and she just got tired of telling herself he was off limits – that she just decided it was time to put herself before other people. By listening I somehow feel I enabled them. I know that she thinks that my being in on it somehow gives her a right to my vote, or something.'

'Oh, stop. That's daft. Hard to believe they've known one another for years and only started bonking now. If that's to be believed.'

'What do you mean?'

'Maybe it's been going on longer and she only just decided to tell you, when things were heating up.'

'No. I know it's odd, but it definitely hasn't been going on for years.' Of course, now that she's done this with the husband of a very close friend, who is to say what she has been truthful about?

'But I really can't believe that you knew she was having an affair and you went along with it.'

'How do you make that out? That I went along with it? I didn't stand there and cheer her on!'

'It's the same thing, though, isn't it? If you don't disapprove, they think you support them. I mean, I wouldn't sit there with any of my mates and listen to them talking about screwing around on their wives, would I? Or it would look like I approved. Maybe it'd look like I even do the same thing myself.'

Make me feel bad, why don't you. 'But I didn't know it was Neil, did I? She said it was somebody called Nick.'

'No, but you knew he was married with a family. You knew he was somebody's husband. Somebody's dad.'

I don't know what to say. Maybe he has a point. He yawns now. Even the dog groans like he's had enough.

'I'm sure he doesn't love her. He probably just wanted to get his rocks off.'

'Don't say that! God, you've got such a way of reducing everything!'

'Well, he must be hard up, that's all I can think. And some blokes, when they just want to get action, they're not too picky.'

'I know you always say she's no looker—'

'A mutt.'

'Don't say that!' I suppose because I know and love my friends I always see them as beautiful. 'And how can he be hard up? He's married! I can't believe he said to Leigh that Wendy doesn't give him everything he needs!'

Rob lies back in the chair, clasps his hands behind his head. 'Well, I'm sure he just added that to get it signed and sealed. You know, the sympathy vote. But maybe she *doesn't* give him what he needs. Maybe she's spent her life resenting not having a career and a life of her own. Maybe he really does prefer Leigh – hard as that is to believe. You don't know what their marriage is really like, Jill. There are three sides to every story. His side. Her side. And the truth.'

'There are only two sides to this story. And hers is both of them.'

He looks like he's moving to get up.

'Where're you going?' I pin him there with my eyes before he has a chance to get any ideas.

'I'm getting Leigh'd out.'

'Stay! We haven't finished!' He obediently slumps back down. 'It's so disappointing, though, Rob. I mean, I always imagined he'd be so upright. I thought they were the perfect couple. I thought I'd actually encountered one.'

'As opposed to us, of course . . .' he says sarcastically.

'You know what I mean.'

'Well, those buggers are the worst, aren't they? The upright ones. The couples who are always holding hands and looking cosy. They're always the ones who are cheating. But he's a good-looking bloke, I'll give him that. I'm sure it's hard for him to stay faithful.'

'But just because somebody's good-looking doesn't make them more likely to cheat, does it?'

'I don't know.' He cocks his head and studies me with interest. 'You're good-looking and you've not cheated. Have you?'

'Well, see what I mean.' I look at the dog.

We go on and on. Forwards, backwards and in circles. The room grows darker. The dog slides off the sofa to the floor. Rob slinks farther down the chair. 'Tell me what to do,' I plead.

'I have. Seventy-five times.'

'That's not being helpful. I feel like I have to do something! I mean, if I hadn't introduced Leigh to Wendy none of this would have happened. And Wendy didn't care for her in the beginning, but I was the one who was determined we would be a jolly threesome. I was the one who kept dragging Leigh to Wendy's exercises classes, including her whenever Wendy and I were going to go out . . . I wonder now if Leigh being all generous and helpful – this rock when Nina died – really was for Wendy or if she was doing it to somehow earn points from Neil, though that's a horrible thought. But it makes you wonder.'

He yawns again, only his yawn has an 'Oh Jesus' tacked on to the end of it. 'It doesn't make me wonder. I'm done wondering. I've had enough.' He moves to get up again. Does he think this conversation's over? I still have another ten miles of it to run.

'Where are you going?'

'Oh, I was just leaving the country.' He looks at me. 'I'm going to get a drink of water.'

I know once he leaves the room I'll never see him again. He'll be like one of those men who go missing and all they find at the shoreline is their shoes.

'I can't believe you're not giving this the weight it deserves!' I say after him.

'Just keep your big nose out of this, Jill. That's my last word.'

I nod. 'You're right.' I watch the dog pad after him across the floor. 'I'll stay well out.'

A few days later I ring Neil.

Thursday lunchtime I am seated opposite him in the stately oak-panelled dining room of the Stannington Hotel. Where businessmen lunch. Or come to have affairs. It feels peculiarly appropriate. The place was his suggestion when I rang him and said I wanted to meet.

Across a white linen tablecloth decorated with white place settings and silver cutlery, I say the immortal words. 'I know about your affair with Leigh.'

I could just as well have said I know where you buy all your socks. He is unflinching. Everything I'd rehearsed I was going to say evaporates into the green walls with their oil paintings of the Tyne Valley. And I see a Neil I've never seen before. A Neil who isn't even trying to look comfortable. Just a curious, cold bastard. Cold, like those glacial eyes.

'And?' is all he says to me. He quickly knocks back his Scotch and soda and waves the approaching waiter away.

'And?' I repeat defensively. I can suddenly picture him as a cop. I bet he can be a mean bastard. I shiver just imagining.

'And you've come to tell me to stop seeing her.' He adjusts his tie then sits back confidently in his chair, crosses his arms, turning the tables on me with just a stare. 'It's stopped already,' he surprises me by saying. 'I mean, it was never really started as far as I was concerned.'

This isn't the Neil I've known all these years. Been on holiday with, for God's sake! The Neil I never quite warmed to, but always wanted to. I always wanted to see in him what Wendy saw beyond the handsome exterior. Yet in all the slightly negative things I berated myself for imagining about him, I never actually imagined him being unfaithful.

He looks at me now. Seems to note my speechlessness. Shrugs. I run my eyes over him. I'm having a hard time picturing this man with his face up Leigh's skirt. In his own house. Bathroom. Bathtub. I always thought he was upstanding.

'That's not how she sees it. She's in love with you.'

His eyebrow shoots up, as though he's mocking the very idea. 'In love with me?' Something in his expression seems to humanise again. 'Argh, well, that's her misfortune.'

I pick up my wine glass. It feels weird sitting here drinking with him, but I need the Dutch courage. 'You are still seeing her. She said you are. So there's no point in saying it's stopped.'

'Well, frankly, my friend, that's none of your business,' he says, with a smug Hollywood flippancy, and I hate him – it's as though for all these years I've been waiting for him to say something odious like that. Even if perhaps I did deserve it. There's a lone crusty bread roll sitting on my side plate, and I feel like pelting it right between his eyes.

'Do you know your wife might not be well?' Around me I hear the chink of crystal water glasses being filled by waiters. Two creases form between his eyes, the only imperfections on his blank, impenetrable, handsome face.

'I don't know what you're talking about.'

Adrenaline rages in me. 'She's been for tests. Did you know that? Why don't you go home and ask her how she is, how she really is?' I bet he never does. I suppose I've always sensed she loved him more.

He knows I know he didn't know. But again he doesn't flinch. But this time his Mr Cool act seems just a touch less convincing; there's a twitch under his left eye. 'She's never said anything to me about any tests.'

'No, because she didn't want you or the lads to worry. That's how strong and unselfish she is. But while you've been busy with Leigh, she's been seeing doctors.' I'm exaggerating, and that feels wrong, even cruel, but somehow necessary.

He flushes under his eye sockets, studies me for moments, as though he's thinking how to respond, then he says, 'Well, then it's good she's got such a good friend in you, isn't it?' And I don't quite know what that's supposed to mean – if he's actually paying me a compliment. If I can take anything he says at face value. Then he leans to one side, slides a hand into his trouser pocket and pulls out some money. Then he stands up. And I realise I've lost. Rob was right. I shouldn't have done this. You can't play cat and mouse with Neil.

'I have to get back to the station, Jill,' he says. Am I delusional or does he say it almost with affection? 'Look, don't worry yourself. Leigh and I . . .' He doesn't finish. He tosses the notes on the table, glances at me with finality, then briefly lays a hand on my shoulder. Perhaps he just can't be bothered to finish the sentence. Or he feels he shouldn't have to. Or does he just mean *it's complicated*?

I watch his confident, unfaltering walk as he cuts a path around tables. A few faces look up as he passes them.

The next day comes and goes, and the wrongness of my confrontation takes root and grows in me. Go to see Neil! Why did I do that? Rob was right. What did it accomplish? Nothing, except to infuriate Leigh – if he tells her. But I'm sure he won't. One thing I've always sensed about Neil: he is too shrewd to say more than he needs to.

Rob keeps asking me what's the matter. 'Been up to anything I wouldn't do?' he says, narrowing his eyes. I go into work and am useless. The good thing is that Irving is off on holiday. Torquay is being blessed with his presence. (I hope he's staying in one of those Fawlty Towers guest houses with Basil after him, doing the goose-step.) So at least I don't have him glaring at me with those large eyeballs. Only a lot of phone calls, and a lot of accounting to do, and a couple of urgent billing matters that he's left instructions for me to handle. 'He discovered you made an accounting mistake just before you went off sick,' Leanne whispers, as though she shouldn't be telling me.

'Mistake?' Shit. I did make a couple, but I'm sure I fixed them. 'What sort of mistake?'

'No idea. He wouldn't say.'

'Well, what did he look like? Was he furious?'

She shrugs. 'But I'm sure he'll let you know about it, if it's anything.'

Damn it. I've never made mistakes in my job until recently. I've always taken such pride in it. Well, I suppose if it'd been anything major he'd have delighted in telling me.

Rob and I seem to heal. Or rather, since the news of Leigh's infidelity, we haven't had a wrong word between us. He doesn't look at me strangely. All that business about the mobile phone and my mood seems to be off his mind. And, strangely enough, the business behind the mobile phone and my mood seems to be off mine. Even though I still have the dim feel of him in my body. And the sense that he's there, waiting to be my next thought, if I let him.

When I come home in the evening, Rob's got dinner made. He heaps spaghetti alla puttanesca on to two plates. The M&S box sits torn up on the worktop. But the pasta, me, him . . . it all feels too easy, this returning to normal. *Affairs are easy,* didn't Leigh say?

We're just eating, and I am counting my blessings yet again, when the phone rings. I pick up and I hear two words. 'You bitch.'

'Leigh!' My heart falls. He did tell her!

'You unimaginable, double-crossing little back-stabber! And to think I thought you were my friend and I could trust you!'

This verbal hail of bullets sends me collapsing on to the kitchen chair. 'Oh, Leigh, I . . .'

'Don't "Leigh" me, you cow! You went to see him to tell him to leave me? After I'd told you I loved him? That I was ready to leave my family for him? You went to break us up?'

'It wasn't like that—'

I'm cut off by her screaming obscenities at me. 'Like you've got some right to start telling people how to lead their lives, you hypocritical little cow. You of all people!'

She goes on bawling me out, but I'm thinking only one thing. I knew I should never have told her. I feel the need to say nice things, to get on her right side again.

'He's ended it now!' She's sobbing. 'Do you realise what you've done? He doesn't want to see me again. Won't even give reasons. He was furious that I told you, and even more furious that I hadn't told him about Wendy and the tests.'

'Well, maybe that's his reason. I mean, the possibility that his wife has cancer and you knew about it while you carried on with him – it is a big enough one.'

I feel her seething. 'Even Wendy says it's more than likely not cancer.' There is uncertainty and a tinge of remorse in her voice. Then she says, 'Well, I suppose you're happy. You've really done it for me, haven't you? Tell me, Jill, what am I supposed to do now? I've already told Lawrence I'm leaving him!'

'That was Leigh,' I tell Rob when I put the phone down.

'Glad you clarified that. I was wondering.'

I regurgitate the conversation.

'I take it you didn't keep your big nose out, then,' he says.

'I can't believe she's already told Lawrence!' This is a disaster, and she's right; I probably have made things worse.

In bed, Rob holds me and says I'm a good person and I tried to do the right thing, even if it was a cockamamie idea in the first place. Then he scratches his chest and says the dog's giving him fleas. His parting words before sleep are, 'You'd better prepare yourself. Something tells me you've not heard the last of this. What do they say? Hell hath no fury like a woman scorned.'

For the next few days Leigh's call haunts me. She's right to hate me. What sort of hypocrite am I? I, a cheat, betrayed a friend who had an affair because I didn't like her choice of partner. And I did it with complete disregard for what this would do to her. And despite what Rob says, I do believe she thinks she's in love with him. And I believe her when she says she really did intend it to end after a few weeks and she never wanted to hurt Wendy. Some people are just naive to think they're never going to get found out. But what troubles me most is that never for one minute did I consider that the affair might blow over, that Leigh would finally see sense, or Neil would dump her, and life would go back to normal again. I never even gave it time to happen. I just barged right on in there and messed everything up.

'Don't feel too sorry for her, Jill,' Rob tells me. 'People who cheat on their partners don't deserve you losing sleep over them.' We're in bed again.

My heart sinks. 'But people stray for all kinds of reasons, Rob. Surely they deserve the benefit of the doubt as we haven't walked in their shoes.' He loosens my tight grip on his chest hair.

'Not when they've been unfaithful. Cheating is a choice. You don't just do it as some spontaneous response to disappointment.'

I am dwelling on these words when he adds, 'You should be furious she ever told you any of this when you were Wendy's friend too. She should never have put you in this position.' And he's right. She shouldn't have. But she did. And I can't use that to justify betraying her. But somehow, I suppose I have.

The next phone call I get, sometime the following afternoon, is from Wendy. I see her number on my call display and think *Oh God.*

'Why did you tell him I've been for tests?' she asks me, in a subdued tone, which is as close as Wendy will ever get to telling you off. 'He said he bumped into you in town. That you happened to mention I was seeing a doctor.'

He lied. And now, by default, I have to. Again. Neil must know that I chose to confront him rather than tell Wendy. So he's using that. He's using me. Expecting I'll keep up the story. That I'll lie to protect my friend, and somehow save his bacon in the process. So my first instinct is to stick it to him and tell her the truth. 'Wendy . . .' I take a bracing breath, then I suddenly see sense. This is not about revenge on him. It's about protecting her. 'Look, I'm sorry. I know I'm a big idiot. It was inexcusable of me. It just slipped out.'

There's a silence. I hate lies. Even the kind ones. 'I'm not sure how it really happened actually.'

'It's all right,' she says. 'I'm not hauling you over the coals.'

'Aren't you?'

'No. Worse things could have happened, couldn't they?'

Really? Like what?

'I better go, though. I've got to clean the house and then get some dinner on, and there's a job in a solicitor's office I'm thinking of applying for. Half of Newcastle is probably going to go for it and get rejected, so I might as well be one of them.' Her humour sounds strained. We say goodbye. It bothers me as soon as I put the phone down. I know Wendy. If she were really furious with me she'd be 'strained'. Then she'd probably freeze me out of her life. So I quickly call her back and apologise again and ask her if we are still friends.

'Of course we are, silly billy. I've forgotten about it already.'

A few days later I have to go to Sunderland to take my parents a piece of cushion flooring I bought for their bathroom, because my mam has been peeing on the carpet in there. I'm just coming back and am stuck on the A1 in traffic when, immediately ahead of me, a BMW rear-ends a VW hippy van. Out of the van pour a fat young girl and a guy who looks like a pack of sausages with a head on – presumably the father. He's a tattooed ball of blubber with a bottle of Newcastle Brown Ale in each hand. And then there appears to be the granny, one of those hardened council-estate hags with smoker's hair, whose face is gradually capsizing into the space where she used to have teeth. And they're ganging up and laying into the driver of the BMW. I thrust the heel of my hand on to the horn. The noise feels nice. They all stop their bickering and look at me, probably wondering what my problem is. I leave my hand there, blaring, staring at them with an intensity that equals the noise I am making. Then it hits me. How am I going to explain to Wendy that Leigh and I have fallen out? What's Leigh going to say to Wendy about it? Our stories won't match. I stop blaring on the horn and put my head in my hands.

The dispute is over. Somebody behind toots at me now, because I'm still sitting there, not moving. I hurriedly get going and am just slipping into second gear, when I see it. In the opposite carriageway, zooming up to pass a slow-moving Nissan Micra, is a beaten-up white VW Golf. I don't see his face, just the flash of him; a blur of tanned skin and dark hair.

My knuckles whiten as I grip the wheel, attempting to drive in a straight line. Of all the cars on the road in Sunderland, what on earth were the chances of that? It's utterly mad and unbelievable. How many more times in my life is this man going to just coincidentally appear?

I get home safe, but hardly sound. Kiefer is going scatty for a walk because I didn't take him to Pause for Paws today. I'm hungry, but I've not been to the supermarket and don't know what we've got in for dinner. All the strands of my togetherness unfurl again. Our answer machine says we have four new messages. What if he saw me and now he's ringing? Maybe all that commotion across the road made him look over. I can't breathe. I let the dog out and go around the sitting room doing a quick nervous-energy tidy, picking up newspapers and putting them in the wastepaper basket, one hundred per cent convinced it's going to be his voice on that machine. Then I finally press 'Play'. The first message is from Rob, saying he'll be late home so not to bother with dinner – maybe we can go out – that he loves me, that he's feeling better about things. Every time I hear Rob's voice, loving and trusting, I fill with a glorious sense of reprieve, a fawning inner gratitude to a God I never knew I believed in until now. If Leigh were going to ring Rob to get her own back on me, she'd have done it already. Knowing her and her anger at me, I can't see her waiting five days, trying to decide whether to tell him or not. So with each day that passes, I am one step removed from my worst prediction. The second message is from Mrs Towers from the puppy obedience class that Leigh very thoughtfully signed us up for. Talk about poetic timing. And the third message is Lawrence. Oh my God! The distress in his voice! 'Did you know this was happening, Jill? You're her friend, are you really going to tell me you didn't know? All those times you went out, were you talking about this all along? Or maybe she never did go out with you. Maybe you covered for her . . . Maybe there were no exercise classes all along.' He is thinking aloud. He sounds beside himself. But even when he's angry he sounds gentle, which makes me bleed for him. 'She's gone!' he says, as though to himself, in disbelief. 'Neil doesn't want her now, and I told her I certainly don't. She's moved in with Clifford.'

She's living with her boss?

He sighs, as it comes out slow and tortured. 'Molly's howling and won't eat. I'm pissed off and I'm confused, and I miss her and I hate her and despite everything I still love her, and I don't know what to do. And I had my parents over, but they didn't really help and they've gone home now and they must have done a lot of furtive, nervous drinking because

I'm finding beer bottles in weird places . . . And I know I annoy her, but I never thought she would do this. And I'm so damned hurt.' He stops abruptly. 'Argh!' he adds, as though he's worn himself out. 'Don't bother ringing back. You're as bad as she is.'

I wonder if she's told him about me. I quickly press 'Delete'.

The last message is from Wendy, a total contrast to Lawrence's. 'Hi, Jill,' she says, her voice flat. 'Give me a ring, will you.'

'Wendy!' I say, when she picks up.

'Oh. Hi there.' Her voice is a mere whisper.

There's a tense silence while my heart beats in nervous anticipation. Something is terribly wrong.

'Wendy, what's the matter?'

CHAPTER SEVENTEEN

We sit in her car around the corner from where she lives, overlooking Jesmond Dene and a group of motley teens smoking behind a wall. She looks raw, like somebody has told her life-changing news. Impassive and empty. Wendy, but not Wendy. As though Wendy has left the building.

She plays me the voicemail on Neil's phone.

Leigh's distraught voice fills the quiet car. 'Neil, you've got to talk to me. You can't just say it's over. This is my life here! I've left my husband for you, you bastard!' She bawls. 'Oh, I'm sorry. I didn't mean to call you that. I love you! I always have. From that day Wendy invited us over for dinner around Christmas I have been in love with you. And I miss you. I miss your face. I miss your body. I miss you in my body. So you can't do this to me, you bastard! You've got to talk to me! Answer the fucking phone!' By the end there she's growling like a wild animal. It makes Alex Forrest in *Fatal Attraction* look civilised.

'I came home from my doctor's appointment. My phone rang as I was walking in the door. It was Neil, telling me I had his phone.' She looks at her bitten fingernails. 'He was right. They look so much alike.' Her throat makes a dry crack. 'He insisted I bring it to him, but I told him I wasn't feeling all that well and I needed to make a cup of tea. I said he'd just have to get it later. Then we hung up and it rang again.' She frowns. 'I saw Leigh's name.'

Wendy, a level, more subdued version of herself, looks at me now. 'Don't ask me how I know his password. I'd rather not get into that . . .'

I sit there barely breathing as she puts the phone back in her pocket, the fine hairs on her arms standing up. The lads by the wall do a catcall after some girls who grin as they walk past.

'You knew, I assume?' She looks me in the eye.

How can I lie? I don't even have to. My hesitation, my silence, answers for me. I quickly add that I knew she was having an affair. I didn't know it was with Neil.

She digests this for a moment; her stillness is palpable. I am waiting for her to get angry with me, but surprisingly she doesn't.

'That's why she's been behaving so off-it at work. She comes in, doesn't even look at me or say good morning, goes into her office and slams the door. Clifford comes in virtually right behind her and does the same thing . . . I thought I heard her crying in her office the other day. I tapped on the door, asked her if she was OK. She didn't even reply. When I tried the door, it was locked. I was thinking she must still be sulking about the stupid store opening, but in the back of my mind I felt it was more than that. Leigh doesn't sit crying very often . . . Then I heard her call "I'm sorry".' She looks at me frankly. 'I put my ear to the door, thinking did she really say that? Who is she talking to? So I said, "What about?" and she just said it again, "I'm sorry" . . . I thought she meant about being a little off with me recently . . . She was really cut up. She was apologising for sleeping with my husband.'

I am a little surprised. I would have expected Wendy to exhibit more shock or rage against Neil, yet she seems more fixated on Leigh's behaviour.

'How long has it been going on?' she asks, now, coldly – as though there are things lining up in her mind, in some sort of order that she needs to clarify.

I recognise that the more I say, the more I betray Leigh. But what am I supposed to do? Wendy is the injured party. 'Weeks,' I say. 'Since June, maybe.' But maybe it was before that. I can't think.

'Weeks,' she repeats, distantly.

'She said it was somebody called Nick. She said he was one of her clients. She only told me it was Neil the other day. That's why I went to see him. I was frightened he was going to do something terrible like—'

'Leave me.'

'I was convinced she meant to have him at all costs.'

She watches one of the lads idly kick the wall. I cannot get over how freakishly calm she is; I am completely puzzled by it. She doesn't comment, just sits for a while – a long while – staring over the top of the steering wheel. Her chest is all that moves, a shallow rise and fall. But her pallor frightens me. Even her hands seem to have lost their tan.

'All the times she kept telling me to tell Clifford that she was out with some client. She was getting me to cover for her while she was having sex with my husband.' She looks at me, vulnerable and baffled now. Then her shoulders shake almost imperceptibly. Her brows knit and form two vertical ridges between her eyes. 'I don't understand. Neil's always said she's brittle and has bad breath.' She searches my face. The intensity of her scrutiny makes me look away.

'Does he know you know?' I ask.

'Not yet.' Splotches of red break out on her forehead.

I want to say, *What are you going to do?* But it has just happened. How can she know?

I feel as helpless as that day when Nina died, knowing no comfort can compensate for the pain she is feeling. I stare at her hands, her platinum wedding band, the only piece of jewellery she ever wears, and I don't know what to do for her. 'Look, do you want to come home with me? Stay with us and we'll work out what you're going to do together?' I don't know Wendy's heart, which in a way makes me realise that I don't know her at all. I can't guess as to what she's likely to do. Maybe she can't leave him. Maybe they'll have a big row, he'll say it's over, she'll get a new job, never talk to Leigh again. Life will somehow mend itself, as my own seems to be doing, after a fashion.

She shakes her head, her eyes still not moving from the scene in her mind. 'I covered for her. I actually covered for her while she was out screwing my husband.'

I am still amazed this seems to be bothering her more than the fact that Neil cheated.

I look at her unblinking profile, the strapping, speckled shoulder nearest mine. As though she reads my helplessness, she looks at me, for a long time, still completely unable to comprehend what Leigh did. Then she says, 'I have to go into hospital. They've found something wrong.' Her eyebrows shoot up and she gives a tiny little huff. A huff that says, completely without self-pity: *Can you quite believe this?*

I follow Rob around the house, breathless in my distress as I tell him. The good thing, apparently, is that the cancer – carcinoma in situ – as she called it, is very early stage. But she has to have a 'procedure' that's supposed to remove the affected tissue. If it works, she's fine. If not, she'll have to have a hysterectomy. 'Have my womb out,' she'd said, and she'd put her pale hand on her belly.

Later, Rob holds me in bed while the word 'cancer' circulates around us, making every other drama pale by comparison. I feel the rhythmic tickle of his eyelashes on the side of my face. 'Rob, I feel like an evil chain letter.'

'Don't be daft. It's not your fault she ended up with his telephone. And if she knew his password, maybe she's used to checking up on him.'

I don't quite follow. 'But if I'd never gone to Neil, he'd have never dumped Leigh, and she wouldn't have rung his mobile in hysterics.'

'Yeah, but she'd have found out some other way. Surely you always know, deep down, if your partner's cheating. People who have affairs always get found out, don't they?'

The next day is a reasonably quiet one at work, thank God. Irving is back from holidays, but he never mentions the error I'm supposed to have made. Nor does he ask how I am, or in any way reference my time off and the fact that I didn't provide a doctor's note. But in some ways all that feels like a long time ago now. I try to get Wendy all day on her mobile, but it's switched off. And she's not home when I call the house. And of course I know she won't be at work. I have a mountain of accounting I've not got done because I've been in la-la land, so I stay until past six to catch up. Then I drive home, after picking up the dog, subconsciously noting every small white car, my new habit. When I get in the house I try Wendy again. She'd usually be home for the lads at this time, making dinner. I'm getting a bit worried now. I have visions of her standing on the Tyne Bridge, staring into the depths of the water . . . a headline on the news . . . somebody witnessing a body, as if in slow motion, fall through the air. Rob and I are in the middle of eating when she rings me back.

'I've thrown him out,' she says. 'I went home after I'd sat with you in the car. Neil came home and I gave him his phone. He went into his study, presumably to listen to his messages, then he came back out again. Seemed fine. Obviously didn't suspect I knew a thing.' She's keeping her voice down, maybe the boys are around. 'The next morning he got up and went to work while I pretended to be asleep. Then I made tea and toast. Then when the lads went out I took four large suitcases down from the cupboard. I packed Neil's clothes, Neil's toiletries, Neil's paraphernalia from his desk drawers, even Neil's dirty laundry from the bin. Then I put Neil's name on some packaging labels and tied them on the cases, got into my car and drove to the police headquarters. I parked across the road and watched the building for a bit. Then I hauled those suitcases across the road, two at a time. I dragged them to a spot right in front of the main doors. Then I turned and . . . I just walked back to my car.'

'Good grief, Wendy! You didn't!' I am visualising this. It's fantastic. 'What did you do next?'

'Nothing. I looked one more time at the suitcases abandoned in the middle of the street. I said "Goodbye, you son of a bitch", and then I drove off.'

'You didn't! What happened?'

'Oh, he was furious I'd humiliated him in front of people at work. I think he was more upset by that, than the fact that I knew about him and Leigh. Apparently seeing suitcases lying outside police headquarters, they were about to call in the bomb squad. Until they saw his name on the label, opened one of the cases and saw a pile of his dirty underwear on top.' She becomes silent for a moment or two. It strikes me as something we'd have laughed about, if it had only happened to someone else. 'I never even thought of that, Jill. I probably should have . . . I just didn't want him in the house and I didn't want to have to see him. By the time he came home I'd had the locks changed.'

'That fast?'

'It was the first thing I thought of to do. Keep him at bay. It was pointless in some ways, though, because I had to let him in. To have a talk. There was no other place to have it. Your home is the only place you can respectfully hurl things at people.'

'You hurled things at him?'

'I did. Yes. A few.'

'Are you all right?'

'Oh yeah. I aimed a few plates at him then he walked out, and you know what he said? He said, "Look, I really don't feel you should be making me the big villain in this".'

'He didn't say that!'

'That's Neil for you . . . I've told the lads that their dad's gone away on business for a few days. I have to buy some time to think how to handle this with them. That is my biggest fear, Jill,' she whispers. 'I don't know who they're going to blame.'

'What d'you mean? Him of course!'

'But I'm the one who's thrown him out. Maybe they think parents are always supposed to work everything out.'

We hold a silence for a bit. Then I ask her, 'So what do you think you're going to do now?'

There's a good pause before she says, 'Sit down and have a cry.'

It strikes me that what I'm doing every day now is living with new information. It gets thrown at me, I intend to try to make sense of it, but it just gets pushed along the great conveyor belt in my head. Because more just keeps getting piled on board, and the wheels of my sanity have to be kept in motion.

A couple of days tick over. Wendy clearly does her grieving in private because when I see her she's in fully-fledged survival mode. 'We've got joint bank accounts,' she tells me. 'And it wouldn't surprise me if Neil tried to do something devious . . . Do you think he can put a hold on our credit card without my consent?'

'I haven't a clue.'

Ring the bank, she writes on a to-do list, which I'm supposedly helping her compose as we sit under the Tiffany lamp of her kitchen table and she sinks three-quarters of a bottle of wine without even registering that she's doing it. 'You know, I can't even remember what accounts we have. I can barely even remember which bank we're with.' Her pale, harrowed face looks at me. 'I've been this cliché of a woman that lets the man take care of all that. But it wasn't intentional. It was mainly because I had other things to do and I just wasn't all that interested in the boring money side of things.' She is now though. She's particularly concerned about the loss of her own pay cheque. 'What should I do? Should I ring Clifford and tell him that for personal reasons I can't come back?' She rests on her elbows on the tabletop, her chin in her upturned palms.

'I don't think you'll have to. Leigh's living with him. I'm sure she's told him everything.'

She shakes her head. 'I still think I should at least email him. He did employ me. I owe him some sort of explanation. I don't want him thinking I'm the bad person in all of this.'

'I don't know why you keep saying stuff like this!'

'I'll think about it later,' she says.

We're just going through a pile of bills when she suddenly drops the pen and stares at me through the soft kitchen lighting. She has black lips from the red wine. She rubs her face hard with both hands, messing up her mascara. 'Jill, I don't even know where the deeds to the house are. Would you think me really stupid if I told you that I don't even remember if Neil put the house in our joint names?'

Some time later, she rings me on my new mobile when I'm at a managers' function at work that I couldn't get out of. 'It's all sinking in now, Jill. All those afternoons when she'd come back from lunch and look at me coyly, secretively; they must have actually talked on the phone while I was in the next room, planned their shenanigans.' I am still puzzled by why she seems more disappointed in Leigh than in her own husband.

I walk outside the functions suite, with my glass of untouched wine, to get some quiet. I remember Leigh telling me they'd had sex in her office. Wendy was at the doctor's, hadn't she said? Although Leigh wouldn't have known why at that point. And that small fact makes her marginally less contemptible.

'Then there was the day when she was trying on underwear in Fenwick's. Do you remember, Jill? She was parading around and acting very strange. She must have been buying them for Neil. She was parading her affair with my husband right under my nose! Who would do that? What did I ever do to her to deserve that? What satisfaction could that possibly give her?'

Lots. Because I think fundamentally Leigh envied Wendy's blithe uncomplicatedness. As Rob once said – and I didn't believe it at the time – Leigh can't stand it if you are happy. Deep down I always knew she was a bit of a foul-weather friend. She enjoyed talking about your misery with you – she was a great listener when you were down in the dumps – but she never much wanted to hear when you were happy. But as in all things, you weigh the good with the bad. Especially as you get older. After all, no one is perfect. You can't design friends to your personal specifications. If you banished people because of their shortcomings, there would be no one left at all.

I put my glass on the windowsill, nod to a few of the footballers who walk past and glance me over, like they think they're God's gift. 'I'm not so sure she was parading it for your benefit, Wend. I think she was just so high on the whole thing that she didn't even register her own inappropriate behaviour.'

'Mm,' she says, not convinced. 'And the barbecue . . . They were obviously carrying on then and none of us were any the wiser. We never saw a sign.'

'No.' But I did, now that I think about it. The way he watched her when she came out of the back door carrying beer. I suppose I didn't want to see it. Or maybe the integrity I credited her with made me blind. Rob was watching her too. But there was something in Neil's face. It was the look of a man rediscovering somebody. The look of a man with a secret.

'It all started, apparently, because she bumped into him in the bank,' Wendy tells me the next day over coffee.

'She told me that bit. Only she said it was a client.' To be saying all this, I have clearly taken sides.

'She asked him if he'd come with her to get a coffee, and then quite out of the blue she told him she'd always wanted him. Ever since day one. She laid this big confession on him in the coffee shop, can you believe! He was stunned. He said he wondered if she was taking some strange pills or something. But then she emailed him at work to apologise, asked to buy him lunch, to make it up to him. He said he didn't want to go but he went. And it kicked off from there.'

He didn't want to go but he went, my arse! And Leigh told me that he had invited her for coffee and she had turned him down, because she was too taken aback by the offer. 'Well, fancy,' I say.

'It's odd, though, isn't it? They've known each other for five years, and only recently they started having an affair.'

Yes! Join the confused club! 'That's what Rob and I can't fathom.'

She pushes her coffee cup away. 'Do you think we're all wrong? That maybe it's even gone on for years and she would never say that because it somehow makes her worse?' Then she adds, 'Don't answer that. If I found that out, I might have to go and kill her.'

And I don't think I want to know either. Though I admit, anything is possible now.

'Neil would never say no.' She rotates her wedding ring on her finger. 'He always loves to be admired. He's as susceptible to it as we all are. Even though it tends to happen every day to him.'

Is she going to take him back? Because she's suddenly seeing him as a victim – of Leigh the devious predator who has been biding her time, and of his own irresistible good looks.

Deception: one's own or other people's; I'm not sure which is worse. Either way, it all gives me a headache. I come home from work emotionally and physically done in. Rob and I eat dinner, then Rob makes me come with him to walk the dog. Kiefer, with his new training collar that the obedience woman recommended (thanks to Leigh), is walking almost like a dream. When we get back to the house I tell Rob I want to go to IKEA to get some more of the water glasses I like that we're running low on, having had some breakages recently, and a few other things that are well priced there. It's not really that I've got some urgent need to shop. I just have to do something normal, ordinary, reassuring, small. He comes with me.

'Do you like the plain ones or the blue ones?' I ask him, holding up one of each.

'Yeah, they're great.'

'Which?'

'Neither. I mean, the blue ones.'

'Rob?' I stand still, holding the blue one. 'Where are the deeds to our house?'

He's bending over to tie the lace of his running shoe, and he looks over his shoulder at me. 'What's that got to do with water glasses?'

'Not a lot, but where are they?'

'In our safe. In the spare bedroom.'

'I don't know the combination.'

'Yeah. Have you ever wondered why? Because knowing you, you'd write it down and shove it in your bag along with the words Bedroom

Safe Combination. You'd probably even draw a bloody map to go with it. And the mugger who nicked your bag would be having a field day by now.'

He stands up and kisses me, and I try to blot out thoughts of the supposed mugger who stole my bag. I wonder if he will remind me of it forever. Then he turns. A pretty young woman goes past in a pair of very tight white jeans, and Rob's eyes follow her.

'Are you looking at her bum by any chance?'

'Never,' he says. 'I mean, who would look at bums when there are glasses to stare at?'

I slap him and he grabs me. He pulls me into him, wraps his arms around me, starts singing one of his little songs – 'My wife, in the middle of IKEA. My wife. Oh how much I really love her' – to the tune of Madness's 'Our House'. A woman holding a glass candlestick looks at us in amazement.

'I was thinking we should take a holiday,' he says, reluctantly letting me go.

'Oh? Really? Like where?'

'Somewhere expensive and tropical.' He thinks for a second. 'Barbados.'

'Barbados? Ha! Well, that would qualify as expensive, I'm sure. Maybe we should sit down and do the sums first.'

'Maybe,' he nods, looking self-satisfied. And then he pulls me into him again, but now he looks so serious. 'I thought I'd lost you, you know. I'm aware this isn't really the place for the conversation, but I know I've been hard to live with lately, for reasons I can't explain. Jill . . . I thought you'd lost patience with me . . . that I'd driven you away.' His warm hands clutch my face; I can feel the calluses on them. 'I love you, Jill. I'd die if we broke up. It'd kill me to think I ever drove you to do what Leigh did. Two out of three marriages here have split up, but I swear I'll never let that happen to ours. You – and us as a couple – mean more to me than anything in this world.' His deep blue eyes plunder mine. 'And I mean that. More than anything.'

I burrow my shameful face in his shoulder. Thank God I never told him. Owning up would have been selfish. Guilt isn't some kind of time-share arrangement. It's something that only I must own the lifetime lease to.

'You'll never lose me, Rob. We've both had a lot of stress lately.'

'Why do you love me when I've been so bad to you?' He strokes my cheeks with his rough thumbs.

I put a hand over his mouth. 'Shh! You were never bad. You deal with things the only way you know how, like we all do.'

'I don't deserve you,' he says and kisses me, an earnest kiss that, by its very nature, is passionate. The woman with the candlestick backs into a pyramid of water glasses, and sends them crashing to the floor.

Later, in bed, I lie with my face on his chest, hating myself, and wracked with guilt that he thinks I'm such a good woman. Occasionally in this life we get a lucky break. What happened tonight in IKEA was mine. But the fact that I've got away with it isn't the blessing it should be. I will hang on to guilt until the day I die. I know myself.

I lie there for ages, listening to the gentle rise and fall of his breathing. Then he moves his head, tilts just his chin to mine. I feel his lips, the light suction of his mouth moving tentatively over mine. For moments we do this gentle, slow, beginner's dance, then . . .

'I can't. I don't know why,' I tell him.

'It's OK,' he says. He plants one of those understanding kisses at the corner of my mouth. 'I just want you to know, Jill, that I promise to be a better husband to you, to be the man I was—'

I stop him by rolling on to my back, pulling him into a position so that I'm cradling his head in my arms, trying to keep the choking sound out of my voice. 'Can we not talk, Rob? Can we just take this slowly? Recover slowly?' And then I hold him there. Until I know that I absolutely don't have an STI, I cannot possibly have sex with him.

I don't know in what order things happen next. What I do know is that it all happens so quickly that I feel like I'm travelling at the speed of sound. My dad rings me at work. My mam tried to iron her petticoat while it was on her body. When my dad tried to stop her, she went for him with the iron. He says there's barely a mark on him, but I need to see this with my own eyes. When I get there he's wearing a long-sleeved shirt, even though it's quite hot out. 'Roll your sleeves up, Dad,' I order him.

'It's nothing!' He hugs himself, protectively.

'I'm not leaving until you've rolled them up.'

He sighs. 'There's nothing to see! Barely a mark.' But he rolls them up anyway. And there, on his right forearm, is the distinct inverted V of an iron burn.

I am so angry at her! But then the rational part tells me it's not her fault; it's not her will. My dad is the victim here because he's trying to be a hero, and in some ways so am I. 'You can't go on like this!' I wrap my arms around him and, for the first time, he lets me. 'If something happens to you it will be my fault because I've failed to deal with it. I've let you convince me you can manage. And I can't take that responsibility. I can't, Dad. As much as this isn't fair on you, it's not fair on me either.'

'I know,' he says. 'It's getting worse and I don't know what to do any more.'

Mam is watching TV, so in the kitchen Dad and I talk about possible options. To his credit, he listens this time, but when he tells me he needs to think about it, I feel we are one step forward and possibly two back. We relocate to the living room, where Mam is quietly sitting on the couch. Dad sits beside her. She must know something is wrong because she keeps watching him, sheepishly, out of the corner of her eye. 'Oh, come here,' she finally says to him in a motherly tone. She takes his limp arm in her hands, and gently runs a finger around the burn mark. He hadn't bothered to roll his sleeve back down once I'd seen it. 'Good heavens! That looks nasty, doesn't it?' I can imagine her having said this a thousand times when she was a nurse. My mother's compassion ruled even common sense sometimes. She tuts, as though some bad person has done this terrible thing to him, and woe betide them when she finds out who it was. Then she lowers her head and kisses the mark.

'You're still my lady-love,' my dad says to her, and it's just about the most heartbreaking thing I've ever witnessed.

I stay a while then drive back home. I hear the date announced on the car radio. August the sixteenth. Damn. Tomorrow is Rob's mother's birthday. I rush to the corner store and grab the first 'Mother' card I find. The checkout girl makes some remark about how she must be a real special old soul as it took me so long to pick the right verse. Then I get home.

I can hear Rob in the kitchen. It sounds suspiciously like he is doing the dishes from last night. Out of habit, I pat the dog and check the pile of post that sits on our hall table. On top of a bunch of already opened envelopes is a white one, marked *Jill*.

'What's this?' It's Rob's handwriting. I walk into the kitchen, opening it as I go. Inside is a piece of folded paper – the receipt for an online booking for two weeks in Barbados at the end of September.

'Good heavens! You've booked it! When were you ever this impulsive?'

'Don't do tomorrow what can be done today.' He casually flings a tea towel over his shoulder and gives me a flirty smile. Then I realise he's actually preparing dinner for us. Out of the corner of my eye I see a bag of lettuce and I believe I smell pork chops.

'It's a whole new you,' I say, playfully. In the rightness of this moment, the sheer perfect fit of it, as I stand here holding a holiday to Barbados, an awareness chimes in me – that, thankfully and miraculously, I have survived. We are fine. I have moved past, somehow sailed through, the worst thing I have ever done.

'These tickets cost a fortune!' I stare at the paper again, properly processing it now.

'You can't put a price on happiness.'

'You're a mass of clichés tonight, aren't you?' I give him a kiss on his cheek. He has even got wine open for us, with two glasses. He never drinks wine. The dog play-growls with jealousy. The phone rings.

'Can you get it?' I walk back down the hall to the cupboard, to hang up my coat.

'Unknown number,' I hear him call, as I'm closing the cupboard door. We usually ignore those calls but, tonight, perhaps he is feeling generous. And then I hear, 'Yes. Ah . . . hello.'

Something stills me at the 'Ah . . . hello'. Doom has a sound of its own.

Then I hear him say, quite soberly, 'She is, yes.' The eerie, flat seriousness of his voice. And I am the subject.

Only one thought comes to mind. Or perhaps it's three.

Hospital.

Mam.

Dead.

The sudden titanic fit of the chills. The hellish race of my heart.

How utterly sure I am of something I can't possibly know.

I creep back down the hall into the kitchen, oddly prepared – haven't I prepared for this? – and yet prepared to come apart. I am telling myself to be brave. I am bracing myself. I am profusely sweating for someone who is usually dry as a bone. Rob's eyes meet mine. For a moment or two we are trapped there in a deadlock, looking at one another, and then he mouths the word: *Leigh*.

I feel like you feel when you're running fast and you fall and there's that stunning smack of concrete.

I haven't time to say *Pass me the phone* because my head is telling me he isn't handing over the phone, is he? He isn't handing it over because the call is not for me.

I take one or two steps back, retreating from the ominous wave of bewilderment that is coming at me from Rob's eyes. I hear her voice, as you do through a phone when it's someone else on it. The mumble of unidentifiable speech. The room is swimming, or I am; I'm not sure. The backs of my legs make contact with the back of a chair. Rob is still holding my eyes. I shake my head, wanting to say something – thinking *Take charge of this! Do something!* – but it's too late. I see it as it occurs. The slow slide of his expression from light to dark. The disbelief and the agony that cross his face.

CHAPTER EIGHTEEN

I am sitting down. Moments have passed. Or it could be days. Time has lost its purpose. Rob is no longer holding the phone. Rob is no longer holding my eyes. Rob is staring at the place where I am sitting, but he isn't seeing me. I know exactly what Rob is seeing. The last ten years of marriage to someone he is realising he clearly didn't know.

'Is this true?' he asks, eventually.

Two tears land on my khaki trousers.

I am aware of him focusing on me now, a slow, pitiably sad study. And my lack of response.

'So she's not lying then?' He leans back against the sink, clutches it, and then says a quiet 'My God. She's not lying.'

'Rob,' I struggle to see through blurred vision. But he's just looking at me with unspeakable disappointment and regret.

I am aware of the space between our words, and the space lengthening between us. 'You know, as I was listening I was thinking maybe she's made the whole thing up. That's what I thought, Jill. I actually thought she was capable of it.' He speaks as though in a twilight zone.

I can't look at him. He's done with me. I feel it in the way he stares at me, in the loss that hangs in the air. I push the heels of my hands into my eye sockets, until I see a kaleidoscope of black stars and flashes.

'Who is he? I couldn't make sense of what she said. Something about you met him in town or at the beach in Sunderland . . .' His voice is ratcheted up with anger and distrust. Not one iota of love is left on his face. I try to swallow, to speak, but my throat feels squeezed. I can barely breathe.

'Who is he, goddamn it? Tell me.'

I clutch my mouth, the urge to vomit at the memory. 'He's . . .'

'He's who?'

'A lifeguard. At Seaburn beach.'

'A what?' His cheeks flush red. A laugh of derision hovers there but dies in him when he realises I'm not joking. 'How old is he?'

'Forty-nine.'

'Forty-nine? A forty-nine-year-old lifeguard! I didn't know there were such things.' His face fills with mocking disgust. Then he strides across the kitchen, clearly not even sure where he's going. 'Jesus. Fuck.' He shakes his head, goes over to the window where he stands and blindly looks out. Next door's kid is chattering away to her dolls in the garden. The air is pungent with my disgrace.

I start doing something that's torn between a cry and a gasp. 'He wasn't some . . . He was a nice man.'

I can't believe that I've just told my husband that the man I was unfaithful with is nice. I realise – insanely – that I'm saying it because there is still a small part of me that needs to believe it, to make it bearable, to mitigate what I have done. I do a single empty retch, where my insides just quietly come up into my throat and slide back down again. He doesn't seem to notice or care.

'Why would she say you met him down the town then? Were there two of them?' He shoots me a look over his shoulder. 'I mean, is that what you did on your Friday nights? You and her? Go scouting for fellas? Were there others?' He glares at me. 'How many others have there been, Jill?'

'Of course there haven't been others! What do you think I am!' He stares at me like he knows exactly what I am. 'Oh, I'm not going to talk about this, Rob, I'm not. Not if you're just going to stand there with some dim view of me—'

'You fucked a forty-nine-year-old lifeguard!' he shouts.

I bawl. 'It wasn't like that!' There was the note on my car, how he remembered me after having seen me twice before. It wasn't like that, but it was. I stand facing him, rail at him. 'You don't understand! Why d'you think I did it? Huh? Tell me why?' My knees buckle. I hit the floor.

For a moment he just looks at me, steadily, as though I am a deranged person, stopping my drama in its tracks. 'I don't know, Jill. You tell me why.'

He hovers over me now. Memories of him tenderly plucking me out of the wardrobe flood me. I'm vaguely aware of incoherently apologising, begging; and of him standing watching me.

I feel my way back to a chair, sit on it. I sit like this for ages and he doesn't speak; still he just stands there. 'I was so lonely, Rob. You pushed me so far away. You didn't seem to see me as a woman any more. I was just this . . . roommate. A roommate you barely spoke to. I was like some wallflower in my own marriage – sitting there waiting for somebody to come along and get me up to dance.'

Just saying it now, it feels so insignificant, like I'm exaggerating it for effect. I'm trying to remember how awful it was for me, to somehow support my case. I'm trying to grasp on to the despair I must have felt to do what I did, but I can't. I don't understand. It. Me. Anything any more.

'A roommate?' he says, sceptically. 'What the hell are you on about? A wallflower?'

'You never touched me!'

'What d'you mean? I always touch you. I hold you. I treasure you. You are everything to me.' He genuinely looks like he has no idea what I'm talking about – despite the fact that just days ago he apologised to me for how he had behaved.

'You never wanted to have sex!'

His waxy cheeks flush with colour. 'Oh, for fuck's sake! So we didn't do it for what, a few weeks? A few weeks in ten years of marriage! So that was enough for you to run off and go screw some loser on a beach?'

'He wasn't a loser! And it was more than a few weeks, Rob. It was months. Over six months.'

Six months. Was that all it was? Now it seems so trivial.

He flings his hands in the air. The dog runs off into the other room. 'I suppose you bloody wrote it in a diary. Six months in ten years of marriage. Good God. I mean, I cannot believe you, you know. How insensitive you could be. What happened to "in sickness and in health"? Did you ever stop to think what I was going through, Jill? How responsible and guilty I felt? How horrible I felt for what I was denying you? Did you ever think that maybe that put me out of the mood? Maybe there was a bit more going on in my head than getting off?'

I have never heard Rob shout. I don't think even Rob has heard Rob shout. We stare at each other, fiercely startled, my heart hammering while he hovers over me in that posture that says he's restraining the urge to kill me.

'Do you know what it's like to come home and lie near naked on the sofa and have your husband have so little interest that he actually walks out of the room? Or to repeatedly try to look nice, smell nice, dress up, plan anniversaries, do stupid belly dances . . . anything to coax life out of the man you're married to, yet nothing works? And he won't even tell you what's wrong. That's the worst part. He won't talk to you. He just seems to act like everything's normal. And your friends and the girls you work with all go on about how they've got to keep fighting their men off, and you just sit there thinking what on earth is wrong with me? What's happening to me? To my life?'

We stand there, eyeball to eyeball, in some grizzly stand-off, fighting for the title of who deserves the pity more. I calm down. 'I know you were going through a lot of pain, Rob. But so was I. And I didn't ask you to feel responsible for being infertile. It had to be one of us. It could have just as easily been me. I told you I wasn't bothered if we never had kids.' Because now, as I'm saying it, I realise I absolutely am not bothered about ever having children. I don't know why it was ever a big deal. 'But you would never listen. You seemed to want to refuse to believe that.'

'Oh yes, I wanted to. I really fucking wanted to.' He rubs a hand over his mouth, shakes his head again. 'Jill didn't want a kid. Jill wanted a kid. Jill doesn't want a kid again. Jill loves kids. Jill hates kids. Jill cries because she can't have a kid.'

'Well, it was the same with you! I distinctly remember you saying there was far more to life than raising little snot noses. Those were your words. Then you even stopped going out with your mates because they were always on at you about when you were going to have kids, and they were all having kids, and kids were all everybody our age was talking about. Every man in the street with his baby . . . it was like walking over a minefield. But try getting you to open up—'

'Yeah, and you would have been so supportive, wouldn't you? You run off with a fucking bloody lifeguard. Thanks. Thanks for the support and the sympathy.'

'It wasn't like that!' I yell as he walks back to the window again, stares out. 'I gave you as much sympathy as anybody can give a brick wall. But what was I supposed to think? That because we couldn't have kids we were never going to have a normal marriage again?' But maybe I could have tried harder. Maybe I should have found some other more effective, less emotional way to deal with Rob's crisis. Did I give up more easily because the Russian came along? If he hadn't, would I have fought harder?

'Don't be ridiculous,' he says calmly, doubtfully.

I put my hand on my chest and can feel my heart pounding against my palm. We're just going round in circles. I don't even know what we're arguing about any more.

He does a sharp intake of breath; moments pass, bringing the tension down. 'So are you in love with him? This lifeguard? I mean, Jesus, Jill.'

'In love? How could you even think that? No! It was only . . . It only happened once.'

He holds up a hand. 'I don't want to know.'

But I know he does. Certainly some things. So I tell him. Briefly. How we met, the coincidence of the note on my car, his having seen me before around the town. About Leigh and my secret envy of her blitheness. 'This man made me forget myself, Rob. He made me feel beautiful. The man I most wanted to find me beautiful was just treating me like a roommate. And until I could decide what to do with that pretty significant detail in my life, I allowed seeing him to somehow save me.' It strikes me that I borrowed that particular piece of poppycock from Leigh.

He stands there, his back to me, in that I'm-not-listening-but-I'm-listening posture, shaking his head from time to time. When I say the bit about him saving me, he groans. I think of us in IKEA, him singing me his little song, and I mourn that little song because I know he'll never sing to me again. 'I never meant for it to happen, Rob. You won't believe that, but it's true. It was just . . . I don't even know how I got in his car.'

He huffs. His hand goes to his face. He wipes his eyes.

'You have to forgive me. I can't really explain how I did it, but I have to know we're not over because of it.' Over. The word kills me. 'It was one time.'

He turns, looks at me, and there are lines on his face that were never there before. Lines I've put there, and tears in his eyes. And I hate myself for making a big guy cry. 'My God, Jill, were things so bad between us? Had you totally given up on us?'

'I don't know. I don't know how I felt then, Rob, because I'm just so overwhelmed with how I feel now.'

Passion. Sex. How trivial it all sounds now, against what I'm standing to lose.

'Why did it only happen the one time?' The question seems to just occur to him. 'If I'm supposed to believe this.' He perches on the windowsill and I can't believe how handsome he is with the sun backlighting him. I cannot lose him.

'I don't want to talk about it, Rob. I don't think I can.' My voice is barely a whisper.

'But I want to know. You're going to tell me. Why weren't there more times?'

I rub my eyes. That tawdry little flat comes to mind, and him banging into me the way he did, the way that Rob never has, like you see them do in bad porn. I nip the bridge of my nose. 'Because it was terrible! He was like some monster.' I realise that's not quite the right word but it's the only one I can find. Part of me can't believe I'm telling my husband about revolting sex I had with some middle-aged lifeguard.

'But five minutes ago you said he was a nice man.'

A small sob reverberates within me. 'I thought he was.'

He's staring at me hard. 'He was nice to me. I was attracted to him so I assumed it would be good . . . But it wasn't. I wanted to stop it, but he was just so carried away. I told him to stop . . .' Even remembering, my memory is unreliable; I think it may have shut down because part of me doesn't want to remember it.

I look at him and wonder how a man who is standing still can suddenly seem to stop moving. 'What're you saying?' A look passes his face, a stunned, sad, horrified, gentle humanity. 'That he raped you?'

Just for one second I think, *Is he going to forgive me if I say yes?* We hold eyes. My heart hammers with the adrenaline of another lie poised on my lips. But he wasn't a rapist. It would be evil of me to try to pin that on him for my own personal gain. He was just a fast, insensitive lover who wasn't even factoring me into the equation; I was just a body part. I misinterpreted the deal.

I shake my head. I see momentary relief in his face, and then a hardening again. 'So it was just bad sex.'

I remember the shock of his private parts touching mine, his mouth on my breast, a strange man trespassing on Rob's territory. The animal-like nature of him. 'I know, Rob, that this will sound like the strangest thing in the world, but I am probably the only woman I know who would take a lover only to lie there wishing it was her husband making love to her instead.'

He looks at me with an odd mix of disgust and curiosity.

'You see, I wanted to feel wanted. But when it came down to it, I wanted it only to be you.' It should somehow make me less unfaithful, but it doesn't.

He sinks down on the chair opposite me, pulling it far out, away from me. 'So I take it there was no mugging. You made that up.'

'I left my bag at his place.'

He processes this, then sniggers. 'So the phone . . . when I rang, it was him who answered?'

'Probably.'

'Him I reported to the police? That's why you were so upset about it?'

I nod, and he says 'Fuck' again. Then there's silence. Then he says, quietly, 'What a fool you've made of me, Jill. What a fool.'

I have. My eyes tell him that, even though I can't.

'I trusted you.' He says it so innocently, frankly, vulnerably. 'If there was one person in this world I'd have said wouldn't have it in her to do this, it would have been you, Jill.' He shakes his head in quiet disbelief.

We don't say much after that. Rob goes upstairs to lie on the bed. Some time later I follow and I stand there and look at him. The sunken shadows under his eyes seem to darken the more I stare at them. I remember my mother once saying that marriage is a series of tests. How's he going to stand up to this one? I am so wrung out. I curl up at his feet, feeling bled of all energy. We stay like this, me waiting for what is going to happen next, vacantly watching the red numerals of the clock click over as though they're the last moments of my life. I am praying for a stay of execution.

'Rob,' I startle him from his thoughts. 'I have to know what you're thinking.'

He stares, unblinking, at the ceiling. Half-heartedly, he says, 'I don't know what I'm thinking. I haven't the first clue. I just need you to go away right now.' He turns his head from me, places his arm over his eyes. 'Please, Jill. Just go away.'

CHAPTER NINETEEN

I sleep in the spare room.

'Do you want me to go stay with my parents?' I ask him after a night of fractured sleep, right before he goes off to work. 'I will for a few days. If you think it's better.' I am trying to be generous. I don't want him to say yes.

'Suit yourself,' he says. So I think, *OK then, if I am to suit myself, I'm staying put.*

When he comes home from work, hours later, he finds me putting together a tuna salad. 'You're still here,' he says.

'Yes,' I reply. 'I live here.'

Rob rakes in the cupboard and opens a can of salmon as though defiantly showing me that he's not about to eat anything I've touched. I abandon slicing cucumber, and sit down and watch him eat the undrained fish that he's just plonked on a plate, complete with bones and skin. Kiefer's moist, black, twitching nose is pushed under his elbow.

'Don't,' he says, quietly, when I follow him upstairs to bed straight after he has eaten. I get under the duvet and try to snuggle him, but he rounds his spine, pushing me away. 'Please, Jill. Just leave me alone.

I just need time to think.' When I don't move, he flings the duvet off, grabs his pillow, storms into the spare room and locks the door.

I spring out of bed, rifle in the wardrobe for a wire coat hanger. Many a time Rob will pick the lock when I'm on the loo. His idea of being funny. I go to the door, and jiggle the end of the wire in the handle. 'Shit,' he says, when I go in. 'If you're going to do this, I'm leaving.' He gets up, storms back into our bedroom, starts filling his sports bag.

I follow him. I cling on to the door frame, feeling close to collapsing. I see him being available for somebody else the second he walks out of this door. Falling in love again. Replacing me. *No!*

'Don't leave me.' I cling to his shoulders as he zips his bag, recognising that every last thread of my pride has come undone. He stands there, clearly not wanting to go – because there really is nowhere for him to go, except to his mother's, and I can't see him doing that and having to explain everything. He abandons the bag, takes hold of me and gently shoves me out of the room and locks the door. I bang on it for a bit, ashamed of my appalling behaviour, but relieved too that he has changed his mind. Then I suddenly feel so exhausted that I slump to a heap on the floor.

In the morning, I wake up still in the same position, sore all down my right side. I can hear him in the shower in our en-suite. When I try our room door, he has unlocked it, so I go in. His bag is on the floor. I go into the bathroom, sit on the toilet lid watching his moving silhouette through the glass door. When he comes out, he towels off, as though I'm not there. I sit across from him in the kitchen as he eats his Rice Krispies. The air has a sad, silent understanding to it. I've been bad. This cold-shoulder treatment is my punishment. I have to weather it because I'm praying that forgiveness is around the corner.

We suffer through one more day and night of this. Rob going out to work. Rob coming home. Rob making his own dinner as though I am not there. Rob locking himself in our bedroom, forcing me to sleep in the spare. Then by the third night when he comes home, something is different about him. He doesn't make for the kitchen to prepare his meal. He sits down in the living room instead. 'Look, what you said . . . about going to stay with your parents. I think it's a good idea. I need time to think, and I can't think when you're here. Either that, or if you won't leave, then I will. But by rights I think it should be you.'

I am astonished. And yet what was I expecting?

'How long for?' I ask, a river of panic coursing through me.

'How can I answer that?' he says, looking at me earnestly. 'I honestly don't know. A few days. A week. A month. I don't know. Until I've thought what I'm going to do.'

'No,' I say. 'Please don't make me. It's better that I'm here then we can talk. We can see our way through this if we just talk about it. I can't leave. This is my home.'

'Jill, I am asking you. I'm asking you to please go, to give me some space.' He speaks very slowly and deliberately, as though trying to reason with an imbecile. But when I tell him I can't do that, he throws up his hands. His face has despair and disenchantment written all over it. 'I don't know why this seems an unreasonable request to you.'

Because I worry that once I'm gone you won't have me back.

'OK. Fine. I'm going out right now.' He stands up, angrily, yet out of energy. 'I need to get out of here. And when I get back . . . please . . . if you care anything about me, just don't be here.'

I pack a small overnight bag. Then I add a few more things, just in case. I don't say a word to my dad, except that I'm staying with him for a few nights just to make sure he is OK. My first night of being back in my old single room, I wake up and it's dark and I don't immediately know where I am. I struggle to sit up and smack my head on a wall that I'm not expecting to be there. As I clutch at the pain, it dawns on me why I am here, and I fill with plain-spoken loss. I peer at my watch in the moonlight. Four a.m. Will he be lying there like me, besieged with grief for us, wanting to run to me, forgive me and take me back? Somehow I doubt it.

I manage this for a couple of days, trying to be handy and help my dad around the garden, but it's almost impossible to be in his company without him seeing through me. So, by day three, when I know Rob will have gone to work, I let myself back into our house. I curl up on his side of the bed, lie there for what seems like hours, then I make sure I'm gone before he comes home, leaving no evidence that I was ever here. I do this for the rest of the week, but on Friday he surprises me by coming home early.

'What are you doing here?' he asks. I am in our living room, just sitting quietly in a chair. He's had the dog at work with him. Kiefer bounds over to me, as though I have been gone half a lifetime, instead of just a week.

'I needed to get some more things,' I lie. 'I'm hoping you've had time to think.' The conversation feels very ad hoc. I wasn't expecting to be having it right this second. Maybe that was the wrong thing to say. Desperately, I add, 'I'm hoping you will say I can come back.'

He sits down. He looks so very sad and rumpled and not himself at all. And I can't believe I've done this to him. Why did I think seven days might have made him see things more clearly, made ten years of marriage stack favourably against this one wrongdoing of mine?

'I have thought, yes,' he says. 'I've done nothing but think. It just goes over and over in my mind, day and night. I can't think of much else.' He shakes his head as though trying to dislodge his thoughts. 'I just keep seeing you with someone else.'

I can't bear his eyes. I have to look away for a moment.

'I suppose what I keep coming back to is . . . I just don't feel I can do it. I just can't' – he looks me fully in the eyes now – 'go on. Forgive. Put it in the past. It's just not going to work.'

'What are you saying?' My voice is scratchy with fear.

His eyes fill with tears. 'I think I'm saying our marriage is over.'

It takes me a moment to fully process it, a part of me rushing to un-hear it as fast as it comes out. 'No! You don't mean that!' He just keeps looking at me. I just keep shaking my head.

'I'm sorry,' he says, sounding not sorry at all.

No, no, no! I shouldn't have let him find me here. I should have given him longer – let him come to me. Maybe he wasn't going to say that. Maybe my being here unexpectedly has suddenly forced his hand. This, again, is all my fault.

But he means what he says. In the next day or two I begin the process of moving out. I pack things that are mine and not ours into a suitcase and a couple of boxes. I am not taking everything. Not my winter coats. Nor boots. Not every last piece of jewellery. Just things I'll need for the time being, and a few mementos that mean a lot to me. I vow that while I am staying with my parents I'll use this time to think how to get him back. But it won't be easy. Rob may be a bit more sophisticated than your average northern male, but like all hard-working men whose grandfathers were miners, Rob is a no-messing bloke. Once he's made a decision, he rarely goes back on it. In ten years of marriage, I can't think of a time when he has.

I stand on the kerb, fish into my pocket for my handkerchief, look back at my house and am hit by a crippling overdose of separation anxiety. I can't do it! I can't just go! I don't blame him for wanting rid of me. I'd be the same if the shoe were on the other foot. But the point is, it's not. And right now I'm not feeling very fair and square and noble. I go back inside and plonk myself on the sofa, wilful, like I've gone on strike, knowing this is the wrong thing to do; I should accept his wishes. I look around at our sparse but solid furniture that Rob made, the bare rectangle on the wall where our framed wedding photo used to hang until I packed it. *No*, I think, *Jill and Rob live here. Not Rob on his own.* I put the photo back up. I'm not giving Rob an opportunity to forget us this easily.

When he comes home he looks annoyed, and sick and tired of my games. 'I thought you were going!'

'Please, can we just talk?'

'No! How many times? I told you! I have nothing to say to you!'

'I think you have.'

He walks past me, his feet heavy down the hall.

'I just want us to talk.'

'I told you,' he shouts, and I hear the desperation in his voice, how close to the end of his tether he is. 'Leave me the fuck alone, all right?'

I drive through to Sunderland. Linda Ronstadt is singing 'Blue Bayou', and I have to switch her off. I don't even notice the traffic light. I sail right into the back of a red Toyota. I register the crunch of metal, the slight throw of myself forwards. The driver, a middle-aged chap with a big gut, is out of his car, having words with my unresponsive face through the glass. As I wind my window down, he mumbles something about having to get to hospital because his wife has just been rushed in. I look at his belly, catch words: damage, insurance, phone number. He waggles a pen and paper at me. My lack of reaction flusters him. I mechanically take his pen. Before he gets back into his car, he looks back at me and shakes his head as though he thinks I'm nuts.

When I get to my parents' bungalow, I put on my big dark sunglasses like a fallen Hollywood starlet. My dad opens the door, does a double take. I peel them off.

'Why the bags?'

'I need to stay a little while longer,' I tell him, hauling my case over the threshold.

'I didn't mean those ones. I meant the ones under your eyes.' He taps his cheekbone. 'What's going on? Something's fishy.'

I just tell him Rob and I have some things to sort through.

I could never tell him. My mother may – and it's a *may* here – have understood. She had a very open mind for someone of her generation and upbringing. And in her eyes I could never do anything wrong. But my dad has some pretty old-fashioned ideas about women behaving like ladies; I can't burst his bubble about me. His lady-love looks up from the telly when I walk into the sitting room. 'Hello, sweetheart,' she says, to my dad. Today she doesn't see me, I am nobody to her, and it cuts to the core. I want her to stand up, hold me and make everything better. Even if we could rewind just a few months, when she would have been capable of doing that. But with her pretty, transparent gaze she feels gone from me. Elizabeth Mallin might be sat here, but she's just a shell in which my mother doesn't live any more.

And that about characterises the next few days. We are shells in which we don't live any more. I try to officially organise a spot for my stuff among the clutter in what used to be my old room. I've brought my own pillow, and as I lie there failing to fall asleep it is not lost on me that I used to lie in this bed dreaming of meeting a man like Rob.

One morning, I come out of the bedroom to find my parents having a fight in the hall. My mother is trying to get out of the door with four carrier bags filled with clothes. My dad has her arms in his grip and there's a tussle going on.

'She's packed her bags and she says she's leaving. She said she's going to stay with her mother in York.'

My mother breaks free of his grasp and reaches for the front-door handle, and I immediately rush to stop her.

'It's locked,' my dad tells her, patiently, but like he's reasoning with an imbecile. 'You can't go anywhere, Bessie. I've got the key.' But my mother keeps rattling away at the handle, like a tormented prisoner who has found a window of opportunity to break out. 'Bessie,' my dad calmly strokes her hand. 'Come on now, love. Come on. Settle down. Come and have a cup of tea.'

'You brought her here!' She shoots a look at me, fixes me with her gaze, which today is unfairly lucid.

'She thinks you're my girlfriend,' my dad explains.

'Tramp!' she spits at me with sharp contempt. 'Can't keep your own man so you want to take somebody else's!'

I throw a hand to my mouth in shock. When I can finally speak, I don't care that she might hear me and understand. 'That's it! I'm calling the doctor! We can't go on like this! This is mad! It's a madhouse in here!' I fight the urge to cry, then flood with guilt. I should be coming down on one of their sides, but it feels like I'm coming down on my own.

'Don't be coming here and ordering us about! If it's a madhouse it's our madhouse, so go home, we don't want you here,' my dad retaliates. Then he says, 'Oh, I'm sorry, lass. You know I didn't mean that.' He wraps my mother in a big cuddle. 'They'll take her away from me!' he wails, and my mother stares out at me, across his shoulder, vulnerable but quietly triumphant.

When she settles down, I manage to get my dad to at least let me ring the doctor. I phone the health centre and they send Dr Reilly, a good-looking young man with smiling eyes and red hair that looks steamrolled straight. 'Irish,' my dad whispers. 'How old do you think he is, thirteen?' Dr Reilly says that the last entry on my mother's file was in 1996. 'That's because our family doesn't believe in doctors,' my dad tells him. The doctor asks my mother her name. And she tells him, 'Elizabeth. Or Bessie, as my husband calls me.' She gives my dad a fond smile. 'Makes me sound like a black Labrador.' After hearing about the day's events, Dr Reilly gives us some pills to supposedly calm her, and suggests we consider booking a visit to the clinic to have her undergo some cognitive tests. He adds that if we're concerned about my dad's ability to look after her here, we might want to consider the option of a home where she will be properly cared for. 'Thanks, lad,' my dad says. 'Thanks very much for coming, and for your sound advice. Let me see you to your car.' Then he takes hold of the doctor by his collar and places his other hand on the doctor's back. He almost frogmarches him out of the door, then down the front path. Free of my dad's clutches, the doctor flees to the safety of his car, turning only once to catch my apologetic expression, and giving me a thin, aghast smile.

I can't face work again. So I ring in sick again. As Irving is out of the office, I rattle off some rubbish to one of the girls about how the bug I've had is stubborn and it still hasn't gone away. I ask her to pass this on to him and say that I'll be back as soon as I am able. When Leanne comes back from her lunch hour, she phones me. I tell her, without going into too much detail, that I'm actually having marriage problems, but I make her promise not to breathe a word. Then Wendy phones. I had almost forgotten about her. So this is where I have to start telling people. I stare at her number on my call display. I don't pick up. I just can't do it.

At some point, I start throwing up – perhaps it's poetic justice, but it seems I have got a virus, and now I don't need to make one up. My dad keeps feeding me tea. Then he messes around in the kitchen and somehow produces mince with carrots and Yorkshire puddings. We eat by the small bay window that overlooks the grassy lawn that's bordered on all sides by old people's semi-detached bungalows. I know my dad is waiting, in these small opportunities, for me to tell him what's going on. But he won't press me; I don't think he's comfortable with it. We are not used to intimate heart-to-hearts. Much as I adore him, my mother was the one I'd always open up to.

'What happened to her place?' I nod to the house across from us, with newspaper up at the window.

'Dolly Oliver? Gone. Stroke. About a month ago.'

I look at my dad's fingers curled around his tea mug and feel a horrible shortening of opportunity. 'Is it strange, Dad, to see people you've known all your life die? People who were young with you, had kids when you had kids . . .'

He leaves his carrots. 'Well, nobody likes to hear that another one's bitten the dust. But it's just life. You get more of an acceptance of it as you get older. We all have to go. As long as we've lived a good life and we've treated those we love well, there's no need to be frightened to leave this world.' He searches my face. I sense he's hinting again. Hinting for me to tell him something. But all I can think is, *Who will I grow old with now if Rob doesn't forgive me?*

More to the point, who will Rob grow old with?

'What are you doing the Ray for again?'

When I cry, I tend to put my sunglasses on, and he'll say I am 'doing a Ray Charles'.

He squeezes my hand. 'She never knew you cared.'

'Who didn't?'

'Dolly Oliver.'

I somehow make it through a week. A week of not feeling particularly well, of my mam's tantrums and my dad's tears, her dirty laundry showing up in strange places, the fire on full blast, the TV blaring, my dad's lectures about not switching the lights on and off as it wastes electricity, or his tapping on the door every time I just get into the bath, telling me he's bursting for the toilet . . . my dad screaming like a banshee in the middle of the night. I'd forgotten about his nightmares. He's had them from as far back as I can remember: the progressively loud squealing that reaches a blood-curdling crescendo, then my mother would usually send her elbow right through his ribcage, and he'd wake up. And then there are the routine comings and goings on the street . . . I feel like I am dying young.

Of course, amidst all this I ring Rob several times and listen to his voice on our answer machine. If he picks up, I hang up. The other day he said, 'Hello? Hello?' And then, 'Jill, is that you?'

'No,' I replied, full of sorrow and self-pity.

'Don't bother me again,' he said. 'Or I will block your calls.'

Since then I've backed off, because I believe him.

But I drive over to our house. I sit parked down our street, staring at the front door, waiting for him to come out. Then, without him knowing, I follow him. To work. To the grocery store. To the park with Kiefer. I reckon that if somebody saw me and tried to have me arrested for it, Rob would probably happily watch as they threw me in jail.

And then I pluck up the courage to ring Wendy. And in the dimness of her Tiffany-lit sitting room, nursing a glass of wine that makes me queasy when I try to drink it, I tell her what I did. She listens for hours, slowly polishing off an entire bottle of wine with a certain mechanical lift to her arm. I have to be a little careful what I say, though. I mean, I can hardly tell her that perhaps I was somewhat egged on or persuaded to do it because Leigh made her affair with Neil look so easy.

But as for what happened in his room – how awful it was – I don't tell her that. I just say it only happened once and I felt too guilty to do it again. Another lie. But one I actually like the sound of, for a change.

Of all people, I would have dreaded Wendy's reaction the most. Yet she listens with an almost therapist-like understanding, completely without judgement, in a way that I wouldn't have thought she'd be capable of, being the wife of a cheat. But she says one thing that stings me to my soul. 'What surprises me, Jill, is that I would have thought nothing and no man would have ever tempted you to go astray. I wouldn't have thought it would even be a last resort for you.'

'But what are you supposed to do in the circumstances I was under, Wendy? When your husband won't touch you and you can't even talk about it?'

She seems to think hard. 'When you know the reason for it? When you know he's just learned some sad news about himself, and you know that fertility is a very tender subject for a man . . . I don't know. I suppose you give him time.'

Time.

Yes. Why didn't I?

Next, I receive the letter. I have to read it a couple of times before it sinks in. My eyes pick up on words I can't fully relate to. Persistent lateness. Unauthorized absence. Incapacity to perform duties to required standard . . . Failure to attend a meeting to discuss my performance – the date of this meeting was a week ago. A meeting I'm only being made aware of now. I have to sit down . . . The paper falls from my hand.

My lovely job at the football club! All my lovely pals I go for lunch with. Leanne rings me a few hours later. She says Irving had it in for me all along. That he supposedly left a message for me to attend a meeting. That she doesn't believe he actually did. She uses words like *recourse* and *tribunal* and *unfair dismissal*, but I barely hear her. Until she adds, 'Why didn't you just get a proper sick note from the doctor? Heather did that when her husband had an affair!'

So she thinks Rob cheated. And, dreadful as it is, I don't feel like disillusioning her. I'm flattered she cares. But I want her to go away.

When I tell my dad that I can't possibly get my head around fighting my termination right now, he gives me a handout from his pension, which I refuse to take, but he ceaselessly forces it on me until I have no choice. 'Don't worry,' he tells me. 'The government needn't know we're splitting it three ways.'

Don't worry, but I do. I worry so desperately about what we're all coming to. I mustn't be hiding it well, because in the dead of night I wake up conscious of a presence in the room. I think I smell her talcum powder first. 'Mam,' I whisper. She hovers above me, then she bends her face to mine, her warm hand lightly touching my cheek. 'No matter what happens in this life, I want you to remember one thing. Nobody will ever love you like your mother.' Then she kisses me, a wet smack of proud ownership, on my lips. And then she disappears as softly as she came, into the still of the bungalow with the fridge softly whirring in the background. It happens so inconspicuously that I almost think I dreamt it.

How fast is a person supposed to recover? Well, I'm not recovering. Wendy tells me I absolutely have to get back up to the doctor's because my face is so gaunt. 'You're remarkably together,' I tell her.

'I'm surviving. I look like this when I'm out doing things. But when I'm on my own with just my thoughts, it's a different story. I'm a lot like you.'

The doctor gives me more than the standard ten minutes, which feels flattering, or worrying, depending on how you look at it. Probably because when she asked what the matter was I burst into tears. She drags down the skin under my eyes, runs a batch of blood tests. I didn't for a minute think I was depressed, but when she suggests prescribing me uppers, this of course sends me into a downer. I tell her I'm not ready to take pills for depression. I tell her that actually I'm fine now. I straighten myself up, walk out of there, and have a fit of tears outside.

At the weekend I go to Seaburn beach – it's what I feel I need to do to try to put this behind me. I know he won't be there, it being September now. In fact, the whole place is a ghost town on this pallid, grey day. Fairground shut. Coffee shops closed. Only Morrisons supermarket ticking away at life. I walk along the deserted promenade and arrive at the bench where we sat when I said those terrible words: 'I've never had an affair before . . .' Staring at the melancholy beach, everything comes back. I relive it, large as life, like I somehow need to, to forgive myself.

It should have just stayed as a flirtation. Nobody can punish you for that. It should have been the summer I almost had an affair. There's a touch of glamour in that. I would have had a whole corridor for my imagination to wander down in my lonely old age, with Rob in the rocking chair beside me.

Speaking of Rob, later in the week I do something brave. I drive home and knock on my own front door, which is a whole other level of weirdness, let me tell you. I barely recognise his face under three weeks' worth of beard and hair that needs a good cut. His dark-blue eyes stare out at me like a man in hiding. Then his gaze drops quickly over me. He leaves the door open as he walks back into the house. I go in. The house feels so empty. It's missing me.

Walking into the kitchen feels foreign, like I've been away on holiday and have to reacquaint myself with my life again. Rob opens a can of soup. I'm amazed how thin he is. The worktops are a clutter of opened cans, empty bread packets, empty milk and juice cartons, food stuck to the hob – his shoes all over the place. 'I want to come home,' I tell him.

He tips the white soup into a saucepan. 'Not an option.' He turns the heat up and watches the soup spatter. Something about his disappearing bum in his faded jeans makes me put a hand over my mouth to stop an anguished sound coming out. 'You'd better stir that or it'll stick,' I tell him, trying some form of cajolery. Like soup pans of the past, I can see this one already with the burnt business on the bottom, waiting for me. And I'd clean it cursing him, resenting the very institution of him, as though this pan was the end of my world.

Why do we let things like that bother us? I'd give the world to have Rob and his gluey pans back, Rob and his dirty underwear on the floor.

He pours his soup into a bowl, takes a dirty spoon out of the dishwasher, doesn't bother washing it, comes and sits at the table. 'I'll go if you want me to,' I say.

He bites into half a French stick. 'Please yourself.' The soup burns his mouth. He stands up and takes a can of pop from the fridge. For a moment I wonder if I'll ever kiss Rob again. But I think I knew the answer the second I saw the state of him at the door. I will never kiss Rob again. Even if he could forgive me, he would never forget how I made him feel.

I watch him skim off the crinkled skin on his soup. I'm not here as far as he's concerned. His body is healing itself and that means voiding me out.

'How's your mam?' he finally asks. Dinner-table chatter of the past. Gets my hopes up.

'Not good. But I suppose not really all that much worse either.' I tell him about my job.

'So what are you going to do then? For work?'

He asks it as though he cares, but as though it impacts only me, not us. It fells me. 'I can't think about that now,' I say.

He studies me unsympathetically for a moment or two then scrapes his bowl. 'Well, what are you going to do about accommodation? I mean, I can't see you wanting to live at the bungalow for too much longer. Are you going to look for a flat or what?'

I stare gauntly at him, disbelieving his cruelty, but he refuses to look at me. My eyes fill.

'Well?' he asks, finally looking at me again. I want his eyes and his heart to melt for me. Aren't I the person he used to least like to see suffer in the whole world? But he looks at me coldly. 'No good crying over spilt milk,' he says, and he scrapes his chair back and goes to the sink with his bowl and runs the tap. I sit there and drop tears into my lap.

'I hate you,' I say, unconvincingly.

'Yeah, well, I'll live.' He starts washing dishes. He's even got the gall to hum a tune.

That's it. This is so belittling. I get up, too choked to even say goodbye. But I register something as I walk down our passage to the front door. He has stopped washing dishes. He's listening to the sound of me leaving.

CHAPTER TWENTY

Wendy and I go for a day out to Durham. It's the first change of scenery I've had in the month since Rob threw me out and I've been living 'on death row at the bungalow', as my dad puts it. Again I note Wendy's conspicuously un-made-up face. But other than that, she's turned out like her old self, and even tries the same carefree smile. We attempt pie and mash in a seventeenth-century alehouse just up from the cobbled marketplace by St Nicholas' Church. We drink draught lager and my misery gets to go first. I fret and she consoles, both of us doing a good job of it. Never once does she pressure me about what I'm going to do, or ask questions she knows I don't have answers to. 'I wish I'd confided in you instead of Leigh,' I tell her. 'It's just you only ever had eyes for Neil . . .'

She studies me wisely. 'You're wrong. I think both you and Leigh wanted to think that about me, but it's not true. There have been, over the years, one or two other men who've caught my eye. With one of them, yes, I suppose something could have happened if I'd wanted it to. But I never thought a fling with somebody who didn't really know me could be better than all the years invested in my body by somebody who did.'

Yet we do, don't we?

Why do we?

'Neil and I were very inexperienced with the opposite sex. I'd only ever had one other lover before him and Neil had had two. We met so young. But that was never a problem for me.'

'Men are different.'

'Are they, though? I think we like to believe they are, to somehow make them easier to excuse or blame. But look at you and Leigh. You both were married.' Then she adds, 'I'm sorry,' when she sees my face. 'I didn't mean it in any recriminating way. I'm just saying I don't blame Neil because he's a man. I blame him because he's Neil.'

I tell her I need fresh air. We walk outside, join the gathering crowd in the market square and listen to a curly-haired student playing 'Clair de Lune' on a violin. A homeless person is sat on the wall. He's swaddled from head to toe in a commercial fishing net, and there's an orange kitten crawling all over it, having a field day. We watch its antics for a while, then leave. We take the narrow high street that's closed to traffic and join the slow, quiet milling people walking down the cobbled bank, gawping at shop windows. I ask her how the lads are doing. 'Surprisingly well. I was honest with them. They weren't going to believe we just weren't getting on so their dad had moved out. They're too clever for that.' She stares off into the distance, and her face softens. 'They're being very protective of me and they refuse to see him at this point, though I am sure that will change.' When we come to Elvet Bridge, we pause to gaze at its unbeatable view of the three majestic towers of Durham Cathedral set high on the green banks of the River Wear. The day is picture-postcard perfect. But it's missing a feeling that neither of us can bring to it. It's even missing Leigh, and the high old times. I experience a wish-I-were-here-with-Rob craving, but push it away. I reckon we have enough missing going on already.

'He's living with her, you know,' she says, eventually, flatly, staring downriver at the rowing boats that roll into the distance. 'He's renting one of those new lofts down the Quayside.'

I am almost too floored, and disappointed, to speak. 'Living with her!'

She plucks ears of grass that jut through the stone wall. 'Neil needs somebody to pander to him. He needs to come home to his comforting pile of ironed underwear.'

'Well, he's picked the wrong girl there, hasn't he?'

'Who knows? She was tired of being the one who wore the trousers all the time. Maybe now she'll be content to wash and iron them.' She looks at me and smirks, and her eyes have colour depths like two dark marbles held up to the sun. 'Isn't that what Denis Thatcher said to a reporter about his relationship with Margaret? That he wore the trousers and he washed and ironed them too? That's about the only thing I remember about a significant era in British politics. Isn't that sad?' Her face quickly takes on that distant, dismantled look again. 'He wants to come home. Came round last night when the boys were out. His words were, "To give it another try".'

I scrutinise her hair, which has been forced into a cute little ponytail that sticks up like a palm tree in the centre of her crown. 'What did you say?'

'I said, "What do you mean another try? We were never giving it a try in the first place. We've been married for eighteen years. We have two sons."' She looks at me with a harrowed expression. 'He said he can't bear her, and now he's living with her, it didn't make sense. Apparently she wants them to buy a house and have Molly live with them.' She goes to bite her nails but stops herself. 'What's really strange about this is that Neil isn't a person to just get bobbed along with the tide.'

'Maybe he just can't be bothered dealing with her right now. I mean, his life has changed radically as well, hasn't it? Maybe he's just catching his breath.'

'Poor him.' That was a rare feat of sarcasm. 'He'll not want Molly. I know how much he didn't want to have a third child, to start from square one again. Sometimes I think he resented being a father because it took him away from the two things he loved most: his job and himself.'

'I'd never have thought, Wend. I assumed he was pleased about the baby when you fell pregnant.'

'I was hardly going to tell you. It doesn't exactly make him look very good, does it? And it's disrespectful to the memory of my daughter, making it known that her own father didn't really want her in the first place.' She straightens up from leaning on the wall. 'Come on, let's walk now.'

We take a stony cut down to the riverbank. Fishermen are casting lines into water that looks like a sheet of opaque green glass. On it quivers the reflection of the cathedral. Wendy stops and gazes out across to the other side, to a neat line of moored rowing boats. 'It's not the first time he's cheated, you know.'

'What?' Peel me off the floor. Her eyes scan my reaction. She almost smiles. She starts walking again, leaving me lagging behind, mouth ajar. 'I don't believe this!' I pad after her. 'Wendy! I had no idea! How d'you . . . How do you know?'

'You just know,' she says. 'I mean, I never had any concrete evidence if that's what you mean.' She pushes up an overhanging bramble and we duck under it, minding our eyes. 'The thing with Neil is he's very good. Maybe spending your career around dishonest people you learn the ropes. You'll never catch him in a lie. None of Neil's behaviour is typical of the cheat. He never gets too nice all of a sudden. Never has strange hairs on his clothing or lipstick on his boxers. He has never gone off sex – quite the opposite. He doesn't make excuses to pop out and be gone for hours. He's not forgetful and I don't have to tell him everything three times.'

She's a walking magazine article.

I look at her profile, the flush of her cheeks, the half an inch of grey regrowth at the temples where her hair needs colouring again. 'Well, how do you know then?'

'Do you want to sit here a minute?' She points to a bench that's covered in graffiti and missing its central plank. We sit. She leans forward, hands either side of her knees. I notice she isn't wearing her wedding ring. When will Rob take his off? When will I take off mine?

'Something happened. Years ago. We'd gone to Edinburgh for his job. We were in a bar.' She looks at me briefly, her neck a translucent peach flush. 'There was hardly anybody in, except this young waitress. She was a cute little thing in a little short tartan skirt, with long, runner's legs and strawberry blonde hair in two low stubby bunches. She was instantly taken with Neil.' She shrugs, straightens her legs, looks at her clean, white running shoes. 'I thought nothing of it. Women always look at Neil. It's par for the course. Anyway, we went and sat down in a corner. It was a nice evening out and it seemed a pity to be in there, but Neil didn't want to leave given the girl seemed so happy to have customers . . . We just ordered mineral water. She brought them to us. Neil gave her five pounds and told her to keep the change.'

That sounds like Neil. A little bit flash, but not enough to be criticised for it.

'So she gets this good tip, and she looks at him. I can still picture her face. Pretty, but a bit hard, like a young Meg Ryan. She stood there chatting with us. Why were we here? Et cetera. Then Neil told her he was a police detective.' Her eyes comb my face. 'Women react to that. Every time.' She swats a fly that keeps dancing before her eyes. 'Anyway, a few more people came in. But every time she walked past us she'd look over, not directly at him, but almost as though she was inviting his eyes on her. And Neil . . . he was talking to me, but it was the same thing: they were very much aware of each other.' She shakes her head. 'Funny thing is, I don't think either of them was particularly aware of me noticing this. We had our drinks and then he asked her where the toilet was. I remember the off-hand way he got to his feet, stood tall and buttoned his jacket, like a man who knows he's handsome does. It was a very assured gesture. Everything about him was confident of himself, I thought, as though he held all the power. The girl said it was downstairs, she'd show him.' Wendy shifts on the uncomfortable bench, hugs her knees so her black Capri pants ride up her legs, which could use a shave – something you'd never see, back in the days of Neil. 'And I'm sat there thinking, *Why does this girl want to show my husband where the toilets are? Isn't he big enough to find them himself?* And I got a really bad feeling. Just' – she punches a fist to her ribcage – 'I don't know, like I was somehow at a disadvantage, helpless. Anyway, she led him down the narrow, dark stairwell. I remember it had prints of jazz musicians on the walls. And just before they were out of sight, I saw her turn and look back at him. And it was all there in her face: that rapt, mischievous, illicit understanding.'

'No! God. Was he gone a long time?'

Her grip tightens around her knees, pushing pockets of muscle out on her arms. 'Long enough.'

'How did he look when he came back up?'

'Well, not like you'd think he'd look if he'd done anything. But I knew he had.'

'How?'

Her pupils drill into mine. 'I knew.'

'So what did you do?'

'Well, I asked him what had gone on. He said I was being ridiculous. It was my bad mind.'

'You don't have a bad mind.'

She smiles. 'I didn't think I did either.'

She gets up now and we start walking again. 'You have to remember, I wasn't looking for anything to upset my world. I had two boys. I loved him. I was very happy with my life. The last thing I wanted was a reason to leave him.' Our feet crunch stones. We pass a fisherman who turns and says 'hello', and three young Chinese girls in a rowing boat whose giggles cut an echo across the still, opaque green water.

'I never actually saw her come back up again.' Our walking trails to a stop, and she seems breathless. 'Whether she left . . . I thought about going down to the ladies', but then I thought, what if she's down there? You know, cleaning herself up, or putting her clothes back on. What'll I do? She'd know I knew then. And I'd know Neil was lying. And I'd have to do something. And I didn't know what I'd do.' The remaining colour drains out of her face.

'My God, Wendy.'

'You always think when you hear things like this, oh I'd flip out . . . or I'd kill her . . . or kill him . . . But when it does . . . I tell you, I didn't know what to do. I was intimidated by the situation. It felt bigger than I knew how to handle.' We start walking again, my eyes on the slow forward-rhythm of our shoes. 'We got back to the hotel and had a massive fight because of course I wouldn't let it drop. But it all boiled down to his word against my suspicions. The way I saw it, I had two choices. I either had to leave him or believe him. So I believed him.'

'This is incredible, really . . . So how did you feel towards him after that, then?'

She laughs a little, humourlessly. 'Alert.'

A picture of Neil flashes up in my mind. Neil, who I have always felt was a little bit unknowable, but that it added to his appeal. Then I think, hell, he's not the man Leigh thought he was either, is he? The loyal man who was only cheating with her because she was special. 'So was that it then? Or did anything else happen?'

'Oh, the phone calls to the house. Hang-ups. There'd be none for ages, then a run of them. A few other things.' She shrugs, and I know she's not going to elaborate. 'In the beginning I'd be checking his pockets all the time, his credit card statements. But not trusting the person you live with is an exhausting way to live. It's completely emotionally poisonous. Besides, I didn't want that sort of unhealthy relationship. That's not who I am.' She stares off into the distance.

'Funny, though, when I found out about Leigh and I asked him how many others there'd been, he hesitated, just for a second, before he said "None".'

'So how many do you think there've been?'

She shrugs. 'Lots.'

'Lots! You're kidding.'

'No,' she almost laughs. 'I know this is a shock to you. And you must think I'm pathetic. And I am. And I'll have to live with that. Or change myself, which I'm trying to do now.'

'Wendy, you never let on . . .'

'I can't. I'm good at being happy, but I'm not good at being a fuck-up.' She looks at me sadly. 'And like I said, there never was any real evidence. I wasn't going to walk out on my marriage and rob my lads of a family on a hunch, was I? Even a very strong one. Or that's my excuse, anyway. But, I don't know, I feel so . . .' She shakes her head, doesn't finish.

I think of that day in the restaurant when Wendy said 'Not always' to Leigh's comment about how she only ever wanted to be married to Neil. Leigh took her two-word response to be – how did she put it when we were talking about it afterwards? – humouring, as though Wendy said it to condescend or just to fit in. But I'm sure she was really just being honest, only we refused to believe it. We've pigeonholed Wendy into being this poster child for happily-marriedness. Why? Maybe to give us some ideal that our own lives fell short of. Maybe to justify our gripes. We walk to the end of the path, and then come back up on to the high street again. 'I did something the other day that I'm quite proud of,' she eventually says, brighter. 'I looked into how I might get to go back and finish my law degree, starting this January.' She smiles. 'It would probably have to be part-time – maybe I could also get a few hours in a solicitor's office as well, for experience – and then of course I'd have to hope I could get a place on the Legal Practice Course, and then I'd be working as a trainee solicitor for two years, but I'd be collecting a salary. After that, there's the Professional Skills Course, but that's really only twelve days.' She looks at me, freshly. 'So, Jill, I just about reckon that by the time I'm fifty I could be a fully-fledged solicitor!' She laughs a little. 'So I think I'm going to go for it. What do I have to lose?'

'That's incredible, Wendy.' And it's amazing that, as far as life goes, she seems to be back on the horse. 'I can see you making a brilliant solicitor.' She analyses the hell out of everything as it is. 'But would it not just be easier to become a legal clerk or something?'

'Yes. But I don't want to be a clerk. I want to be a solicitor. I think I always did.'

I mourn my own job. The job I was happy in. Wendy has a path now. What's mine?

'My problem is I always tend to need to do things well. So I was a good parent, a good wife. But the whole ultra-domesticated thing has really been something I've taken a false pride in. It's not really me. It never really was, much as I thank God for my lads . . . I don't know, I suppose if I'd never had children I could have still been happy. A part of me has always felt I short-changed myself by marrying Neil, even though I've always convinced myself that by landing him I'd hit the jackpot.' She huffs, shakes her head. 'Neil knew about my law ambition, but he showed such little encouragement that he even managed to convince me that I wasn't really interested in it myself. Because Neil has to be top dog. But I think it's because, deep down, if he didn't trade so much on his good looks, Neil's not really a confident man. And men who lack confidence in themselves don't want successful wives; they don't want wives with brains. Besides, he detests lawyers. Always says they get the bad guys off. So imagine how ironic it'll be . . .' She looks at me, widens her eyes.

We walk to Crook Hall, the medieval manor house that serves a fabulous home-made afternoon tea, as she tells me the ins and outs of the studying she'd have to do, the courses she's most looking forward to. We claim a table in the shade in a pretty little rose-filled courtyard by the fountain. Then she's flat again. 'Where do you suppose they went to do it? Leigh and my husband.' We've already had the conversation about how we can't believe she made up the name Nick, which is so close to Neil, and she managed to call him that without a slip of the tongue. But then again, she didn't really use his name all that much, I don't think. It was usually *him*. Come to think of it, I didn't really ask all that much about him. And I was so trusting of her that I never looked for flaws in anything she told me. But now I'm ashamed that I believed so convincingly in the existence of a person who wasn't real. I should have seen some sort of sign. 'I always wonder that about people who have affairs. Where do they go?'

She holds my eyes before I drop mine. I know where they went. 'I have no idea, Wendy. Probably to a hotel. Isn't that what people do?' People. Adulterers. Me. The judge and the judged.

I feel her probe me with her gaze. 'What, Newcastle people? Maybe the ones on the television, but this is real life, Jill. In real life people have bills to pay. Responsibilities. They don't run around throwing money at hotels for cheap sex. Neil wouldn't.'

She knows I know where they went. But she has too much class to press me.

'You always liked him, didn't you? You and Leigh,' she says after a bit as we stare at a three-tiered tray of baked goodies that's been set before us. She picks up the teapot to pour herself another cup.

'Yes. I suppose it's because he's so damned good-looking, Wendy. You don't see past it. You see his looks, the job he does, and you imagine everything else must be great about him too. And it didn't help that you seemed so besotted with him. He was so perfect in your eyes, so that made him doubly perfect in ours.'

She gazes through the spray of the fountain and we listen to its silvery sound. 'I adored him.' Her face pales and those red patches appear on her forehead again. The fine hairs on her arm stand up. She looks cold. She has to put the teapot down. An inch of milky liquid sits in the bottom of her rose-festooned cup. 'In a way I got my own self-esteem boost by knowing I was with him. But you're wrong thinking I thought he was perfect. I was never blind to his shortcomings. I just thought him . . . essential. Essential to me. Isn't that weak?'

I pour her tea for her. 'Well, maybe now you regret not having acted on your instincts, but that's only because what he's done now makes what you thought he might have done back then more likely. Wendy, you stayed in a relationship mainly for your kids. You booted him out the second you found out he was sleeping with Leigh. And you're forty-two and thinking of going to become a solicitor. Weak is the last word I'd use to describe you. You're probably the strongest woman I know.'

She pulls a wry smile and I know she's thinking about her diagnosis. She picks up a Yorkshire ham and brie sandwich. 'I only ever exercised for him, you know. I hate bloody exercise! I thought that if I looked as good as I possibly could it would give him less reason to stray. Can you believe somebody could be so soft? I kept thinking that by marrying me so young he'd missed out. And I knew he got opportunities with women far better-looking than I am. I almost felt sorry for him at times.'

'But he married you because he wanted to. Nobody put handcuffs on him.'

She gives a wry smile. 'I know. And he loved me. And he was attracted to me. And I know he still is. He just . . . Neil has to live on the edge. That's why he's so good at his job.' She looks around the small cobbled courtyard, tilts her sad face up at the rowan berries drooping from a tree above us. 'Oh, we shouldn't be talking about this. Not here. Not today. Look at it, it's too nice . . .'

It's odd, but I feel closer to her now. With Leigh, I suppose I had to know her really well to learn that we were strangers. Yet Wendy has had to open up to me, to let me know that we really are friends.

Her sandwich sits on the plate with just a half-moon bite out of it. 'I'm all right though. I am. I've spent a lifetime suspecting him of being unfaithful. Finding out that he actually has been is surprisingly not that much worse.'

'Why haven't you had it out with her?' I have to ask this, because this is what surprises me most. Along with the fact that Leigh still hasn't phoned and apologised to my friend or offered any explanation. She has just disappeared. It's as though the last decade and a half of our friendship had an embolism and dropped dead.

Wendy shrugs coldly, stares at the bread she's absently poking holes in. 'I can't. I just can't see it happening – me in one corner of the boxing ring and Leigh in the other. Can you? All this over him.'

'No. You have too much dignity for that.'

'I don't have the balls,' she says, surprising me. 'Mind you, if she'd rung me I'd probably have let her have it. But am I going to ring her? Say, *Oh, hello, Leigh, I heard you've run off with my husband . . .* It's like being back in that bar again, all those years ago. It fills me with paralysing dread.' She shakes her head. 'Besides, I don't want her explanation. I just want never to lay eyes on her again. Him neither. All that counts is being there for my boys now. They're at that age where sex and life, it's all just starting to make sense, and they're getting slapped with a harsh truth. That people who we think would be the last to fail us sometimes go ahead and do it, and leave us with this legacy of never being able to trust. You know, this is the age that I really do believe shapes who we become, whether we become cynics or not, later on.'

'Don't think like that. They've got your influence as much as his – maybe more.'

She lays both hands on her stomach. 'Jill, I don't want them being brought up by his example.' She looks at me vehemently. 'And I never want them living with Leigh.' She says it in a way that suggests she's going somewhere, and I know what she's referring to.

'Don't talk like that! They're never going to live with Leigh. They're only going to live with you – always – because you're their mother.'

She looks at me and I see a glint of humour saving the moment. 'Well, not always. I mean I do eventually want them to get married and move out. Imagine if they were both fifty and still living at home. And I was the breadwinner – the eighty-year-old solicitor, hacking away at a living.' We chuckle. We walk out through the rose garden, leaving a tray of goodies we're too full to eat. 'You know, I spent years thinking if I left him, where would that leave me? Who would I have? And the funny thing is now I know the answer. I have me. You're born just you, and you go through life buffered by other people, but first and foremost you are just yourself. And then you die just you. So the sooner you get used to yourself, the better.'

Her words won't leave me. She drops me off at the bungalow, gives me a kiss. I watch her pull off in her car, suddenly very moved by our day. I sneak in the front door and am just picking my way across floorboards when I hear a quiet 'Goodnight, lass' from my parents' room. I'm thirty-five yet my dad still waits up until I'm home.

'Goodnight, Dad,' I whisper. I climb into bed and lie there staring at the ceiling, wide awake.

Maybe that's exactly what I am now.

Just me.

CHAPTER TWENTY-ONE

I drive along the A19 with the radio on. I'm going to look at a flat for rent in Jesmond. Wendy told me about it. Somebody she knows is moving out. I drove by our house again the other day. I keep visualising a 'For Sale' sign on the lawn. At some point it's going to be inevitable.

I pull up at the house; number thirteen – lucky for some. It's one of those white stucco three-storey Victorian terraces with tended gardens and quiet children playing on the path. I park across the street and sit staring at it.

'You can have both tickets,' Rob said on the phone when I rang him the other day about our Barbados holiday, which is supposed to be this Saturday. 'Take your Russian.'

'Don't say that!'

'Well then, take somebody. Take Wendy. In fact, I'm emailing you them now, as we speak.'

'You take them. You go. Take a mate. The holiday was your idea.'

'Well, maybe I will,' he said.

'Or' – I took a big breath – 'given that the tickets are in both our names, and it would be a hassle to start changing them, we could both go. I mean, we could get separate rooms. But the point is we'd be there together, away from here, we could talk, maybe a change of scenery would help us sort all this out.'

'Get serious,' he said.

I was being serious. And I didn't mean forget it ever happened. I just thought there was a chance; after all, he hasn't triggered divorce proceedings yet. 'Well, I don't want the tickets so you do with them what you will,' I said, and hung up. Even though I'm the bad guy in all of this, I am getting truly sick and tired of shouldering the entire blame. Two minutes later, his email containing the online booking reference arrives.

I stare at this house now, the top window, which is the floor that's available. It's so weird sitting here, looking at a room to rent as a single person when two minutes ago you were a couple and you owned your own home. I can't go in. I know he told me I should probably find my own flat, and perhaps he wasn't just being petty, but if I actually do it, then it truly will feel like there's no going back.

I go back to the bungalow, lie on the bed and stare at a single crack on the ceiling. Sometimes, like now, my memory of kissing Rob is so real that I have to stop what I'm doing and recover from the effect of it. Today I tell myself I'll do this one more time then I have to stop thinking thoughts that will continue to buckle me.

Wendy asks me if I want to borrow her *Divorce for Dummies* book. Strangely enough, I actually manage a smile. 'Maybe you should become a divorce lawyer,' I tell her. She screws up her face. 'No,' she says. 'I'd have an unreasonable urge to castrate the husbands.'

On September the twenty-fifth she has her 'procedure'. I go with her and am the first face she sees when she wakes up. 'No sex for two weeks. Doctor's orders,' she tells me, and she manages a pained laugh.

I stay over for a few nights at her house to help out. When the lads go to bed, we sit up for hours nattering, her at one end of the sofa, me at the other. You'll never hear Wendy say anything self-pitying, but somewhere in the scheme of things she feels it was a cruel blow to have lost a child, a husband and now – if her op isn't a success – a womb. 'I've been dreaming about that strange experience I had when I was pregnant. Remember?'

'I do.' It always gives me the creeps. Wendy was about six months pregnant with Nina and she was in a yoga class doing a relaxation at the end. The instructor asked them to picture a scene – some personal place that gave them calm, be it a beach, a spot of sunlight cracking through trees. Wendy couldn't think of one. But then something came to her. She saw it as clear as if it were real. A dark, silent, open space, and in the centre, risen earth topped with a spray of white flowers. It took a while for her to realise that she was seeing a burial place. 'That's how I knew that something awful was going to happen,' she told Leigh and me, after little Nina died.

'Jill, I keep dreaming of that feeling I had. When I felt there was something awful going to happen in my womb.'

I squeeze her hand. 'If you lose your womb, Wendy, it's only a very small part of you that'll be taken away. It's not your brain. It's not your heart. It's not the air in your lungs. It's a small price to pay for still getting to have your life. And your dreams and ambitions.'

She nods. 'You all thought I got pregnant with Nina by accident, didn't you?' She looks at me, her eyes blazing secrets. 'So did Neil. But I didn't. I stopped taking the pill. I think part of me was scared my lads were growing up and motherhood was all I knew. Plus, I had thought that when they were older, maybe I would leave Neil. So perhaps having another baby was my way of putting that decision off for a while longer. Who knows?'

The next night she says, 'You know what bothers me the most when I think of them together? It's not the sex. It's the thought of them talking about me. You know, intimately. Discussing my body, what I'm like in bed . . .'

'You don't know they will have—'

'Oh, come on. She'll have coaxed stuff out of him. I can imagine her wanting to know things about me. Very private things. Wanting to hear how she compares.'

'No,' I say. But I'm thinking, *Yes*. Because I can see a person with dodgy self-esteem behaving like that.

'I'm angry,' she says suddenly. 'Oh, Jill, I'm hopping mad about her.' She gets up, clatters glasses and bottles in the drinks cabinet and pours us both a large something.

'Maybe you shouldn't be drinking, Wendy, with the pills . . .'

She stands in the centre of her sitting-room floor, drinks it quickly, then refills her glass. 'Fuck the pills,' she says; I have never heard her swear that way. 'I'm angry, Jill. I'm so angry I want to kill her. I have this inner rage. I want to critically harm her. Isn't that awful?' She bites the outer edge of her hand. 'I want to ring her and call her a thin, ugly-hearted, tit-less, decrepit bitch.'

'Do. Tit-less and decrepit would probably be enough to kill her. But not tonight. Not while you're so mad. And not right after your op. It'll do you no good. Come on.' I pat the seat beside me. 'Sit down.'

'Tit-less and decrepit,' she chants again. Then she puts a hand on her lower stomach, winces. 'Oh, that hurt.' She sinks into the sofa. And it comes out in a distraught whisper. 'I loved him.' She looks at me. I get the feeling this is the last time she's ever going to say it. For one last time, the room seems to fill with the ghosts of a bygone marriage.

My house must feel like this, to Rob.

I set the chenille throw over our legs again and sink the brandy she's poured for me – and then the measure she's poured for herself just to stop her having it.

'You know what I could never get over about her?' Wendy says calmly, some time later, when our voices have become tired and a little tipsy. 'Why she didn't get those horrid little teeth fixed. I mean, she made all that money, she'd buy those bags and fancy watches, yet she'd live with those funny-coloured teeth.' It's true. Leigh doesn't have great teeth. She claimed it was enamel erosion from taking asthma medication as a child. She often joked that she hoped her adopted identical twin had a better set.

I can't help but have a small chuckle. I've never heard as much bitchiness come out of Wendy's mouth, and I love her for it. 'We're talking about her as though she's dead.'

'No,' she says. 'I wouldn't want her to be dead. I think of what a good friend she was to me when I lost Nina. Both of you were.' Then she looks at me. 'Besides, death would be too kind. Let her have Neil. How long do you think it'll be before he cheats again?' She cocks an eyebrow. 'Judging by how deliriously happy he is to be living with her, I'd say not long.'

'And she once told me she could never, ever, be with a cheat,' I say. 'She said her self-esteem just couldn't take it. It'd kill her. She said that's why she'd married Lawrence, because he was a sure, safe bet.'

'Oh, well. Poetic justice. What a shame.'

Another night Wendy's son Ben walks into the room just as Wendy is busy enlightening me on the fact that Neil didn't have half as big a penis as Leigh made him out to have. Wendy had just been telling me that the lads seemed more shocked that it was Leigh than anything else. Not because she was a friend, but because, as their Paul said, 'Gaw! I thought when married people have affairs they're supposed to, you know, upgrade the model. Park the Peugeot in the back alley and take the Ferrari out for a spin.' Then he told Wendy that she is far better-looking than Leigh. Any day.

Neil will try to get custody, Wendy told them. But their Ben said, let him. There was no way they were going to live with him. And, as Wendy said, they're big lads. Try making them.

'Make way, make way,' Ben says now, and he's holding something at arm's length, pulling a face. It's a sock – obviously one of Neil's. We watch in disbelief as Ben walks over to the kitchen bin, puts his foot on the pedal, and drops it in there with a 'Right then'. He dusts his hands off, nods to us, then goes back upstairs.

'It's all an act,' she whispers. I think it's so sweet how they keep taking turns at making sure she takes her painkillers. 'They hug me and ruffle my hair, want to watch TV shows of my choice. But I see it in the strained silences as we try to rearrange our simple little routines. Like who gets to drive whom where, now that we have to factor Neil – and a second car – out. I see it in their bitter little grunts about how they're never getting married.'

'They'll be all right.' I envy Wendy her lovely lads.

On my last night there I get a surprise. Well, two. The first is that we're sitting chatting away and in the background the North East News is on telly with the sound down, and we suddenly see a gaggle of naked bodies outside a store. Wendy fumbles for the remote control. We just get it turned up to hear the newscaster talking about how two-hundred-pound Madge from Cleveland was the first person over the threshold when the new *Fatz* store opened at the Gateshead Metro Centre. Madge, whose bare arse looks like curdled cake batter, pads like a pet elephant into the store to claim her prize. Wendy and I have a good chortle.

Then . . . over chicken pie and bagged salad, she generously offers for me to move in, as a temporary alternative to staying at my parents'. The lads say they're all for it. For a minute it feels like I'm even being strong-armed. And for a minute it's tempting. But a connectivity of adultery runs between our mutual circumstances. And as long as we're together under the same roof, it's all we talk about. And I'm sure that in the long run it'll pull us down more than it'll help us move forward.

Speaking of moving forward, I finally manage – miraculously – to get my act together enough to actually go to work. I've got a temp secretarial job through an agency. It's at the Newcastle Jobcentre, which is, let me tell you, nothing like working for the football club. No office hilarity or sexy footballers here! The employment agency said they just want somebody short-term, so that suits me fine, because I'm just taking life day by day at the moment. Since going back to my parents and not having Wendy to distract me, I'm not so good again. But I go through the motions until five o'clock. Strangely, it helps. Then coming back to the bungalow pitches me back into despair. But I see it as a sort of halfway house. If I'm there, instead of in some flat I've signed a lease on, I am halfway back to Rob.

The next day in work something terrifying happens. The manager of the Job Centre, Bill Crushing – an intense, overly affable chap who's on Prozac – asks me out. His wife left him for another man. He's not bad-looking for a middle-aged civil servant, but nobody you'd set your sights on. I wouldn't care – I've not even been looking nice lately. I know I still look exhausted because my dad will keep gawping at me like I'm the Bride of Frankenstein, and when I glower at him he quickly pretends he wasn't doing it. And unlike at the football club, which was a bit of a daily fashion parade amongst the girls, I've not been wearing my smart clothes to come here for fear the punters might think I have it too good.

If only they knew.

But he must have sniffed out my situation, this Bill, and he wants a kindred soul in misery. He hovers at the side of my partitioned cubicle. I stop him mid-sentence, tell him, nicely, that I've only been separated a short time; that I'm nowhere near ready to date again. Voicing the *separated* word freaks me out. He looks mildly embarrassed. I go and hide in the toilets. Am I back on the dating scene, after thirteen years? Will I have to dodge predatory divorcees on the happy pills? Is this the type who is going to set his cap at me? That I'll somehow end up being grateful for? I'll have to tell them, won't I? That I cheated. Then the nice guys won't want me. I'll become, in their minds, somebody I don't recognise.

All I can say is I'm pleased that I told work and the agency that I'm going away on holiday for two weeks. Even if I'm not.

Friday night, I'm pacing the bungalow manically twirling my hair because tomorrow's the day that I have to decide whether I am going to use the ticket. I sent Rob a text reminding him that we both have access to the online booking, we both should be adult about this and just go on our holiday rather than waste that money. 'Get on that plane regardless, if he doesn't come,' Wendy told me. 'Have a holiday,' she said. 'Relax. Come back afresh, maybe seeing things a little differently.'

'It's a nice thought,' I said. But it's not.

The flight is in the morning at ten. I go out by the dustbin to get a bit of privacy and make an impassioned, pride-swallowing call to Rob's mobile. Of course he's not answering because he probably sees my number, so I leave a message: 'Look, Rob, I don't for a minute think this is really going to do any good . . . only I have to try, this one last time.'

I take a deep breath. I have vowed I'll not cry or be 'a drama queen' as he sometimes calls me. So I say, 'Rob, I wish I could say I've moved on. I wish I could say I've stopped punishing myself. But neither of those is true. I am so, so sorry for what I have done. I always will be this sorry. Every day we don't talk is a day I feel I'm giving you to get over me. And I should let you do that, but I can't let you do that. I can't let you get over me . . .' My voice cracks now with a jagged ache. 'Rob, I've apologised so many times that it's starting to sound too easy, like I don't mean it.' I pause and snivel. 'Well, anyway, without grovelling, which I know you wouldn't respect, I'm just going to say this one last time. Rob, please forgive me. Or at least give me another chance – for the happy couple that we were for ten years, not the people we became for a few months.' I get a blast of cheery strength in my bones. 'We have tickets to go on a holiday tomorrow. I, for one, am going to be at that airport, and I . . .'

I what? I beg you, I want you, I need you . . .

'I hope you'll be there too. Let's go on our holiday, and let's see if, away from all this, we can talk better and maybe give ourselves a chance to work this out. And if we can't, and you can't forgive me, I promise I will accept that, and I'll leave you alone and you will never hear from me again.' I grimace and bite my lip. Please, God, don't hold me to that, or I'll never get into heaven. Not that I hold out much hope of getting in, in any case. I'm sure there's a separate loading dock for cheaters, and there's probably a big bin they throw them into first, and it's full of boiling tar and feathers, and they even feather your eyeballs. 'Right then.' I draw breath. 'I've said my piece. I'll leave it at that. Like I've said, I'll be there tomorrow. Eight a.m. I'll be waiting for you. So I'm hoping and praying that you will come.'

Somewhere in there towards the end I'm convinced I've heard a beep and I've been cut off. So I ring him up again and leave the message all over again, a shorter version.

When I hang up, I lean back into the wall, stare up at the stars and make an impassioned plea to God, my new best friend, to deliver Rob to the airport tomorrow morning. Mrs Parker next door – nosy parker, more like – is peering at me out of her window. She may have heard every word. Now the whole of the neighbourhood will know and my dad will never dare show his face in the pub again.

Saturday morning I barrel out of bed, and throw on the cargo pants and navy tank top I laid out the night before. It feels, ridiculously, like going on a blind date – only blind as in he may not be there. What am I doing? He's not going to come, is he? I mean, it's mad even thinking it. Going there, hoping he might, is like admitting I don't really know the man I was married to for ten years. But maybe there are such things as miracles. So I have a quick cuppa, brush my teeth, and tell my puzzled dad that I may or may not be going away on two weeks' holiday.

'When like?'

'Now.'

'What d'you mean now?'

'I'm leaving for the airport in three minutes.'

'I'm confused,' he says. I tell him it's a long story and that one day I might share it with him, but that day is not now.

'Be good,' he tells me, as I venture outside into the autumn air. 'And if you can't be good, be happy.'

I get to the airport early. Now that I'm actually here, I know for sure that Rob is not going to come. I imagine him sitting at home thinking, *Is she really sat there at the airport waiting for me?* But still, I pass my ticket information over the counter and go through the motions. If he doesn't come, I know I won't board.

I go to buy a Costa coffee hoping the caffeine will pep my flagging adrenaline. I take it to a bench that faces the revolving door and watch the bustle of the holidaymakers. It always fascinates me what passionate places airports are. The goodbye kisses that make the disenchanted-and-trying-not-to-be-cynical among us roll our eyes. The Orange People coming from the arrivals level, fresh from their two weeks on a beach in the Algarve. I get carried away watching a couple my age with their little boy in the check-in line. The wife is toned and lovely with her belly-ring and blonde and black streaks and her little cropped tank top. She's having a disagreement with her sexy hunk of a hubby about whether little Nathan should take his big coat on the plane or not. Deciding not, she bends over and shoves the coat in the luggage, and her hubby's hand instinctively touches her bum when she stands up. She gives him that smile and a quick, promising kiss. It's lovely. They are lovely. And I wish I could just lop their heads off and stick Rob's and mine on to their bodies and their lives. For some strange reason I think about that time when Leigh, Wendy and I, and the hubbies and kids, went on a trip together. We rented one of those honking great caravans in St Ives.

Imagine all of us in a caravan, no matter how big. Oh, it was hell. Rob got gastric flu on the way down, and by the end of our first day there so had Wendy's lads and Lawrence. Then the toilet in the caravan backed up, so Lawrence, who was the last of the four to fall ill, had to trek across a great big field to use the site's facilities. In the middle of the night he was crawling his way back, clutching his poor gurgling belly, when he realised he'd left the door key in the loos, but he didn't have the strength to go back for it. He didn't want to wake us all up by knocking, so he peeked in the window where he thought Leigh's bed was. Only he had mistaken some other caravan for ours. What he saw was not his sleeping wife, or a sleeping any-of-us for that matter, but a man and his wife having sex. Oh, it was like a Carry On film. The moment he saw them, they saw him – the woman, to be precise, who was on top – and then, oh dear . . . The husband ran out of there stark naked, jumped on Lawrence and gave him a hiding. We all woke up with the commotion, hearing somebody calling somebody a fucking Peeping Tom. Rob tried to pull the husband off Lawrence, but it was Neil who eventually split it up. Poor Lawrence ended up in a police holding cell! Neil had to use his influence. Lawrence spent the rest of the trip in the caravan, manically locking doors and peeking around curtains and doing his business in a bucket. We laughed about it for years. Even Lawrence eventually saw the funny side.

Argh. What will never be again! I feel it like a great big pain of absence. I have to plant my fist in my ribcage. We were all just individuals toeing the line of life, and then our lives somehow became connected up, and deep investments in friendship were made. I cannot accept that they suddenly all count for nothing. Or that we'll never all be friends again. Or that I've lost Rob. I stare out of the glass doors, at arriving cars, coveting some vision I have of him pulling up in a taxi, leaning forward, reaching in his back pocket to pay the driver. And then he'd climb out, hair cut, beard shaved off. The gorgeous, immaculate

Rob of old. The sexy apprehension in his eyes, which would turn to look for me. And then he'd see me, standing by the door. A sea of people would bob between us, but they wouldn't be able to separate our gaze. Nothing would. And in that moment we'd know: that our love was stronger than whatever came to divide it. And Rob would smile, a happy-ending smile. And I would run to him.

I shut my eyes now. And I will that when I open them, what I have imagined will be real.

I open them. Nothing. I look at my watch again. It's twenty past. Our flight leaves in forty minutes.

If he's coming, he's cutting it fine.

CHAPTER TWENTY-TWO

The baby is born in May. I name her Hannah, after my mother's mother. We bury my mam one week after the birth of her only grandchild. The grandchild she saw, but never knew was hers. My mam surprised us by dying in her sleep the day before she was to be admitted into a home; I had finally got my dad to agree to it. People made the same remark at the funeral: about one life ending to make way for another. I could never have imagined I'd look at my mother's dying like that – as though you somehow trade in a mother for a daughter – but, strangely, in a way, it helps to.

It turns out that's why I hadn't been feeling too well, the episodes of throwing up. The doctor left a message to call, but I never did. A combination of me just not being very 'with it' at the time, and maybe fear that I was going to be told I'd caught some kind of sexually transmitted infection after all. Who knows? But I never, ever, thought I could be having a baby. I was pretty certain of my dates. I'd taken the morning-after pill! Of course, the doctor never mentioned the failure rate. Anyway, I found out I was pregnant soon after Rob never showed up at the airport.

The airport. I'll never forget how I felt when I stood there and watched that plane take off without us both. I couldn't pick my heart up off the floor on the Metro back through to Sunderland, carrying my suitcase, my bag full of hope.

It was an awful shock at first. Andrey's baby. A child who would be forever attached to a terrible memory, and the one mistake I would undo if I could. A baby who came along when I was quite sure I could live happily without kids. And a child that meant Rob would never have me back now.

But I try not to think of that any more, or of the past, or the life I had and what I've lost. At some point you've just got to stop punishing yourself. I still feel bad about cheating and always will, but that's just me and my strong, but momentarily misguided, morality. But I've got over punishing myself. And I don't wish it had never happened. Not when I look into Hannah's little face and see her flex her moist little pink mouth that I keep dropping kisses on. Or I feel her little sausage fingers tighten around mine. I can only thank God for her. I can't imagine my life without her.

The loss of Rob is the gain of Hannah. A weird way to look at it, but such is life.

But even if I wanted to pine and mourn and beat myself up, there really hasn't been time. Between working, being fired, being pregnant, being hired somewhere else, being split up, being shacked up in the spare room of a senior citizen's bungalow, I've been very much just coping with life as it's been flung at me.

The flat I moved into before Christmas is hardly my dream place to live, but at least it's in a nice part of Gosforth. I'm on the first floor of a three-storey townhouse owned by a couple of retired teachers who live downstairs. I was worried at first about the baby crying, but they don't have grandkids and said they actually find the noise quite soothing. Which is more than I can say for myself. Hannah does cry a lot. But nowadays, strangely, I don't. I often wonder if she detects sadness in me and decides to cry to save me the trouble, if this little bundle of baby is somewhat telepathic.

I tried to find him: Andrey. It's odd calling him that. I like to think of him as nameless, faceless, everything-less. That was a hell of a decision to make. I didn't think he'd care to know that he was a father; he certainly didn't strike me as the family type. But I felt his right to know was bigger than all my reasons not to tell him. But the main reason I did it was for Hannah. I just had to think of Leigh or Rob to know how hard it was to grow up knowing nothing about your own dad. I remember Rob's speech to me about the fractured family. I didn't know where to start, of course. I couldn't go knock on his door because, strangely, I've never had any memory of where he lived. Certain events of that episode are just locked out of my mind. So I went to the Civic Centre, his employer, and managed to find out the sort of confidential information they're not supposed to tell you, but if you catch the right girl on the right day and tell her your life story, you might get lucky. She was a single mother herself. Yes, she said, she remembered him: lovely-looking bloke. Turned out, Andrey left his job at the end of last summer. She believed he moved out of the area. That was pretty much in keeping with what I knew about him. I was ready to leave it at that, but then I placed an announcement in the 'Personals' of the *Sunderland Echo* and the *Evening Chronicle*. For a second I wondered if Rob would see it, but I couldn't really see Rob looking in a newspaper to find love. It was a very weird message to write, and what I ended up writing sounded crazy, really: *To a certain Russian on a beach. You have a daughter. From a woman who you once thought would be impressed by a fancy car.* He'd get that, if he read it. I included a PO box so he could get in touch with me, dreading that he actually would. I still check it. Seven weeks on and I'm still getting post. Mind you, it's very bizarre stuff.

Men wanting to meet me, take me on holiday, marry me. One who sent me a picture of his penis! Someone who claims he's in the Rolls-Royce Club of Great Britain. A lesbian couple who offered to buy Hannah for ten thousand pounds. A very old man who sent me a picture with the caption: *Let me be your sugar daddy.* There's a lot of oddballs out there. But one day, when my daughter asks, I'll be able to look her in the eye and say that I tried to find her father. And I'll probably tell her stories about how she's related to Princess Anastasia, the only vaguely interesting bit of Russian history I ever remember.

As for her ever calling anybody else Daddy, I don't hold out much hope there. It's been ten months since Rob and I split, and I've never as much as thought of another man. On the rare occasions I do think of sex, it's still sex with Rob. This doesn't bode well for my future. I don't know how I'll ever move on to anybody else. Because Rob was, and always will be, my one and only. In my heart – if not, alas that one time, in places farther south. Has Rob moved on to someone else? Somehow I doubt it. Interestingly, in all this time he still hasn't made a move to file for divorce, and obviously neither have I. I don't take encouragement from this. He'll be working hard. I'm sure he just hasn't made time for it, and he has never been a lover of procedures and paperwork. But every day when I check the post I expect to see an envelope.

Speaking of moving on. Wendy is doing surprisingly well. The operation was a success and she's been given a clean bill of health. She's got a job working part-time for a solicitor – a much older Jewish gentleman who she says, with great understatement, is a very nice man in a 'father-figure' way (to translate: I think she might actually have slept with him). And back in January she resumed her law degree course, part-time. I'm convinced that before she's fifty (as she joked) she really will be a solicitor. Then it'll be the old middle-finger salute to Neil. I can tell that she's dying for that day. Revenge, even to good people like Wendy, is essential somehow.

'Sometimes I still have to take time to mourn him,' she'll occasionally say. 'But mourning him is good because it means he is fully dead to me; there's no going back.' Her lads are doing well, although Ben developed psoriasis, something that the doctors say can be triggered by stress. Wendy says they regularly spend time with Neil now, and she wouldn't want it any other way.

Leigh and Neil are a bit of a different story. They ended up having a massive bust-up and she went home to Lawrence. Lawrence, not surprisingly, when I think of his phone message that day, took her back. But only for about a week. So Leigh went back to stay with Neil, who still says he doesn't want her, who still makes the occasional pitch to Wendy to take him back. Molly is living with her dad, until Leigh sorts herself out, although she sees her mother every weekend. But apparently Leigh isn't sorting herself out. Wendy saw her by chance in the town centre and said she looked almost unrecognisable: grey hair, no make-up, dark glasses and gaunt.

I received a card from her. A *Congratulations on the Birth of Your Baby* card. She could have only found out via Neil, through Wendy telling him. Perhaps it was an olive branch. I'm sure that in her own way she loved us, as we once loved her. Although she still hasn't apologised to Wendy, and I doubt she would think she ever needed to apologise to me. But she did send Wendy a Christmas card, saying *Wishing you Peace from Leigh*. Not Leigh and Neil. And *Peace*? It doesn't even sound like something Leigh would say. Wendy and I tried to fathom it, but, as usual when the subject comes to our once best friend, we can't.

What Wendy and I do know is that we have zero desire to ever look Leigh in the face, or to speak to her again. Wendy, because she just won't lower herself. Plus she wants to send a message: *Be in no doubt – I am glad that he's gone.* But for me, I have thought about this many times. What happens when I accidentally bump into her? It's surely inevitable. What do I say? I have never needed to ask her why she betrayed me. I know why it was; it was tit for tat. Would I argue that my betrayal of her wasn't nearly as big as hers of me? It's true. I only talked to Neil to try to halt what was happening. But she would never understand – as evidenced in her continued silence. If she had wanted to apologise, she would have. If she had thought she had done a bad thing, Leigh would be out with it; that much I give her credit for. And then again, to sit down and talk to her would be to what end? I don't want her back. I don't need closure. The friendship door was closing the moment she told me that Nick was really Neil. It slammed shut and was padlocked forever when she rang Rob. Besides, I just keep coming back to the fact that I still feel such shame for what I did. And seeing her, talking to her, would just be a reminder of it. I can't face being reminded that we're just the same. I don't want her repeating how I'm just as bad as she is. One day, maybe, I won't be as emotional or as vehement about this, and perhaps I will gain some balance, and perhaps there will be room for a modicum of healthy, internal forgiveness. But that day is not now. I need all my energy to be aimed in positive directions at the moment.

But once in a while I am blindsided. I can think of her without a burning sense of bitterness. How could I not when we were so close? I've run the gamut of emotions, but in the end I just come back to pity because Leigh was, is, and always will be, a very damaged person. And, as much as I've tried to blame her for perhaps egging me on to go astray, I know deep down that I can't pin that on her. I was a big girl. My actions were all mine. And even if she'd never ratted on me to Rob, I'd still have got pregnant, so he'd still have left me. Once in a while I'll catch myself smiling over some of the silly little laughs we had. There is a massive void in my heart where a good friend once resided. I miss her. Or, rather, I miss who I thought she was. Sometimes it saddens me because I think I'll never put that sort of faith in a friend again. A part of me will always be guarded. But maybe that's not a bad thing.

As for myself, Rob still won't talk to me.

I had to tell him I was pregnant, of course, because I was sure he'd find out. The North East, as I learned the hard way, is a small world. In light of our history, it seemed like a very cruel blow that the man I was unfaithful with should succeed where my husband had failed. There was a big silence down the phone when I broke it to him. And then he said, 'Well, be a mother and be happy, Jill. Don't have any regrets.' And then he hung up.

Ironically, today happens to be our anniversary. Hard to believe how different my life was a year ago. Today is also Hannah's baptism. I wasn't going to bother with all that business because I've never been what you'd call religious, so it seemed hypocritical. But my dad nearly had kittens: 'You have to christen her! Or you know what she'll be, don't you?' he whispered. 'She'll be a bastard.' My dad still sometimes gets things a little wrong, and he still doesn't know that Rob isn't the father; I want him to leave this world still having some respect for his daughter. The most I have ever told him is that our marriage just wasn't working, and, sadly, there's no going back. But one day I caught him stuffing photos of Hannah in an envelope with Rob's address on it. I snatched the package off him. 'Don't ever do anything like that behind my back, Dad!' I said, so annoyed that it must have raised a red flag. I caught it in his eyes. Bewilderment followed by a realisation waiting to land and be verbalised. But he never said anything. That's just his way. And I silently thank him for that.

But my child will never be fatherless. I plug her arms into the cream-and-white knitted cardigan that she's going to be wearing over the cream-and-white knitted dress that was mine when I was christened. I will be mother and father to her. And whenever I've got my 'Dad' hat on and I don't know what to do, I'll try to imagine what Rob would have done under the circumstances, and I'm sure we'll bluff our way through it somehow.

Hannah is taking my last name: Mallin. I wrote it down before I chose it, liking the flow of it, the rhythm, the n's and the l's. When I married Rob I kept my own name. I foolishly thought it was a way of retaining some of me in our coupling. I regret that now, though. I regret not taking all of him while I had the chance.

Rob. Still his name resonates in me with loss, after all this time. I pick Hannah up and squeeze her to me by her podgy little shoulders. Sometimes I get moments where I don't believe how my life has turned out. This is one of them. Hannah starts to cry.

My dad taps on the bedroom door. 'You're ready? We're going to be late.' He comes in. I look at him, dressed in his suit and cheerful mauve tie, which has already got a tea stain on it and he's only had it on two minutes. My dad, who lost my mother and acquired a single, unemployed daughter with a baby, and has never for a moment been anything other than a trooper. 'No more doing the Ray Charles . . .' I keep hearing him say, a thousand times a day, even when I was just thinking of doing the Ray Charles, and it makes me smile. Yes, family sticks. Friends don't always. Not even husbands. But I thank my lucky stars that I was born of a close family. I lift little Hannah above my head, and jiggle her there.

'She's a beautiful little baby, yes she is!' My dad coos to Hannah and he thumbs her little cheek. My daughter's head is eggshell pale and smooth. Her skin, with its flush of pink cheeks on cream, is just like my mother's. But in every other respect – her eyes, her nose, the shape of her face and her mouth – she is, uncannily, the image of her father. Every time I look at her, I see him, and I probably always will.

Sometimes I'll catch my dad staring at her. 'She's the living double of Rob, isn't she?' Then he sends me that look. Clearly he only says it because he knows damned well that she isn't.

I often wonder, though, if he connects it all to the Russian, and our day out at the beach. My dad has always been a man to know more than he'll ever let on.

I settle Hannah on my shoulder, patting her big, square, nappied bum, and she pulls a handful of my hair. I walk into my parents' bathroom and look at the two of us in the mirror. I did get my figure back quickly, all but a few pounds. Although nowadays I really don't care. I think of all the time I spent focusing on my imperfections. Don't they say that sometimes you just need something bigger than your biggest problem to realise you never had anything to worry about? However, considering I sleep only about two hours a night because of all the crying she does, I actually think I look pretty good.

I am both excited for this and dreading it. Last time I went to our local church it was for my mam's funeral. Even in my grief I still found myself looking around for Rob. I know how much he loved my mother, so I couldn't imagine him not coming, and I was looking around, asking myself where he was. But then my dad said he did come! He was standing at the back of the church. He nodded to my father as we were all walking out behind the coffin.

Rob. My head floods with him again, like it's prone to do at all the worst times. Hannah lets out a great big bawl. Saves me the trouble.

'Do you remember this?' my dad says. He is holding a small book. 'I found it in a drawer.'

He hands it to me. And then it dawns on me. 'I remember it!' My mother's. A small, ruby-red, leather-bound notebook that she used to write in. Quotes and things. Quotes about love.

I open it. I can feel my dad watching me closely. I scan the first few pages quickly because we don't have much time.

The most powerful symptom of love is a tenderness which becomes at times almost insupportable. Victor Hugo

To love a person is to learn the song that is in their heart, and to sing it to them when they have forgotten. Anonymous

I ask you to pass through life at my side – to be my second self and best earthly companion. Mr Rochester in *Jane Eyre*, Charlotte Brontë

I loved her against reason, against promise, against peace, against hope, against happiness, against all discouragement that could be. Great Expectations, by Charles Dickens

I look at my dad. 'Why are you giving this to me now, Dad?'

He appears to think. Then he shrugs. 'Actually, I'm not sure. I just . . . I found it the other day, and I thought your mother would have wanted you to have it.'

He meant well. But as we drive to the church, I cannot get the Charles Dickens quote, and Rob's face, out of my mind.

The church isn't exactly packed, but there's enough of a turnout for it to have an intimacy as we enter it. I decked the aisles out with strings of white roses. Before we buried my mother, I was a child when I last came here. Now I come here today as a mother myself, with my own child. Something about that gets me right in my gut. Hannah starts to cry again.

Wendy is holding Hannah. I gaze at the small stained-glass rose window while the vicar does a reading and his voice drifts peacefully through me. The organist sits studying her fingernails. There are four other babies getting christened today. All of their names have been printed into a small, white booklet with a flocked cover, which I stare at as it sits open on my knee. *Hannah Mallin.* I look down the list of names, and my eyes keep coming back to my daughter's. It's by far the best, of course. I hope I'm not going to be one of these obnoxious mothers who other mothers hide from at school functions. *No*, I think, looking at her and just wanting to plant kisses on every square inch of her little sausage body; *I hope I am.*

I take my daughter from my best friend's arms, my friend who very bravely accepted the role of godmother to my daughter, despite having lost a daughter herself. I look down the short pew at my dad, his gnarled hands resting on his kneecaps as he listens solemnly. *This is all that matters now*, I think. This moment that I wouldn't change if I could; not all the things that I would change given half the chance. It's all water under the bridge. My dad looks across at me. His eyes are full of tears. I know it's hard for him. I know he's thinking of my mam.

I pass Hannah to the vicar when he nods to me. She scowls and twists and puckers her mouth. I look up at the stained-glass rose window again. The vicar starts giving her his blessing and I'm lost on a sentimental journey of thought about this weird state of screwing up we all go through until we finally accept that life is just something we have to take, however we get it dished up, with all its associated baggage, pitfalls and mistakes. That I am a mother freshly shocks me again. The vicar is just at the point where he asks for her name, when something strange happens. I hear a dog bark. I mean, you couldn't really miss it. It's such a loud, crisp bark, a get-right-on-your-nerve-ends bark.

I've heard that bark before. It seems to stop everything, including my heart.

My head instinctively shoots round to the back of the church, and just as it does the door opens, giving one of those low, burring groans I remember from when I was a child.

Rob pokes his head around the door.

I gaze across a sea of curious faces and look at my husband.

You could hear a pin drop.

'I'm sorry,' Rob says, looking even more Heathcliff-like with his wild hair, his arms cocked stiffly by his sides. 'I thought I'd get here and catch you before you went in.' He looks around, self-consciously. 'Can I speak to you outside?'

How did he know about today? I look across at my dad, who's looking at me, with 'OK. So Shoot the Messenger I'm Nearly Dead Anyway' written all over his face.

I look back at Rob. He's dressed in his old jeans and navy GAP sweatshirt. After a quick glance at Wendy, I step away and follow Rob outside, aware of a sea of bemused faces behind me.

I'm hot. There's a ticking of blood in my temples. 'What are you doing here, Rob?' I ask him when we're outside in the bright sunshine on the narrow, gravelled drive framed by headstones. I can hear the quiver in my voice. I look at his pallor, his pained eyes. I've never seen Rob look so changed. The last time I saw him was that day I went round and begged him to let me come home. I imagined in all this time he would have been back to his old self again.

He kneads his temples with one hand, blows out a big breath. 'I've come to give Hannah my name. I want to be her dad . . . if you'll let me.'

He looks right at me, his pupils latching questioningly on to mine. A breeze rustles the trees, and it takes a moment or two for me to speak. 'But you said you didn't know if you could love someone else's child.'

He shakes his head, turns from me, props himself against the dark-blue church door with an outstretched arm, and looks down at his feet. 'Am I not allowed to be wrong?' His forehead rests now on his arm. I wonder what kind of a drama we must look like.

As much as I've dreamed of this moment, of course never expecting for a minute that it would happen, there's another force going on inside of me: the mother in me. I can't have Rob barging in and testing the waters of forgiveness at Hannah's expense. 'You don't mean this,' I say, stupidly. It feels too good to be real.

He nods. 'I do.' His eyes meet mine now, and birds tweet in the trees behind us. 'Of course I'd have loved a kid of my own. I never realised how much until I couldn't have that. But I can't have that.' He smiles. 'But I've come to see that having one that's yours is the next best thing.' He touches a stray bit of my hair, tucks it behind my ear;

his eyes soften. He scours my face again. 'And I want you back. If you'll have me back.' He takes hold of both of my hands. 'I love you, Jill, and I'll love your baby. I wanted you back the second I made you go. But a part of me thought maybe I should try and live without you because I was so damned hurt by what you'd done. I just couldn't understand it. But now . . . I don't know, in some ways maybe a part of me does. Or maybe I just don't think it matters as much as I always thought something like that would.' He shakes his head, and the birds leave the trees with a flurry of wings. 'I'm just not happy without you. These last ten months . . . I'm a very sad person. And I don't want to be sad any more. I keep waiting until I'm going to feel better, until I'm going to come home and not register your absence as I walk in that door.' He digs the heel of his hand into his eye socket. 'I miss you more than I ever imagined I could. And I just want us to be a family again.' He squeezes my hand. 'The three of us.'

I choke with love for him, and disbelief. I cannot speak. It's only then that I register Kiefer, who is tied up to a tree. When I look at him he wags his tail and barks.

'He passed his obedience training with flying colours,' Rob says.

I laugh.

He is looking at me like a man who has fallen in love all over again. 'You know what was on Metro Radio the other night?' he says. 'Before the phone-in? That song, you know? Bonnie Tyler. The one we danced to at the wedding. "If I Sing You a Love Song".'

I nod because I can't speak. Because I remember that song very well.

'It was a nice song,' he says. 'It's our song.' He wraps his arms around me and pulls me into his chest.

I rest my head against him and hear his heart thumping. 'So you've not met anybody else in all this time?' I ask.

I glance up at him, and his eyes ooze with love for me. 'I never even looked.'

I'm terrified a breeze will stir up and this moment will be blown away on the back of this fateful summer day. 'But it's his child, Rob. How will you ever be able to forget that?'

He cups my face in both of his hands and lightly squeezes. 'I can forget it, Jill. Whose child it is – it's just biology.'

I know Rob wouldn't mess me around. If he's saying this, he's given it a hell of a lot of thought and he means it. 'Oh, Rob . . .' I squeeze my arms tightly around him, lay my face against his shoulder again, claiming him, slightly panicked that he's going to suddenly change his mind. Maybe he'll say, *Look, Jill, now that I'm touching you, now that you're in my arms, it doesn't feel the same, and I've made a mistake coming here . . .*

But when he plucks me off him, he's smiling. He doesn't look pale any more. More like flushed. He gets down on one knee, and at that exact moment, through the sunshine, it starts to rain, a fine showerhead sprinkling.

'What on earth are you doing?' I press my tear ducts to try to stop the flow.

He looks up at me, quietly doting. 'Jill Mallin. Will you be my wife again?'

I pull him up by the shoulders of his sweatshirt and wrap my arms around his neck. 'I've never been anything else.'

ACKNOWLEDGMENTS

I am endlessly fascinated by the dynamics of female friendship, in particular how we recognise, or erect, boundaries – what we tell our friends, what we hold back and why. This book was inspired by a conversation I had with a friend many years ago – a friend who was contemplating having an affair. At first I was curious, but then I realised I didn't really want to know if she ended up doing it. It made me think about loyalty – to our friends, family and spouses, and the tests we face and how we handle them. *The Secrets of Married Women* was a very fun novel to write because I found myself answering so many *what ifs* that made me grateful this was only fiction. I don't really know anyone like Leigh or Wendy or Jill, and yet in some ways I feel I know them on a very deep and personal level. My hope is that you might, too.

Huge thanks to my publisher, Lake Union, and everyone who had a hand in making this book as good as it could be, and bringing it to the attention of readers – in particular, thanks to my editor Sammia Hamer, and to Victoria Pepe and copyeditor Julia Bruce. I have a fantastic agent in Lorella Belli, and I am so lucky to have her always enthusiastically nudging me in the right direction. I am enormously thankful for my mother, Mary Mason, who always encouraged me to read and who has such a wonderful way with words herself that I'm guessing my writing inclination came from her. And I will always be indebted to my husband, Tony, who supported my dream to write and never suggested it was time to give up – even when the one year I took off work to try to get published turned into several.

ABOUT THE AUTHOR

Carol Mason was born and grew up in the North East of England. As a teenager she was crowned Britain's National Smile Princess and since became a model, diplomat-in-training, hotel receptionist and advertising copywriter. She currently lives in British Columbia, Canada, with her Canadian husband.

46334356R00153

Printed in Poland
by Amazon Fulfillment
Poland Sp. z o.o., Wrocław